Praise for USA TODAY bestselling author

Kasey Michaels

"Kasey Michaels aims for the heart and never misses."
—*New York Times* bestselling author Nora Roberts

"Known for developing likable characters and
humorous situations, Michaels adds an element of
danger and suspense to this sexy romp."
—*Romantic Times BOOKreviews* on *Dial M for Mischief*

"Michaels demonstrates her flair for creating likable
protagonists who possess chemistry, charm and a
penchant for getting into trouble. In addition, her
dialogue and descriptions are full of humor."
—*Publishers Weekly* on *This Must Be Love*

"Michaels has done it again…. Witty dialogue
peppers a plot full of delectable details exposing
the foibles and follies of the age."
—*Publishers Weekly*, starred review, on *The Butler Did It*

"Michaels can write everything from a lighthearted
romp to a far more serious-themed romance.
[She] has outdone herself."
—*Romantic Times BOOKreviews* on
A Gentleman by Any Other Name (Top Pick)

"[A] hilarious spoof of society wedding rituals wrapped
around a sensual romance filled with crackling
dialogue reminiscent of *The Philadelphia Story*."
—*Publishers Weekly* on *Everything's Coming Up Rosie*

"Nonstop action from start to finish! It seems that
author Kasey Michaels does nothing halfway."
—*Huntress Reviews* on
A Gentleman by Any Other Name

"A cheerful, lighthearted read."
—*Publishers Weekly* on *Everything's Coming Up Rosie*

Also available from

and HQN Books

Kasey Michaels

Mischief 24/7

HQN™

Recycling programs
for this product may
not exist in your area.

ISBN-13: 978-0-373-77366-4
ISBN-10:   0-373-77366-8

MISCHIEF 24/7

Copyright © 2009 by Kathryn Seidick

www.HQNBooks.com

Printed in U.S.A.

Dear Reader,

Sometimes a story unfolds in real time; a man and woman meet, fall in love, overcome obstacles both interior and exterior, and we have our happy ending. But sometimes things don't work out that way; sometimes the obstacles are too great, the desire bringing them together not as strong as the problems tearing them apart.

This was the case with Jade Sunshine and Court Becket, who met, succumbed to their strong mutual desire—and then realized that desire wasn't enough to hold their union together in the face of life in a world not designed for lovers.

But had theirs been simply physical attraction, the proverbial fire too hot not to cool down? Or had there been more? With their divorce about to become final, that question lingers for both of them.

When Jade's father is buried after an assumed suicide, Court races to Jade's side, whether she wants him there or not. Jade and her sisters believe Teddy Sunshine has been murdered and are out to prove his innocence by capturing the real murderer. But the Sunshine sisters didn't know Teddy the way Court did, the way all the men in the Sunshine sisters' lives knew the enigmatic man who had been part loving father, part manipulator.

Mischief 24/7 is a story told in real time, but also a story told within that story—memories of a hasty courtship, an impulsive elopement and the clash of two strong personalities all unfolding as both Jade and Court look to the past to find their future, together.

Join me as we retrace the steps that led Jade and Court to where they are now, looking for love amid tragedy and danger, even as we race through a nonstop twenty-four hours of dangerous mischief.

All the best,
Kasey Michaels

Mischief 24/7

To John Edward Groller.
Welcome to the world, Johnny!

THE TIME IS NOW, the place, the City of Brotherly Love. And the crime is murder.

Murders, actually. Murders old, murders new.

Retired Philadelphia homicide detective Teddy Sunshine had been working four cold cases whenever business was slow at the Sunshine Detective Agency. He'd been conducting a routine semiannual updating of his files on those cases when he was found dead in his home office, an apparent suicide.

But Teddy hadn't eaten his old service revolver, the police said, until after he had strangled the woman he'd been stalking for three weeks—Melodie Brainard, the wife of the leading mayoral candidate.

His three daughters aren't buying that story. They can't. They loved Teddy Sunshine.

One by one, Jolie, Jessica and the oldest, Jade, who had been partnered with Teddy in the

Sunshine Detective Agency, took on the cold cases and worked them the way their father had worked them, sure one of the cases was connected with their father's death. One by one, the old cases were solved, leaving only two: the surely un-solvable tragedy of a high-school scholar athlete gunned down in a drive-by shooting, and the sad haunting case dubbed the Baby in the Dumpster.

But every answer the Sunshine sisters found seemed to raise new questions, and while the girls have felt cheered by their progress with the cold cases, they still can't prove Teddy's innocence.

Jade, even more than her sisters, feels a re-sponsibility to clear Teddy's name. But will her obsession with the old cases, old hurts, past mistakes, risk her future with the man she had always loved, the man she'd thought gone from her life after their short, troubled time together as Mr. and Mrs. Court Becket?

The clock is ticking….

SUNDAY, 11:06 P.M.

THERE WAS A SUMMER thunderstorm making it a noisy night outside the suburban Philadelphia mansion belonging to antiques importer Samuel Becket. Sam wasn't there, however, having traveled to California with his on-again-off-again and now on-again fiancée, movie star Jolie Sunshine.

He'd invited the three Sunshine sisters—Jolie, Jessica and Jade—to stay at the mansion as long as they liked, since their family home had been damaged by a suspicious fire shortly after the death of their father. Sam's sprawling, securely fenced-in estate, complete with a gatehouse manned by intrepid former professional wrestler Carroll "Bear Man" Yablonski, was now Operations Central for the Sunshine Detective Agency, or what was left of it.

And what was left, now that Jolie had been forced to return to California, were TV cable-news journalist Jessica and Philadelphia homicide detective Matt Denby, Jade, and Sam's cousin from Virginia, Courtland Becket. Court, owner of an almost embarrassing empire of five-star hotels, among his other assets, had flown immediately to Philadelphia when he'd heard about the alleged suicide of Teddy Sunshine. He wasn't going anywhere as long as Jade needed him. Even if she said she didn't.

Jade closed her cell phone with a snap and looked blankly at her ex-husband as he entered the living room. "I don't believe it."

Court, casually elegant in belted, pleated tan slacks and a form-fitting navy pullover too expensive to sport a label, tipped his head to one side inquiringly, and then headed for the bar in the far corner of the large room. "For the sake of harmony, neither do I. Ginger ale for you, right? Considering the tone of your voice, however, I think I'll have a beer. Oh, and what don't I believe?"

"Jessica, of course," Jade said, thinking about her baby sister, who had left the house not four hours ago on what she had called a *mission*. "Poor Matt."

"Poor Matt? That doesn't sound good." Court returned to the conversation area with their drinks and sat himself down on the facing couch. "When we discussed this earlier, I thought the idea was that your sister was going to give him some space. What was it she was going on about? If you love someone, let him go, et cetera, et cetera? In which case, might I point out, you obviously adore me."

"Not now, Court, please," Jade said, getting to her feet and smoothing down the wrinkled skirt of her simple shirtwaist cotton dress. She was bone-weary and definitely rumpled. Only Court could still look fresh, and heart-crushingly handsome, this late in the day. Or maybe it was a gift bestowed only upon those who were born to generations of money.

Not that she wanted to think about that right now, either. She needed to pace, to work off some of the tense energy that had driven her these past weeks. Not even two weeks, in fact, since she'd come home to find Teddy's body in his office, the back of his head blown off and his service revolver on the floor beside his desk. And yet sometimes it felt like an eternity. "The bottom line is, Jessica and Matt are together again, how I don't know."

"You're talking Jessica when you say you don't know, right? As to that, Sam and I have a theory that might apply here," Court said, speaking of his absent cousin. "We've decided that your baby sister is a witch. The good, G-rated, pretty, blond, nose-twitching kind. But still a witch."

Jade smiled in spite of herself. "You and Sam might have a point. In any case, they've gone off somewhere together. To celebrate before the rest of the world knows anything, which they will, soon, from coast to coast and in several large foreign cable markets—and that's as close to a direct quote as I think I can get. She won't say where they've gone, but she did say to hold the fort and that they'll be back tomorrow night sometime."

Court took a long pull on his beer, then smiled up at Jade. "Gone? Really? Let's do roll call, Jade, all right? Sam and Jolie? In California, getting ready to fly to Ireland to shoot your sister's next movie. Matt and Jessica? Whereabouts unknown, although the words *hotel suite with a king-size bed and room service* seem to be one fairly plausible conclusion. They should have called me and I could have arranged for the penthouse downtown."

Jade winced inwardly. She remembered that penthouse very well. She tried to cover her sudden discomfort by saying brightly, "Ah, but then we'd know where they are, and I don't think Jessica wants anyone to know."

"Good point. In any case they're gone, they're not here. Jessica took our new friend Ernesto home earlier, where he is even now packing to leave for college on Tuesday. Mrs. Archer has the weekend off, although she may have come back by now. Still, her apartment is pretty isolated. Bear Man is in his gatehouse at the end of the drive, most probably standing in front of a mirror as he strikes a few muscle-popping poses. Leaving this very large house—and you and me. For the first time since we got here, Jade, I think I like the odds."

It was tiring, always fighting Court—fighting herself actually—so Jade gave in. "You forgot Rockne," she said, smiling as Teddy's beloved, aging Irish setter snored in front of the cold fireplace. "He's my chaperon-slash-bodyguard. Rockne! Sic him, boy!"

Rockne's left ear twitched a single time, but his eyes didn't open.

"I suppose you could go see if Mrs. Archer is available. She's probably deadly with a rolling pin at twenty paces," Court suggested. "What do you say, Jade? Can we put the cases to one side for one night? Just one?"

Jade returned to the couch and sat down, not to agree with Court, but to reach for the file folders that had been piled on the coffee table. "We're getting so close, Court. I mean, taking the process of elimination into account, I should be able to wrap this all up in a few days."

"*You're* going to wrap this all up in a few days? Just you? Who solved the case of the Vanishing Bride?"

"Jolie and Sam," Jade said, shifting the manila folders on the tabletop. "With a lot of help from Teddy, who nearly had the whole thing wrapped up before he…before he was murdered."

"Steady, Jade," Court said, leaning across the table to squeeze her fingers. "Let's move on. And the Fishtown Strangler case?"

"Jessica and Matt. Except that's not completely solved, not if Herman Longstreet is telling the truth about Tarin White not being one of his victims, remember?" She put a hand to her head. "Sometimes it's like we're going in circles, you know?"

"Look, I don't want to push this, but every day you look more…well, fragile. Your hands look a lot better since the night of the fire, but the burns still have to be tender. You don't eat enough, I don't know when you sleep, and when I think maybe you're taking it easy for a while, I find you in the workout room running on the treadmill. You've got to slow down, Jade. Stop beating yourself up."

Jade pulled her hand free of his. He was wrong. The burns she'd gotten trying to put out the fire were completely healed now. It was the rest of her that remained wounded. "That's just crazy, Court. I'm not beating myself up. Why would I beat myself up?"

"Oh, I don't know. Because you didn't come home earlier that night, find Teddy while he was still alive and draining that bottle of Irish whiskey, talk him out of what he was going to do?"

"Teddy did *not* kill himself!" Jade clasped her hands together in her lap because her hands were shaking and, otherwise, Court would see. He already saw too much.

"All right. Fine. He didn't kill himself." Court rubbed at his own forehead now, and Jade suppressed a guilty wince, knowing that he was as tired as she was. They were all tired.

"I'm sorry, Court. I know what it looked like. I was there, remember? The door to the office closed, Rockne shut outside that door, whining and agitated. The nearly empty bottle of whiskey for liquid courage. Teddy's body on the other side of that door, slumped back in his chair, the gun on the floor beside him after he'd…after he'd been shot. I know, Court. I know how it looked. I'll never forget how it looked."

"And the front door locked, the alarm on and no signs of forcible entry anywhere," Court added, his voice tight, as if he didn't want to say what he was saying, but likewise, knew that some things had to be said.

"I don't *remember*," Jade told him. "Honestly, Court, I don't. Is that it? Have you been thinking that I lied to you all about that? About the alarm being on or off, the door locked or unlocked? Do you think I only said I don't remember about the security code because otherwise the verdict of suicide is impossible to argue? How long have you thought I've been lying?"

"Not lying, Jade. Not intentionally. But sometimes we do forget what we don't want to remember."

"Then I should have been able to forget finding Teddy like that. Holding Rockne back so he couldn't contaminate the scene when all I wanted to do was go to Teddy, shake him back to life. Calling Jolie and Jess and telling them our father was dead. Living through the hell of the medical examiner and a bunch of cops poking around the house for hours, all of them talking about Teddy and other cops who couldn't take civilian life and ate their guns," Jade said, blinking back tears. "Why can't I do that, Court? Why can't I forget any of that? Why can't I forget that Teddy went to his grave labeled both a murderer and a suicide, disgraced, denied the departmental funeral his long years of service to Philadelphia demanded?"

Court had gotten up from the couch and come to sit beside Jade as she spoke. Now he gathered her close. "I'm sorry, sweetheart. I'm a jerk for bringing it up at all. I'm so, so sorry."

"But you've been thinking it," Jade said against his chest even as she put her palm against his shirtfront and pushed herself away from him. She dipped her head forward, allowing a curtain of long, golden-brown hair to fall forward and hide her profile. "Sam, too? And Matt?"

"We've discussed it. But two things still can't be explained. One, Teddy didn't leave a note, and we think he would have done that. And two? You're right, Jade, Teddy wouldn't do that to you. He wouldn't have let you find him. If he were going to kill himself, he wouldn't have done it where you could see what he'd done. He loved you too much."

Jade wiped her eyes with the handkerchief Court had passed to her. "Thank you. Unfortunately those conclusions come from our feelings. The cops worked with what they saw. Just the way they saw Teddy on Melodie Brainard's front-door security cameras, the last visitor the camera picked up before she was found doing the dead man's float in the swimming pool." She made a face. "I'm sorry, I shouldn't have said that. Although dead woman's float doesn't sound any better."

"You were around Teddy all the time," Court reminded her. "Sometimes you sound a lot like him."

"And that's a bad thing," Jade said, sighing, willing herself to be composed, or to behave as if she were. "Or at least, it wasn't a good thing when I met your friends. Savannah Harper? She was always after me to tell her stories about how to shadow a cheating husband."

"She would be, considering she's done some fairly extensive cheating of her own on poor Buzz."

Jade allowed herself to be diverted. "She got caught?"

"Caught, forgiven, and she's back at it. Jade, many of the people I associate with are simply social or business acquaintances. Not my friends. You knew that. But I did pretty much toss you into the deep end with their wives, didn't I? I'm sorry about that."

Jade moved to return his handkerchief, but

then reconsidered, and blew her nose into it. "It's all right. It was even fun at first, listening to them, sorting them out. But I wasn't built to be a society wife, Court. We both know that now. It wasn't that I couldn't fit, because I think I could, if I worked on it. I just didn't want to fit. Country club lunches and charity balls? They're not my thing."

"You were bored."

"No, Court, I was being *smothered*. Melting away, losing myself. There's a difference." She looked at him, felt a small catch in her belly and reached once more for the stack of files. Those files were the only things she could hold on to right now. Solving the remaining cold cases, praying one of them led to Teddy's killer.

"I was a jackass, only thinking of my own happiness," Court said, and she sliced a quick look back at him, seeing the hurt in his face.

Such a handsome man. That's what had caught her attention at first, his dark good looks, but his innate goodness had been what held that attention. She couldn't stand to see him hurting.

"I should have told you I was unhappy—that was unfair of me. And we were both pretty stubborn, as I remember it. You were always gone on business, and Teddy needed help back here until he could replace me. One thing led to another, didn't it? But that's all water under the bridge, right?"

"Is it?"

"Court, I…" She dumped several files in Court's lap. "Let's do this now, clear off Sam's priceless antique table, sort out what we need and don't need. I can't count on Jessica having her head anywhere near the game for at least a few days, and I think we're getting too close to slack off while she walks around with stars in her eyes."

"We're going to have to talk about this sooner or later, Jade. You do know that. I love you. I've never stopped loving you."

"Court, please," Jade all but begged him. "Not now."

"Not now. That's becoming a familiar refrain."

"I'm sorry, Court. But I really can't do this now. Every day that Teddy is believed to be a murderer is one day too many. If we're…if I'm to have any future, I've got to correct the past."

"Sometimes that isn't possible, Jade. Sometimes we simply have to close the door and move on."

"Like we have? Our divorce was final almost a year ago. Have we moved on, either of us? Would you be here now if Teddy hadn't died? Is it time we gave up, Court, and closed the door on us?"

Court looked at her for a long moment, his deep brown eyes unreadable. "Point taken. Pass me one of those folders."

Jade handed him one of the files, blindly, as she couldn't read the words on the tab through the tears in her eyes, and then pulled another file onto her lap. She opened it, staring at nothing as she felt Court's assessing gaze on her, burning into her. What was he thinking?

THE BECKET PHILADELPHIA

Two years earlier

IT WAS THREE DAYS after Christmas. Court sat at the hotel bar with Sam Becket, watching as his cousin made a valiant attempt to drown his sorrows with gin and tonic. Clearly not a dedicated drinker, his cousin, or else he'd go for a single malt, neat, and doubled.

"Tell me again why you didn't just go after her?" Court said, thinking it might be a good idea to keep Sam talking, instead of drinking. "You know, fly to the Coast, grovel, plead, grovel some more?"

"I told you," Sam said, lifting his glass and looking into it, frowning. He set it back down. "I don't even like gin and tonic. Teddy warned me away."

"Teddy. That's the father, right? Jolie's over twenty-one, isn't she? It wasn't as if you needed his permission."

"Jolie's his daughter. He knows her better than anyone. Obviously better than I do, or I wouldn't have offered her money."

Court picked up his own glass. Bottled water with a twist of lemon, as he had elected himself designated driver, even though he was staying at the hotel and that meant driving Sam back to his own house in the middle of a snowstorm. But these were the sacrifices one made for family. "I have to hand it to you, Sam, that's unique. Here's money—marry me. Yet slightly lacking in romance, I'd say."

Sam shot his cousin a sharp look. "I offered her money to live on while she waited tables or whatever it is out-of-work actors do to survive while looking for their big break. She threw it back in my face. Literally." He pushed back on the bar stool. "Damn it, Court, I was trying to help."

"But that help came with a time limit. I remember this part. Go to Hollywood, Jolie, fall flat on your face—but eat well while you're doing it—and then come home at the end of one year and marry me. You ought to think about a career in the diplomatic corps. Especially since, last I heard, she's still out there and you're still here, kicking yourself in the backside."

"I'm done kicking myself for that one, Court. I've done something else since that fiasco. The dumbest damn thing I've ever done."

"Dumber than the day you pinned a pillowcase to your shoulders and *flew* off the garage roof?"

Sam smiled at the memory, rubbing the arm he had broken in the fall into some saving shrub. "I was seven. I had an excuse. I don't have an excuse for this one. I know a few people out there in La-La Land and I...I bought Jolie's way into the worst movie ever released straight to video."

"Porn?"

"Very funny. No, Court, a horror flick. You know, kids out for a night of necking in the woods, the obligatory masked madman running through those woods, chopping up teenagers with a souped-up Cuisinart or something. She had a few lines and then got some pretty good close-ups where she had to look scared and scream a lot."

"All right, I think I'm beginning to follow this," Court said, commandeering a bowl of peanuts from the bartender. When you own the hotel, someone is always watching, ready to supply anything you want. "The film bombs, Jolie bombs, and she gives up, comes home to pick out china patterns. So? Tell me about the flaw in this master plan, because obviously there was one."

Sam ran a hand through his already mussed dark blond hair. "So this big Hollywood type saw her, said he'd never seen anyone the camera loved more since Julia Roberts, and signed her to a three-picture deal. The first one isn't out for another month or so, but according to the grapevine, she's brilliant in it."

"Ah, hoist with your petard," Court said, toasting Sam's debacle with bottled water. "Or something like that. Now what?"

"Now I face the fact that I've lost and I've got

to learn to live without her, that's now what. Now I keep doing what I've been doing."

"Burying yourself in work," Court said, thinking of Sam's legacy separate from the Becket family inheritance, a large import/export antiques empire that had its beginnings nearly two hundred years ago and, in the past few years, a steady increase in high-end retail antique stores. Court had leased him a large area inside this same hotel and many of his hotels around the world. "How's that going for you?"

Sam held up his glass. "How does it look like it's going? But enough of me crying in my gin and tonic. How are things with you? I know you just flew in from somewhere. Where was it this time? London? Paris?"

"Rome. You'll be happy to know that your share of our latest acquisition to the Becket family portfolio includes an owner's suite overlooking Vatican City. It's yours to use whenever you want."

"Sweet," Sam said, clinking glasses with Court. "I propose a toast. To Ainsley Becket and his entrepreneurial spirit. Shipbuilding, land, thoroughbred horses, banks, developing industries. He was a man ahead of his time."

"He was a privateer and a pirate, chased out of his own country before he could be hanged," Court said, smiling. "Come to think of it, so are we. Pirates, that is. We just play more within the rules than he did two centuries ago."

"Good, because I don't think getting hanged from some yardarm is on my to-do list for the New Year. How about you? Court? I said, how about you?"

"Hmm?" Court had turned on his bar stool, his interest caught and held by the woman just entering the bar. He watched her steady progress toward him, everyone else in the crowded room fading away as if a spotlight was on her, moving with her.

She was stunning, from her unbelievably long legs to the artlessly piled honey-brown hair that made him itch to find the pins that held it in place and slide them out one by one, all those warm-looking curls cascading down over her bared breasts. The clear mental image surprised him. "A couple of days after the fact, but better late than never. Thank you, Santa Claus."

"Santa Claus? What the hell are you talking— Oh, damn it all to hell. What's she doing here?"

"You know the lady?" Court asked, dragging his gaze away from the woman who was heading for a bar stool two down from him. A good thing he was civilized, or he'd push the guy next to him to the floor so she could sit beside him. "Talk to me, cousin. If I'm going to propose marriage to the woman, I probably should know something about her."

Sam kept his head down, a hand raised to shield his profile. "That's Jade Sunshine. Jolie's older sister. She works with Teddy at the Sunshine Detective Agency. She's a PI, Court. And you'd have about as much luck trying to tackle a porcupine. Maybe more luck with the porcupine, come to think of it. Trust me. You don't want any part of that."

Court was silent for a full three beats. "Really. She's a private detective? Do you think she's here on a job or something? At least she isn't a high-class call girl, which would have ruined everything. You know, thinking ahead, for when one of our kids asks how I met their mother."

"Which one of us was drinking tonight? Look, Court, give me your elevator key. I don't think I should drive tonight, so I'll crash with you."

"Oh, I don't think so. I may have plans for that suite. Believe me, cousin, they don't include you as a roommate."

"You're casting Jade in that role?" Sam peeked out from behind his hand to grin at his cousin. "I've got fifty bucks here that says it doesn't happen."

"Just go to the front desk and tell them I want you set up in a room, all right? Now, if you're not going to introduce us, just go away. If you two don't like each other, you won't be any help, anyway."

Sam slid off the stool, his head still averted. "It's not a question of dislike. It's just that I hurt Jolie, or at least that's how Jade sees it. Stick to first names," he advised quietly. "She hears Becket, and you can kiss any ideas you've got goodbye."

But Court was barely listening, as he was already tuning in to the conversation going on between the middle-aged man next to him and Jade Sunshine.

"And you're sure I can't buy you a drink, honey?" the guy was saying, his back to Court. "Something *real.* Who comes to a bar to drink ginger ale?"

Jade stirred her soda with the plastic swizzle stick, the ice clinking. "I like to start slow and then build from there. In my business, a clear head is a part of the service."

Court liked her voice. A little bit low, slightly husky. Definitely sexy. And he was pretty sure she knew it. The guy next to him was nearly drooling.

"And what is your business, honey?" the guy asked her.

Jade kept her right hand on the swizzle stick as she gracefully swiveled on the bar stool and carefully crossed those long legs beneath the short, black sheath. Court swore he could hear the silk of her stockings whisper with the movement.

She reached out with her other hand and stroked a finger down the guy's tie. "I thought I told you, handsome. Service. You see, honey, I serve people. Should I *serve* you? I'd really like to serve you. What's your name, honey?"

Court lowered his head and let his breath out slowly, wondering why the ice cubes in his own glass, and in every glass in the bar, hadn't melted yet.

"I…I'm Harvey," the poor sap stuttered. "If…if,

uh, we're going to get to know each other, um, *better,* maybe you should tell me your name?"

"Sure thing, honey," Jade said, her hand leaving the man's shirtfront to slide down his thigh and then onto her own knee. "I'm Lucy. Lucy Lawless."

"But isn't that the name of that actress who… Oh. Oh, right. I guess, in your line of, uh, work, names aren't real. I should have thought of that. But I *am* Harvey. Sorry."

"Don't be sorry, Harvey, honey," Jade soothed, inching up the already short skirt of her dress. Her other hand had left the swizzle stick and now rested on Harvey's jacket lapel. "It's a great name, Harvey. What goes with it?"

Out of the corner of his eye, Court saw the bartender moving down the bar, probably to eject the obvious hooker. Court shook his head slightly, warning the guy away.

Harvey's eyes were all but glued to Jade's leg as she slid two fingers beneath her hem and slowly headed North. "Hubbard. I'm…I'm Harvey Hubbard. Should you be doing that here? I've got a room upstairs and…"

Court caught a mind-blowing glimpse of black lace garter as the blue-cover-clad tri-fold appeared from beneath Jade's hemline. At the same time, her other hand grabbed at and pulled on Harvey's jacket front, and an instant later the obvious summons was in his inside jacket pocket.

"Harvey Hubbard—honey—you can now

consider yourself *served,*" Jade said, getting to her feet as she let go of him.

Harvey wasn't too quick on the uptake, at least in Court's opinion, but he certainly reacted pretty quickly to what had just happened.

"You *bitch,* I'll *kill* you," Harvey muttered murderously as Jade turned to walk away. He flew off his bar stool and clapped a hand on Jade's shoulder a split second before Court was off his own stool and reaching for him.

Court shouldn't have bothered. He'd already had a front row seat for the show from where he'd been sitting. In fact, he almost got his nose in the way as Jade rounded neatly on Harvey, her left arm—fingers together, palm rigid—cutting through the air like a whip. Well, like some sort of efficient judo move, anyway, but who needed particulars?

Harvey sure didn't. He simply went down like a felled tree. It was, Court had told Sam later, a thing of real beauty to watch. Poetry in motion.

Court raised his left hand slightly and pointed toward the crumpled Harvey, and two bartenders quickly hauled the man up by his underarms and half carried him out of the dimly lit bar. Most of the patrons, intent on living their own lives, hadn't even noticed anything unusual.

Leaving Court and Jade facing each other. She tipped her head to one side, blinked and then just stared at him as he stared right back at her. She had to feel it. The attraction, the pure, physical pull between them. But she didn't flinch, didn't run away. She just lifted her chin slightly and continued looking at him.

She was tall, but he was taller. Their bodies would fit together like a song, a symphony. Did she hear the same music?

Her eyes sparkled. She was very obviously on a natural high after serving Harvey—or maybe it was taking the guy down that had gotten her blood flowing hot in her veins. She probably needed an outlet for all that pent-up energy, and Court felt it only his duty as a good host to help her out there.

"Hello," he said at last, pushing back the bar stool recently occupied by Harvey. "I'm Court Becket, the owner of this hotel."

Her chest was still rising and falling fairly rapidly from her recent exertion. "Good for you. And you want me to leave your hotel."

"No, I'm pretty sure I want to marry you. Which means we probably should get to know each other a little better. We could do that here, or up in my suite. There's a fantastic view of the city skyline, including City Hall. Billy Penn's wearing a Santa hat. You should see it."

"That's sacrilege—on all counts—and he is not."

"How do you know? You haven't looked. As for the first part, yes, I am. Going to marry you, that is. Would you like me to go down on one knee? I mean, I'm game if you are."

She didn't move. She also didn't look away

from him. He imagined she had learned every inch of him and committed it all to memory.

"I saw Sam trying to avoid me. I'll assume you're related to him."

Court took a single step forward, not quite invading her space, but close enough to smell her perfume. "His cousin. And you're Jolie's sister. Consider us destined, if you want. You. Me. This time. This place. Not Harvey, though." He lost his smile. "Whatever works for you, Jade Sunshine."

Something moved through her magnificent sherry-colored eyes. A decision made? A bridge crossed?

Her voice took on a new huskiness. Low and intimate. "This isn't a good idea, Court Becket."

"I've had worse."

"Nothing's going to happen, you know."

"You don't believe that any more than I do," he said, holding out his arm to her.

She slipped her arm through his. "You saw me take Harvey down."

"I'll consider myself warned," Court said before they walked out of the bar in silence, toward the last elevator on the right side of the lobby, the one that served only the penthouse.

The first hairpin dropped to the carpeted floor of the elevator almost before the doors had whispered shut….

SUNDAY, 11:42 P.M.

"WHAT'S WRONG? Court?"

Court blinked, then rubbed his eyes. "Excuse me?"

"You…I think you groaned," Jade said, looking at him. "Is it something in that file?"

"No," he said, looking adorably confused, or at least as confused as an intelligent man could look. "I was just…my mind was wandering, that's all. Sorry."

"And you tell me I need sleep?" Jade took the file that was still closed on his lap and frowned at it. "This is the Vanishing Bride case. It's already solved."

"Really? I guess I didn't notice."

Jade looked at him again, and she was surprised she could resist putting a hand to his brow to check him for a fever. "You've been sitting here for nearly forty-five minutes looking at a solved case?" She put the file on the coffee table and stood up. "Come on, let's go."

Court got to his feet. "To bed? Would it be too tacky to say that your wish is my command?"

"Yes, and we're not going to bed. You're coming to the kitchen with me. I think you need food."

"Sustenance of some sort would probably be helpful, yes," he said as she led the way into the large kitchen. "What are you going to cook for me?"

"Cook for you? Are you crazy? It's nearly midnight," Jade said, her head half inside the large refrigerator. "You'll get whatever I can find in here and like it." She heard her own words and bit her lips together, turned to look at him. "Sorry. I just had a flashback, I think. Suddenly you were Jess or Jolie, demanding to be fed long after I'd cleaned up the kitchen for the night. I had to keep reminding them that I wasn't their servant."

"Did it work?" Court had sat himself on one of the stools at the large granite island.

"Not in my memory, no," Jade said, making a face. "They always asked, and I always gave in. For one, Jolie was too skinny, anyway. And Jess? She'd just look at me with those big puppy dog eyes, and I'd melt."

"You're their sister. You sound like their mother. Where was your childhood, Jade?"

She turned back to the refrigerator. "PB and J on white bread," she said, avoiding his question. "Take it or leave it."

"I'll take it. And I'm sorry if I'm opening an old wound here. But you never talk about what it was like for you after your mother left. I spoke with Jessica about it the other day, and she had what she called a small epiphany. It's her conclusion now—besides the notion that your parents never should have married in the first place—that she and Jolie were spoiled brats and that you got a raw deal. I'm betting you don't feel that way."

"Don't count on it. There were times I hated them all, even as I played Frankenstein to their monsters." Jade opened cabinet doors until she found the jar of peanut butter and set about making them each a sandwich. "Looking back from where I am now, I'd say that I played the cards I was dealt the best I knew how at the time, that we all did. Pretend I'm a teenager again, however, and that changes. At times I felt like running away and leaving them to realize how they'd be lost without me—but that would make me just like our mother, so it wasn't an option."

"Much better to emulate your father? Did you

ever wish you'd been born a son, instead of a daughter?"

"I'll ignore that."

"That's probably good. Go on."

"I will, since you started this. At other times, I liked being the one in charge of everything and wouldn't have it any other way. And I was in charge, Court, at least in the beginning. Teddy… poor Teddy just fell apart when he finally understood that our mother wasn't coming back this time. I had to stick close."

"*Our* mother? As in, to all four of you? You know, to an outsider, it could almost look as if you raised all *three* of them, Teddy included. But eventually Jolie and Jessica went to college, and Teddy managed to get his act back together. And yet still you stayed home."

"So? I have an associates degree and my PI license," Jade said, knowing she sounded defensive. Which was probably because she *felt* defensive. "I wanted to work with Teddy, so I didn't need anything else. Jess and Jolie did." She slid one of the plates across the granite. "Here. Eat."

"So you didn't have any idea of what to do differently with your life once the others were established? You always wanted to work with Teddy?"

"Who said I wanted to work with… What is

this, Court? An interrogation? Exactly what was Jess saying to you when you two had your little talk? And for the record, I don't appreciate being the topic of conversations going on behind my back."

"I'm sensing that, yes. Good sandwich, but it's missing something." Court walked around the island to take a carton of milk from the refrigerator. He poured a glass for each of them and placed one in front of Jade before returning to the other side of the island. "Nothing better than ice-cold milk with your PB and J. Drink up, and as long as you're angry with me, anyway, let's do a hypothetical, all right?"

"I don't deal in hypotheticals," Jade told him nervously. "I deal in facts, evidence."

"Tell that to someone who isn't working these cases with you," Court told her as he put down his glass. "We're working with about forty percent hypothetical, and another forty percent hunch. Leaving not a lot of room for facts, if you're adding up numbers on your fingers."

"You have a milk mustache," Jade told him, wishing he'd leave her alone. Leave her alone, or take her in his arms and run off with her, the way she'd sometimes wanted to run away from all her teenage responsibility. "All right. A hypothetical. One, and then it's back to the files."

Court wiped his mouth carefully, as if mentally forming his question, the single one she'd allowed him. "All right," he said, putting down the napkin, "here goes. If—*if*—your mother hadn't left, how would your life be different? In other words, and still the same single question, would you still have joined Teddy in his private-investigator business or would you have pursued another dream?"

Jade felt a stab of regret, then quickly pushed it aside. "Sure, Court, there was something else I wanted to do. I wanted to go out West and be a cowgirl. Right after I was the first female astronaut to step on the moon. One small step for woman, one giant leap for womankind. Come on, let's get back to work."

"Stay where you are," he said, and something in his voice told her he wasn't going to let her get away without giving him a straight answer.

"Why, Court?" she asked him, nearly pleaded with him. "Why this question and why now? What I want, wanted, has nothing to do with what happened then or with what's happening now."

"True enough. But someday this is going to be over, one way or the other. What are you going to do then, Jade? Run the agency by yourself?"

She shook her head. She'd wondered when he'd get around to asking this particular question.

"No, that's not possible. Teddy was the heart and soul. I was just the nuts-and-bolts person, working the computer and hardly ever going out into the field. I don't have...I don't have his flair. The Sunshine Detective Agency is officially out of business."

"Leaving you free to go out West and be a cowgirl or fly to the moon. Which will it be, Jade?"

Did he have any idea how much he was hurting her? Tears stung her eyes, and she blinked them away as she cleared the counter. "Neither. I suppose I'll have to find a new dream."

"Or tell me the real one," Court said, finishing his sandwich. "I'm guessing 'chef' isn't on the top of your list."

Jade smiled at his attempt to lighten the moment. Obviously he did know he was hurting her. Yet he kept on pushing. Maybe if they'd talked more before they'd married, they wouldn't have fallen apart at the first obstacle. Maybe...

"You're not going to stop, are you? You're going to push at me and push at me until I tell you what you think you want to know."

"That's the general plan, sweetheart, yes," he said, following her back into the living room. "Is it working?"

She stopped and turned to face him, surprised that he had been walking so closely behind her. "A doctor. I thought I wanted to be a doctor when I grew up, all right?"

Court just looked at her, his expression unreadable. "What kind?"

Jade sighed. "What do you mean, what kind? A doctor doctor. Okay, so I thought I wanted to be a pediatrician," she said quietly. "From the Christmas I was six and got a play medical kit and practiced on all our dolls. And on Jessica and Jolie, whenever they'd let me. It's all I'd ever wanted. And then our mother took a hike and I had to have other priorities. Now I'm edging into my thirties and too old to think about years of medical school, specializing, going through an internship and residency. A dream, that's all it was back then, and I've put it away. Happy now?"

"No, I can't say that I am," Court told her as he reached out a hand and gently stroked her cheek. "A pediatrician. Because you love medicine and you love kids. Ah, baby, it still hurts, doesn't it? All these years later, and it still hurts."

She longed to melt against him, feel his arms tight around her, his strength supporting her as she let go of some of her grief. For Teddy. For everything she'd lost. "I told you, Court, medical school was only a childish dream. I'm too practical to live in dreams. I needed…I wanted to help Teddy."

"Because he needed you. Because he relied on you. And you let him steal your dream."

"No, that's not true!" Jade bristled, probably because she'd sometimes thought the same thing. "My mother was gone. She didn't care enough about me…about us all, I mean, to stick around. So maybe I needed him, too. Maybe I needed to feel indispensable to someone. Did you ever think of that? Don't dissect me, Court. I know I'm not perfect, I know I've got what shrinks call baggage. But it's *my* baggage and I can live with it. And we made it work, Court. Look at Jolie, look at Jessica. Look at their successes. We made it *work*."

"Not to belittle your achievement with your sisters, Jade, but to hell with Jess and Jolie. I'm looking at you, I'm looking at us. But there is no *us*. I never really fit in there anywhere, did I? Yet there I was, at least for a little while. Jess and Jolie grown and gone, and you still here, still mothering the bright, personable, but always needy Teddy. What was I for you, Jade? Your one stab at rebellion, at adventure—at independence?"

"You're wrong. It wasn't like that between us. It couldn't have been like that, damn it." Her eyes shifted involuntarily to the left—according to

Jessica, a sure sign someone is at least searching for an alternative truth—so she quickly looked at Court again. "Don't cheapen what we had, please, or try some psychobabble explanation to explain it. I loved you."

"I hope so, Jade. I really hope so. I hope that, somewhere inside, you still do." He leaned in and kissed her. On the cheek. Like they were friends, pals. Former lovers, one-time mates. "Come on, let's do what you really want to do. Let's get back to work."

Jade nodded, unable to say anything, and Court took her hand and led her back to the couch, back to the stack of files on the coffee table.

He picked up the Vanishing Bride file and tossed it to the floor. "One down. What's next?"

"The Fishtown Strangler," Jade said, willing her mind back on the cases. The cases, and solving them, clearing Teddy's name, that's all that was important now. Later, when the nightmare was over, when she'd fixed things—yes, *fixed* things, the way she always did—only then could she think about what Court had said to her. "This is where it all gets tricky, doesn't it? Jess and Matt found the killer, but he denies that Tarin White was one of his victims."

"The man's a terminal AIDS patient in Graterford Prison. His confession to Matt and Jess could almost be called a dying declaration. There's no reason not to believe him. And no real reason for him to lie, come to think of it."

"I know," Jade said, looking at the photograph of Tarin White. "Yet the MO, on the surface, is so similar, right down the line. Raped, strangled, dumped in Fishtown. The same brand of plastic wash-line cord used to bind her wrists and ankles, everything. Allegedly a prostitute, just like the other victims, and smack inside the time frame when the Fishtown Strangler was active. So what makes her different?"

"Which of Jess's many theories do you want to run with?" Court asked her, picking up a legal pad with Jessica's neat notes written on the top sheet, the main points highlighted in pink. "Crazy as it sounds, I pretty much favor the one where Tarin White dovetails somewhat into the Baby in the Dumpster case."

"I know, me, too. Tarin as the dead baby's mother," Jade said, nodding. "Farfetched, but possible, especially since the infant's body had been frozen, making time of death impossible to determine. Nobody ever claimed the child, no one reported a child that age missing. With Tarin dead, who could?" She reached for the Baby in the Dumpster file. "Give me the date of Tarin's murder again."

After a few moments Court told her the date on the medical examiner's report. "Does that work?"

"It's the same year, the same summer. About three months give or take between the day of Tarin's death and the discovery of the baby's body. But anything else is conjecture, just another of Jessica's theories. Let's review what we actually know, okay?"

Court ripped off the page of Jessica's notes and picked up a pen, ready to start a new list. "Whenever you're ready."

"In a second," Jade said, shuffling notes and papers. "So much is fact and so much is conjecture. It's becoming difficult to sort them out in my head. Okay, let's start just with Tarin."

"Prostitute."

"We don't even know that for sure, do we?" Jade asked, looking at the photograph again. Tarin White had the face of an angel, her dark eyes and dusky complexion surrounded by a halo of soft black curls. "Her former landlord disputes that and told Jessica and Matt that Tarin had a boyfriend. As in singular. Write her name, write prostitute on the first line beneath her name, but put a question mark behind it."

"You want strict outline form, Roman numerals, that sort of thing, Ms. Sunshine, or do I just wing it?"

Jade finally smiled. "I'm giving orders, aren't I? I'm supposedly very good at that, being bossy, Jolie says, although I've never really noticed. Sorry."

"All right. And I'll be sorry that I'm not very good at *taking* orders and do what you want, even as I add a second line—mother of dead baby, question mark."

"That's out of order," Jade said, and then bit her lip. "No, no, that's good. Now let's go back to more on Tarin as Tarin, not as prostitute or as anybody's mother. We know from her autopsy report that she had extensive dental implants, high-quality work."

"Unusual for a street prostitute, correct," Court said as he wrote on the pad. "And thanks again to Jessica and Matt and to one intimidated dentist Teddy found just before he died, we now know that Joshua Brainard, mayoral candidate and husband of the late Melodie Brainard—who, it turns out, is your father's supposed victim—paid for that extensive dental work."

"Which still totally blows my mind," Jade admitted as she turned over pages in the Fishtown

Strangler file. "The connection is definite, easily proved with the dentist's records, and Brainard has to know that. You'd think he'd be running scared, not running for mayor. But now we get back into conjecture. Like, Tarin wasn't a prostitute at all. Like, her boyfriend was the very wealthy, handsome Joshua Brainard, just out of grad school, married, and up-and-coming-man-about-town back then, Philadelphia's fair-haired son now."

Court consulted Jessica's notes. "While talking about Joshua Brainard, we have to take into consideration that he and his father were present at the gravesite when Tarin was buried. Jessica and Matt got the tape from her studio archives and there they were, front and center. Them, and a few prostitutes. We think we might know why Joshua was there, but how do you explain the prostitutes?"

"A show of solidarity? They assumed Tarin was one of them, because all the previous Fishtown Strangler victims had been working girls?" Jade shrugged. "And the Brainards were there because Daddy Brainard was a member of the mayor's commission pulled together to help solve the Fishtown Strangler case. That's their story, and they're sticking to it. And to be fair, the rest of the commission was also there."

"But that doesn't explain Joshua. He wasn't on the commission."

"He was lending his father moral support, or at least I'm sure that's what he'd say if anyone asked. I don't know why he was there, Court. Maybe because he was Tarin's married lover. Maybe he paid for her dental work and fathered her child and then killed both of them because Tarin was suddenly more inconvenience than potential life partner. Maybe because he'd figured out that with his looks and Daddy's money and position, he had a big future in politics. He didn't need the baggage, Tarin didn't want to go away quietly, so he chose a more permanent way of saying farewell to young love. That's the conjecture part."

"Mixed with the facts. Like the dental implants."

Jade toed off her shoes and tucked her feet beneath her on the couch. "Here's another fact. With Clifford Brainard as one of the commission members, sonny boy would have had access to anything his daddy brought home from the office. Like, for instance, how the other women died. Right down to the brand of rope used to tie up his former lover, beat her, rape her and then strangle her—and, by the way, strangling someone isn't easy. It takes time, lots of up-close-and-personal time, so strangling someone is actually pretty rare, rare enough to brand a killer. Strangling someone you once loved, someone who bore you a child, takes a special sort of sadistic bastard, Court. Except…"

"Go on."

"Matt told me something a few days ago," Jade said, frowning. "And he took the medical examiner's one-page summary out of Tarin's file so Jessica wouldn't see it and go ballistic, so don't bother looking for it. According to the medical examiner, Tarin wasn't raped and then killed. She was killed—strangled—and only then assaulted sexually with a foreign object. Like, you know, the other victims were raped, so Tarin had to appear to have been raped, as well, to keep with the MO. Which is why Matt and I weren't as surprised as the rest of you when the Fishtown Strangler denied that Tarin was one of his victims."

Court sat up straight. "What?"

Jade nodded. "I know, I know. It sounds crazy. The other victims were raped perimortem—we know that from their autopsy reports, just like we know from Tarin's that she'd given birth not too long before she died. Maybe a couple of months,

Matt told me. Making it possible that she's the mother of the Baby in the Dumpster."

"You really think Joshua Brainard murdered Tarin White in a copycat killing?" Court frowned and then held up his index finger, as if asking her not to answer him yet as he was still working it all out in his mind. "If there was any physical evidence left behind by the rapist, that evidence couldn't differ in Tarin's case, correct? So he couldn't rape her. He couldn't take that chance. But she still had to appear as if she'd been... violated."

"Exactly. And one other thing. Herman Longstreet is a nonsecretor, meaning they can't get a blood type just from bodily fluids. That was in the police files from the get-go. You can fake a lot of things, but you can't fake that. So first Joshua kills her and then he sets the scene, simulates the rape. According to Matt, the police weren't all that concerned with the victims back then, as the killings were still going on and all the victims were assumed to be prostitutes. If they'd found a suspect, if a case had gone to trial, *then* the discrepancy in Tarin's autopsy would have immediately become apparent. But there never was an arrest."

"You're sold on this, aren't you? That Joshua

Brainard murdered Tarin White and made it look like she was one of the Fishtown Strangler victims."

"He killed Tarin *and* the baby. Don't forget that poor baby. And yes, I do believe it. Because then the rest makes sense. Think about it, Court. Teddy was investigating all these cases for years, right? He'd pretty much solved the Vanishing Bride case before Jolie and Sam took it over. I love Jolie, I really do, and I'm proud of what she did, being a complete amateur detective, but she and Sam really fell into solving that case. Teddy even had the plane ticket so he could go see for himself if he was right."

Court shook his head. "No. We're back to the Vanishing Bride case? Sorry, I'm not getting where you're headed on this."

"I'll explain. Why wouldn't Teddy have gone flying off the moment he thought he'd figured it all out? I mean, after all the years of chipping away at these cold cases, he finally makes a breakthrough on one of them. He had to be over the moon with his success, so why wait to see if you're right? Why make airline reservations a week or more out?"

"Because he thought he was also close on another case? Or even better, on two other cases that had suddenly rolled into one?" Court said, and Jade wanted to kiss him. He was so smart.

"Where was Teddy seen the night he was killed? At Joshua Brainard's house, right? Teddy wouldn't have gone there looking for Joshua, because Joshua had some speaking thing going on in Kensington, and Teddy would have checked that out easily enough. No, he went there at that time, at night, expressly to see Melodie Brainard without chancing that Joshua would also be there."

"All right. That makes sense."

"I know, scary sense. What did Brainard tell Jolie? That Teddy had been *stalking* Melodie for a couple of weeks, right? The card Matt found in one of Teddy's shirt pockets, the one with the dentist's name on it? Teddy had been to see that dentist around two weeks before he died. That made the connection for him. After all these years of schlepping himself from dentist to dentist throughout the greater Delaware Valley and parts of New Jersey, flashing that photograph of Tarin, hitting dead end after dead end, he finally struck pay dirt and landed on the guy he'd been looking for. He finally found out who had paid the freight for Tarin's pretty smile."

"Joshua Brainard."

"Exactly. And suddenly, dotting the final i's and crossing the final t's on the Vanishing Bride case had to take a number and get in line, because this was big—huge. He tried to see Joshua at his campaign headquarters, but the great man was too busy with his race to be elected to see him, so Teddy went after the wife, Melodie. Teddy was on to something, Court, he was close. Close enough to call attention to himself. And Joshua Brainard has a lot to lose, doesn't he?"

"Do you think Melodie told Teddy anything?"

Jade shook her head. "I don't know. The better question might be—what did Teddy tell *her?* Let's switch to what we learned from the girl who shampooed Melodie Brainard's hair about ten days before the murder. She told us about the bruises on Melodie's neck and cheek, the ones Melodie tried to cover with makeup, remember? And then that business about that same shampoo girl overhearing Melodie telling her hairdresser she wasn't going to take it anymore, who did he think he was…whatever that was all about. So, yes, Teddy might have told her something, and maybe she repeated what he'd said to Brainard, who went ballistic on her."

"All of this taking place about two weeks before they were both dead. Teddy kept going back to see Melodie, didn't he? Including that last night. He had some information or some plan we still don't know about, didn't he?"

"But I think we do know about it, Court," Jade said, her heart pounding so hard she was surprised he didn't hear it, and comment on it. She still couldn't believe she hadn't noticed anything different in Teddy's behavior, or that he hadn't chosen to confide in her. When adding up her list of hurts, those two things pretty much topped the list. "I think I suddenly understand why Teddy kept going back to Melodie Brainard, kept working on her, and why he needed her."

Court laid down the pen. He'd stopped taking notes long ago. "Feel up to sharing?"

Jade pressed a hand to her chest. "I'm sorry. I feel like Jessica, jumping to conclusions—and thank God Matt has put so many stars in her eyes that she hasn't seen this yet for herself, not that she won't soon, which is why I'm actually glad she's gone right now. But I think I know better how Teddy operated, having worked with him. I think I know what he was after. If he had connected the cases, that is. I mean, the idea that the baby's body was frozen for all those months? What other reason than to disguise the time of death, make it unlikely that Tarin's death would be in any way connected to the baby's death, correct?"

"Is this all coming to a head anytime soon? Like Jolie and Sam and Jess, I also don't have my PI license, remember?"

Jade closed her eyes for a second and then looked at Court. "I'm betting Teddy was after Brainard's DNA. The man's staff wouldn't let Teddy near him, so what better way to get it than to ask the little wife's help?"

"Why would Melodie Brainard want to *help* Teddy?"

Jade shrugged. "It wasn't a happy marriage? Remember the bruises, Court. Teddy and I worked a lot of divorces, have met a lot of wronged wives. He'd have picked up on Melodie's unhappiness in a heartbeat, and then worked it to his advantage. That's what he did so well, turning on his Irish charm for the ladies who felt neglected and abused. You'd be amazed to watch him work a divorce case. Even in a no-fault commonwealth like Pennsylvania, smart wives know that having a little leverage, be it a mistress or some iffy business dealings, can go a long way in fattening up the private divorce settlement."

"Is this where I thank you and Teddy for not putting me through the wringer in our divorce, even though I kept telling your lawyer that anything I had was yours? Not that I had anything to hide, mind you."

Jade made a dismissive motion with her hand, her mind locked tight on where she was going. "Shh. I'm on a roll here."

"I'll make a note not to get back to that subject later," Court said, grinning at her. "All right, Nancy Drew, carry on. I'm impressed, I really am."

"I'll ignore that crack, too. We know the marriage hadn't been real for a lot of years. Brainard was being all boyish and penitent to Jolie and Sam, blaming himself, their inability to have children, all that stuff. He didn't just hint or suggest, he came right out and said it. Honest Joshua, Philadelphia's next mayor, confessing that he and his wife were the best of friends in an otherwise loveless marriage. Jolie said she wanted to puke, except the guy is so good at coming off all boyish and sincere that she was mad at herself for disliking him. Oh, damn it…"

Court covered her hand with his own. "What's the matter? Something's bothering you. What are you thinking that obviously hasn't occurred to me?"

"What if Melodie saw her chance to lord it

over Joshua, and *told* him she'd given Teddy some of his hair, his toothbrush, whatever? No, maybe not that. That would be stupid, because then she's smack in the middle of a public scandal. She wouldn't have wanted that. I mean, she would have left Brainard long ago, right, unless there was something in the marriage for her. Money, position, that sort of thing. Less stupid, making it plausible, is that she *threatened* Brainard with something Teddy had told her, in order to scare him. Sort of an 'I know what you did' kind of threat that would get her something she wanted. Blackmail. People are that kind of stupid all the time. And it always backfires."

"What would she have wanted?"

"Like maybe she was tired of playing the game of public happy family, lousy private life, and she wanted a divorce after the election and half his considerable wealth in exchange for her silence? Or maybe she was a romantic, still loved the bastard, and the demand was that good old Josh keep it zipped and come home once in a while. Maybe Tarin was the only straying he ever did— but I'm doubting it, not if he and Melodie weren't living as man and wife all these years. The guy's ego couldn't take not having it, and other parts of him, stroked on a regular basis."

"Sometimes I feel like I'm in the middle of a TV cop show, do you know that, Jade? Who writes your dialogue?"

Jade felt herself blushing. "Sorry. Cop talk again. It can be a little raunchy, but it doesn't really mean anything and keeps a person from feeling too much when *facts* are what we need to concentrate on. Teddy didn't bother to watch his words around me. But let's get back to this, okay? Does anything I said make sense to you?"

"I think so, yes. Especially the part about Melodie trying to hold what she thought she knew over Brainard's head and Brainard deciding that his wife—and of course, Teddy—had to go. Kill one, blame it on the other one, play the grieving widower all the way to City Hall in November. The press has already all but ordained him, his wife's murder passed over in favor of concentrating on the bereaved husband who will press on through this personal tragedy for the good of the city. Very neat, a tidy, convenient solution to all his problems."

Jade closed her eyes for a moment. "Kills Tarin, kills his own son and then stands there as Tarin is buried, not even blinking. Nearly two decades later, another problem slams him in the chops. What can he do? So he thinks, hey, if it worked once to solve his problems, murder, that is, why couldn't it work again? They say it's the only thing that gets easier the more you do it— killing people. Joshua Brainard is a monster, isn't he? A sociopath with no heart or conscience."

"If we're right, yes. If we're wrong, he's the wildly popular and lovable guy with a fistful of top-tier Philadelphia lawyers ready to strip us all to our skivvies in a civil lawsuit. Which begs the question—what next? We're still working on that slim margin of facts up against a ton of conjecture."

"Yes, but what if we're right, down-the-line right, start to finish? I don't think this can wait for Matt and Jessica to get back. We can't hold off a moment longer than we have to, not with the news about Tarin White not being a Fishtown Strangler victim going to hit the papers at any time. We've got nothing to connect Brainard to Teddy's murder, not a damn thing. We need a confession."

"Back to Teddy. Right. Nothing like keeping our priorities straight."

"Don't do that, Court. *Yes,* back to Teddy. What happened to Tarin and her baby was horrible, but Teddy was my father, damn it. Tarin is our one big piece of leverage there and I don't want to lose it. I think we have to confront Brainard immediately, Court. Just go right in, head-on, and slap him with what we do know, and hope he slips up, says something incriminating. We get that, and it's like dominoes—they all start to fall."

"Fine. With one caveat. I want to wait until Jessica and Matt get back. You said they'll be home tomorrow night. Excuse the cop talk, but it always helps to have a badge along."

"No, not Matt. He's already skating on thin ice with the department, according to Jessica. We'll do it ourselves, tomorrow morning. Unless you'd rather not go with me, and I'd certainly understand if you didn't want to. I can take Bear Man with me. As Sam said when Jolie pulled one of her stunts that backfired on him, you have to do business in this town."

"Now I guess I'm caught between bragging— saying Brainard can't hurt Becket Hotels—and being a wimp and pointing out that, if we're wrong or just can't prove what we're saying, Brainard will use all his political clout as mayor to drive me crazy with inspections and zoning changes and you name it every time I want to put up a new towel rack in the hotel. Let's stick with bragging—I'm going with you."

Jade quickly closed the file in front of her and stacked all the folders together on the coffee table. There was still one more case, the most personal of the cases—that of scholar athlete Terrell Johnson. But that had to wait. "Your call, Court, but thank you. I'm going to go upstairs and check Joshua's official Web site, see where he's making campaign appearances tomorrow."

"Out of curiosity, what do you plan to say to the man?"

"All right, let's review."

"Please. I like to think I'm a fairly intelligent man, but I have to tell you that it's getting so a man can't tell the players without a scorecard. You want to be the one who tells him about Tarin, correct? That's your opening?"

"See? You do know what I'm planning. Matt said it will be a day or two before the press learns that Tarin White was not one of the Fishtown Strangler's victims. Knowing how City Hall leaks, knowing that Brainard's father knows everyone down there, I'd say one day. I think I want to be the one who breaks that particular piece of news to Joshua Brainard. I want to tell him we know he paid for Tarin's dental implants—that should work for starters—and then hit him with the rest. I'll be able to tell a lot from his reaction to those two facts. Then I'll pile on a little with one other piece of information— that we know he donated the plot for Tarin's burial so that she wasn't buried in a potter's field like some charity case."

"When did we find that out?"

"We didn't. We just know some anonymous donor came forward and fronted the money for the private plot. We just *say* we know it's him, and maybe he admits it, maybe he doesn't." She rubbed her palms together carefully as, yes, they were still tender. "I'm glad Jessica isn't here. I've been sidelined long enough with waiting for these burns to heal, and then with chasing my tail trying to get somewhere with the Terrell Johnson case. I can't wait to go at Brainard tomorrow."

"Wait a minute, Jade, I think I might have found a flaw in your plan," Court said. "Brainard isn't in town, remember? After his father's collapse at that political rally last week, he took the old man to some vacation home they've got out west. We don't know if they're back yet."

"Damn, I forgot that part," Jade said, clenching her fists. She was so ready to go after the man. "You know, I still think Clifford Brainard is much too protective of his golden child. That was a pretty convenient collapse, just as reporters were asking him questions about Melodie's murder seeming a lot like the Fishtown Strangler had struck again. Man, when Jess lies, she lies for effect, doesn't she? I still can't believe she got her reporter friend to print that one."

"You think Clifford Brainard knows his son is a murderer?"

"He wouldn't be the first parent to protect a monster of a child. Yes, anything's possible. But that's a good thought, Court. We need to meet Joshua *away* from Daddy Brainard."

"Cut the calf from the herd, you mean. I think I remember now that the Brainard vacation place is a working cattle ranch. Sorry."

"You're forgiven. I'm still going to go check Joshua's appearance schedule on his official Web site. Leading in the polls or not, he can't stay off the campaign trail too long. I'm betting he's back and will resurface at some point tomorrow. Breakfast at seven?"

Court stood up just as she did, his body close to hers once more. "That sounds reasonable. I have one or two calls to make, playing time-zone tag with a few investors, so I'll be up around four. It's almost a waste to try to sleep now, although going to bed remains an option."

Once again Jade's eyes pricked with tears. How long had she been holding back the torrent of tears that kept prodding her to let them fall? "Big game tomorrow, coach," she said, trying to keep her voice upbeat as she pushed a smile onto her face. "No sex before the big game. It's a team rule."

She stood on tiptoe and kissed him the way he had kissed her—quickly and on the cheek. "Which doesn't mean we can't celebrate a win when it's over."

"As pep talks go, that one was pretty short, but definitely full of incentive," Court told her, matching her smile for smile.

His smile didn't reach his eyes any more than she knew her smile had been anything more than lame window dressing. Their smiles, even their banter, only covered a much deeper problem that hadn't been solved by the two of them sharing a bed the week before, an impulse move that would only make her miss him so much more when he finally went back to his life in Virginia.

But Jolie and Sam were happy again, and Jade had met Jessica in the hallway that night last week, her younger sister more than willing to share that she and Matt had *plans* for the evening. Why should she, Jade, sleep alone, when Court was so close? As she'd thought at the time, what could it hurt?

Yet it had hurt, badly. She'd never felt more alone than in the days since she'd knocked on

Court's bedroom door, let him take her hand and lead her to his bed.

"I need…please, Court."

"I know. Teddy first. I'm familiar with the drill."

She tried for humor. "Maybe I'm just not good at multitasking."

"Will I always come in second to Teddy, Jade? Even now? I want you, sweetheart. I want to hold you, love you. Even if it's only a temporary solution. We can work on the rest."

"Can we? We still live in two very different worlds, Court. Last week was a mistake and we both know it. So are we going to fight again now? Because I really don't want to fight now."

"No, sweetheart, we're not going to fight now. I already lost, more than a year ago. Sometimes I just seem to have a little trouble believing that. Maybe I'm a poor loser. Was it so bad between us, Jade? Sharing my bed again, letting me love you?"

She felt Court's gaze on her.

It was his eyes that had gotten to her the first time they'd met, those dark, soulful, old-as-time eyes. She had fallen into them without a thought, without a backward glance.

How easy it would be to simply slip into his

embrace the way she had last week, let him hold her, make love to her, even take her with him when he went home—the whole fairy-tale line of *Take me away from all of this.*

But she'd tried that once. Court didn't know how right he'd been to call himself her *rebellion,* and she'd be an idiot to make the same mistake twice. She loved him, but going with him now would be using him, trying to build something together on yet another shaky foundation. Court deserved better from her. Maybe even she deserved something better from herself.

"Good night, Court." Jade quickly made her way out of the room and toward the staircase in the foyer.

THE PENTHOUSE

JADE LAY intimately sprawled on Court's chest, her legs tangled with his, her chin in her hands. "Do you know, I think you have gold flecks in your eyes. I hadn't noticed that until now. No, don't close them, let me see. Yes, definitely gold flecks. That's very sexy, Mr. Becket. I think they turn me on."

"Is that right, Ms. Sunshine? In that case, I'll be sure to wear sunglasses whenever I'm around you. Out of concern for you, I mean. I wouldn't want to tempt you at inappropriate moments."

"Sure you would. You'd make a point of tempting me." Jade made a small purring noise in her throat as Court's hands slowly slid up and down either side of her spine. She couldn't remember ever feeling this content, this complete. Why, they were even talking as if they had a future together, which was insane. "You're very good at it, by the way."

"One can only try one's humble best. Now what are you doing?" His hands pressed her back down as she tried to push herself up and off him. "Keep moving your body like that against me, and we'll miss hearing the knock from room service.

A man could starve around you, Jade. Not unhappily, I'll admit."

"We haven't left this bed in over twelve hours, Court. I need a bathroom, a shower—do you happen to have any spare toothbrushes you keep around for your overnight guests?"

"Becket Hotels prides itself on thinking of every personal comfort," he told her as he let her go. She dragged the soft cotton top sheet with her and stood next to the king-size bed, watching him watch her wrap its length around her body. "You don't need that sheet, Jade. There isn't an inch of you I haven't already seen and appreciated."

Jade thought she should tell him he could allow her at least the illusion of feminine modesty. But once you've had your legs scissored around a man's neck while his mouth and fingers took you past the point of rational thought, flew you up to a world you hadn't known even existed, had you calling out his name over and over and over again as you mindlessly begged him not to stop, not to ever, ever stop? After that sort of carnal intimacy, seriously, what was the point?

"I still don't believe any of this," she told him honestly as he propped up his head on one bent arm, doing nothing to cover his own nakedness. She'd never believed the sight of a naked man was all that men would like to think women thought it was. Until now. "I don't even know you."

"We knew enough last night, Jade," he told her

quietly. "I knew the moment I saw you. I'm going to marry you. It's that simple."

"Don't say that. It…it makes me nervous."

"I would have thought the same thing twelve hours and five minutes ago, before you walked into the hotel bar and figuratively punched me in the solar plexus." His gaze went toward the living room of the suite. "That's room service. The food will stay warm while we both shower. You'll find a robe in the bathroom closet."

Jade watched, not moving, until Court stepped, naked, into the slacks he'd worn last night and pulled them up over his hips. Only then did she come to her senses and run for the bathroom, locking the door behind her.

After all, if he thought they were going to shower together, no room-service covers would be enough to keep their food warm for the next two hours. The penthouse suite was huge; there had to be another bathroom somewhere. Probably three or four of them.

This bathroom had no windows, but the overhead lights, including a crystal chandelier that was just downright decadent, came to life the moment she'd shut the door.

Jade dropped the sheet she'd been clutching around her and caught a glimpse of her reflection in the freestanding full-length mirror in the far corner.

No, that couldn't be her. But then, who was

that rather exotic stranger looking back at her as she advanced across the room? Look at the way she moved, like a cat, sure of herself, aware of her every nerve ending, her every sense.

Not a facade, not a role she was playing for the job, the way she'd done last night with Harvey What's-His-Name. This was real. The way she felt was real. *Sexy.* Her. Jade. Not Jessica, the blond bombshell, or Jolie, the strikingly different. But her, Jade. Simple, practical, no-nonsense, boring-white-bread Jade. She was looking at a sensual being, only recently awakened and glorying in newfound freedom.

Court had done this to her. A near stranger had awakened her, when she hadn't even realized she'd been sleepwalking through her life.

Her hair was a wild tangle that cascaded over her shoulders, so unlike the way she normally wore it. Her brown eyes seemed almost smudged, but not with last night's makeup. The darkness came from within. Her mouth looked fuller, the lips subtly swollen, pouty.

She looked like a woman newly risen from her lover's bed. And she liked the way she looked.

Jade struck a pose. Being silly, being stupid, moronically carefree. Her left arm bent to cover her breasts, her right hand lowered to her center; Botticelli's famous *The Birth of Venus.* Or as Jolie had called the painting when she'd nearly flunked her college Art Appreciation course, *Venus on the Half Shell*.

Jade bit her lip to suppress a giggle.

What was wrong with her? How had she lost her mind this way? This wasn't her. She wasn't this kind of woman. A fall-into-bed-with-strangers kind of woman. She was responsible. Clearheaded. Dedicated. She didn't go in for one-night stands. She wasn't the type.

Then again, she also knew she'd never felt this good before, not in her entire responsible, clearheaded, dedicated life. Jessica, the romantic one, would say that Jade was in love, that it had been love at first sight between Jade and Court.

Which was ridiculous. *Lust* at first sight? Yes, that sounded more plausible. Physical attraction, pheromones, whatever, it had been an instant *crash* of mutual desire and need, that was certain.

The question now was what to do about it.

There was a knock at the door. "I don't hear the shower running. Are you ready to eat? I don't know about you, but I seem to have worked up quite an appetite."

Jade dropped her irreverent pose and headed for the oversize shower stall. "In a minute!"

"All right. Do you like strawberries dipped in dark, warm chocolate?"

"What? Do I…for *breakfast?* Um, yes, sure, I suppose so. Why not?"

"Good, because I'm working up this fantasy

where you lie with your head on my lap as I feed one to you, and then you return the favor."

"Sounds, um, sounds like a plan?" Jade fussed with the taps, wondering why anyone would need so many controls to turn on a simple shower. Except this wasn't a simple shower, not with all those extra showerheads. "Just give me five minutes and…and we'll talk about it."

She didn't wait for the water to turn warm, but stepped quickly under the cold sprays that seemed to come from everywhere, teasing at her already sensitive skin. She had to get her head back on straight, was what she had to do. She had to shower, find her clothes, make up some sort of excuse and get the hell out of here.

If she didn't go, now, she'd never want to leave. As it was, she was fairly certain that the memory of last night, of Court Becket and his bottomless brown eyes, the wild abandon they'd shared, would haunt her for the rest of her life.

MONDAY, 4:16 A.M.

"No. Not yet, not yet, you idiot…don't leave yet, don't go…" Jade pleaded, keeping her eyes firmly closed, trying to recapture the dream. No, not a dream. A memory. Her life, the one she'd had within her grasp and then so carelessly thrown away.

She gave up and opened her eyes, silently cursing the ringing phone that had awoken her, sparing one of her choicest swear words for Court, who seemed to think nothing of doing business in the middle of the night. The least he could do was answer the damn phone.

"Four o'clock?" she muttered, aiming her outstretched arm toward the nightstand. Her fingers closed on the receiver and she pulled the phone onto the bed with her as she fell back against the pillows. "Mr. Becket will be with you in a moment," she half slurred into the phone, praying she was right. Otherwise, she'd have to get up and go hunt Court down. And then kill him.

"Which one are you?"

Jade pulled the phone away from her ear and squeezed her eyes shut tight for a moment, hoping she'd feel more awake when she opened them again. The voice was deep, most probably male and obviously disguised by one of those electronic devices anyone could pick up on eBay. Probably the same guy who had called before, the one Matt's friend Ernesto had thought was a kid playing phone pranks.

Fully awake now, Jade held the phone to her ear once more. "Screw you," she said, and then winced. Obviously she couldn't be as awake as she thought she was. *Screw you* wasn't exactly the snappiest comeback in the books.

"Okay, you're the bitchy one. Jade, right? Not the actress? I'll bet most of your callers want to talk to the actress. Too bad, but as long as I have you, how about we just chat?"

"How about I just hang up and you go seek professional help?"

The caller went on as if Jade hadn't said anything. "Brains are messy, aren't they, Jade? They hit that knotty-pine paneling, and then they slide down it, the bits that don't get hung up on the pieces of skull stuck in the wood like shrapnel. No, never mind. You don't have to answer me.

You know how it looks, Jade, don't you? You saw how it works."

Jade quickly covered her mouth with her hand, afraid she might vomit. Then she took it away and sucked in a lungful of air, letting it out again slowly. She had to calm down, refuse to let this guy get to her. They'd had a million phone calls since Jessica had the bright idea of putting their number on the air during her news-magazine show, asking for help from the public. What they'd gotten were whack-jobs. One good lead with Melodie's shampoo tech, granted. But most of the calls were like this one, complete with electronic voice disguisers. So many sick tickets out there with time on their hands. "And *you'd* know this how?"

"How do you think I know?"

She should just hang up, but she was too angry. "Are you confessing to killing my father? Hey, terrific. But first tell me what you did with Jimmy Hoffa. Is he really buried beneath the goalposts at the Meadowlands?"

"Back off, shut down that smart mouth of yours, or else I'll *show* you how I did it. I can get at you, any one of you, anytime I want. For instance, do you know where your blond-bimbo sister is right now? I do. Should I reach out and touch her, or are you going to behave?"

Okay. This had never been funny, but now it was turning ugly, and Jade was beginning to get a cold, sick feeling in the pit of her stomach, because she *didn't* know where Jessica was right now. She was already half out of the bed when her bedroom door opened and Court stepped inside, a cordless phone to his ear. He lifted one finger to his lips and then motioned to her to keep talking, keep the caller on the line.

"It's a little late at night for fairy tales," she said as she subsided back onto the bed, her eyes on Court as he advanced across the room toward her and squeezed her outstretched hand. "Or should we just call that threat what it is—you're blowing smoke."

"Am I? Do you really want to find out?"

Oh, my God oh, my God oh, my God. Jade began to rock back and forth on the bed as Court put down the cordless and fished his cell phone out of his pants pocket. She knew what he was doing. He was calling Jessica's cell, or Matt's. *Hurry hurry hurry. Make her answer make her answer.*

"All right, you've got my attention now, so talk to me," Jade told the caller, clutching at anything she could think of to say, hoping to keep the monster on the line. Joshua Brainard? Was she talking to Joshua Brainard? No, that wasn't likely. What were the odds? Jess had said something about the whole world knowing something soon. Whatever she and Matt had done, were doing, might already be public knowledge. "Why are you calling me? What do you want?"

"You know what I want. I want you and your sisters to stop digging where you shouldn't be digging. Parading yourself all over television and the newspapers, crying about your poor dead daddy. A person could get hurt sticking her nose where it doesn't belong. Your old man is dead. You don't really want to join him, do you?"

Court smiled and held his cell phone to Jade's free ear.

"Hello? I said, *hello!* Do you have any idea how scary it is to hear a phone ring at four in the morning, Jade? Damn it, Jade, talk to me, and if someone isn't bleeding to death, I'm going to—"

Jade sagged in relief as Court pulled the phone away and walked to a corner of the room to tell Jessica what was happening. Matt was with her. Matt was a cop, he carried a gun. He'd protect her.

"Party's over," Jade said to the anonymous caller. "We won't say it hasn't been fun, you getting to play with your little electronic toy and pretend you're a real bad guy, just like in the movies, but I'm hanging up now." Jade climbed out of bed, her fears all turned to cold, hard anger.

She'd decided it was time she took control, control she had ceded to the man the moment she'd picked up the phone, and got rid of this squirrel once and for all. If it *was* Brainard, she knew where to find him. But chances were it wasn't—Brainard was too smart to play phone tag with her. "Look, hey, before I go, let me tell you something. Call here again and I'm going to make finding and prosecuting you my own personal project. You got that?"

She slammed the phone back down even as Court took her in his arms and held her trembling body close against his strength. "Good girl," he crooned into her hair. "Good girl. That had to be an idiot with a sick sense of humor. Matt warned us this could happen again. Not that the bastard didn't have me going for a minute there. I think it's that electronic disguise of the voice that makes it all sound so real."

"That's the whole point of it, to weird us out that way. I should have hung up the minute I realized it was a wacko with a hard-on for causing other people misery," she said against his chest before pushing herself away from him to begin pacing, burning off her adrenaline-burst of energy.

"It's that he had Sam's private number—that's what kept me hanging on the phone. This makes twice he's called. Not your average squirrel, like Matt said, and he really had me going, too, when he started asking if I knew where Jess was. There are some badly bent people in this world."

"Matt got on the phone with me once Jess calmed down. He said you and I are to stick here at Sam's until he gets back," Court told her, watching her from the bed. "They're in South Carolina, by the way, but they'll definitely be back tomorrow night, as promised. Tonight, actually. Or sooner, if they can get an earlier flight. Not that I hadn't already half planned to call Matt before this phone call and get him back here, in case you hadn't figured that out on your own."

"I did. But I was hoping you wouldn't do it."

Court ran his fingers through his already mussed hair. "I know how much you want to confront Brainard on your own. I was still wrestling with my conscience when our new friend called."

"Pretty much taking the decision out of your hands, at which point you told Matt everything. I understand." Jade stopped pacing to look questioningly at Court. "South Carolina? What in hell are they doing in South Carolina?"

"I'm not supposed to tell you, but they're down there meeting Matt's mother and father," Court said, smiling. "That's where his dad retired when he left the force, some rural area that took them a plane change to get to, he said. According to Matt, Jess has already charmed the socks off them, even if they had to drag themselves to the airport at midnight to pick them up. I don't understand the rush, but Matt said something about it all going public on television by tomorrow morning, anyway, just as Jess hinted to you, so he wanted to get to them first. I didn't pursue it. They're already planning the wedding, Jess and Matt's mother. Oh, and Matt sounds a little…dazed."

"I wish I'd taped her show tonight. I have a feeling it was pretty good." Jade tried to smile. She was happy for her sister, both her sisters. Out of tragedy had come Jolie's reconciliation with Sam, and Jessica's meeting Lieutenant Matthew Denby could almost be seen as Teddy reaching down from heaven to make sure his Little Princess would be taken care of now that he was gone.

Leaving her, Jade, to wish she could see the same sort of happy ending for herself. But again Teddy had left her with the responsibility, hadn't he? Just as he'd left her to find him in his— "*Oh, my God, Court.*"

Court was on his feet immediately. "Jade? You've gone white as a ghost. What's wrong, sweetheart?"

Jade began pacing once more, her mind racing. "I was only half-awake when the phone rang, still fighting off a dream I'd had about… Never mind. It's my only excuse. I was only half-awake and I was mad, not thinking clearly. How else did I miss it? He was trying to scare me, sure, but he slipped up, said too much. Cocky bastard, blowing his own horn. He said knotty pine, Court. *Knotty pine.*"

"Damn it, you're right. I heard that, too, but I didn't pick up on it. Teddy's office had knotty-pine paneling. Jesus, Jade." Court pulled his cell phone from his pocket once more. "I'm calling Matt. He needs to get back here now, even if he has to charter a plane to do it. He can do things we can't. He might even be able to find out where the bastard was calling from."

Jade raced over and closed the cell phone, torn between relief and a new urgency. "No, please don't do that. He tried doing that after the first call, and it didn't work. These guys use throw-away cell phones now and we can't trace them. Besides, it's already almost morning. You said they'll be home tonight. Don't bother them."

Court looked at her, his expression tight. "I

never thought you believed me to be stupid, Jade.
I know what you're thinking, and you're not still
doing this on your own, not after that call. Not if
I have to tie you to the bedpost."

"Don't be silly. I'm just going to talk to
Brainard, in his office, in a public place. That's all,
Court. The plan hasn't changed. What else would
I do—go in there with my six-guns blazing, like
we're in the Old West?"

"I don't know, but whatever it is, you're not
doing it. This call changes everything, and you
know it. You'll look at him, and he'll see that you
know, that you're a real, imminent danger to him,
and suddenly the target is pinned to *your* back.
He's talked to you now, he knows you're no
pushover. That surprise element you're hoping for,
charging in there and springing what you know
about Tarin White? That's all gone now, Jade. Hell,
if he's got a brain at all, he'll simply refuse to see
you."

"I can play a role. I've done it before. You've
seen me do it." Jade winced, as they both knew
she was referring to the night they'd met.
"Besides," she added quickly, "half of being a PI
is acting."

"You're not Jolie. Besides, nobody's that good
an actor. You won't let me contact the police, and

I understand why you're against that after the way you were treated the night Teddy died, which means we'll wait for Matt. So scratch any visits to Brainard's campaign headquarters, his house or anyplace he might be later today giving one of his speeches. You're not going, it's not happening. I forbid… Oh, damn. I should have quit while I was ahead, shouldn't I?"

Jade smiled at him. She couldn't believe it, but she actually felt…happy. They hadn't discussed it, but both she and Court knew what hearing the words knotty pine really meant. Just those two small words, and everything had changed. Those words meant that Teddy hadn't been alone when he died and he hadn't killed himself. The call also meant that they were getting close, really close, and it might have been Jade who'd felt spooked by the call, but it was the killer, it was Joshua Brainard, who was really spooked. She felt like rubbing her hands together in glee like a mad scientist. She felt like dancing a jig—which was stupid.

"It doesn't matter where you quit, Court, because I'm still going to do what I'm going to do. You know that. I know that. That call didn't change my plans, it just made them more urgent. We're almost there, Court. We're already looking at the right answers, and Brainard knows it. I can't not confront him—we have to end this."

"I agree that we're close. I'll give you that much."

"Good. So, please, let's not argue. Although, if you want me to yell at you, you could always try that 'I forbid it' line again. Now excuse me, I'm going to go shower and look over the files one last time. I'm betting we have more of the answers, more of the puzzle pieces, than we think we do, more fact than conjecture. I can't sleep anymore, anyway. Besides, don't you have phone calls to make?"

"I do, unfortunately," Court said, and sighed. He looked rumpled, and worried, but Jade could see that his sharp mind was also considering the ramifications of the phone call. "He did say it. I heard him. Knotty pine. He could have said 'the wall,' or even just 'paneling,' but he was specific."

"And, according to the decorating magazines, knotty pine isn't exactly a big trend out there right now."

"And probably hasn't been since the middle of the last century. Teddy's whole office was one big time warp. Brainard really slipped up with that one. What I'm not quite getting is why he's making these calls at all. I mean, what's the point?

Nobody ever backed away from something important because of a threatening phone call."

"Maybe not you, Court, not a *man*—but a woman might," Jade pointed out sarcastically. "At least that's how a man who has no real respect or regard for women might think about it. The calls make for one more nail in Brainard's coffin—something else that leads straight back to him. I'd say he's afraid of what we're doing, but even I don't completely buy that one."

"I understand. He's worried, but he still thinks he's in the driver's seat."

"His ego again, right. He thinks he committed the perfect crimes all those years ago, and again now. Reaching out to touch us, talking about seeing Teddy? That was arrogance, Court, plain and simple. And a man who can't stand not being in control, not being the one giving the orders. He almost told us who he is with this latest phone call, although I doubt that was part of his plan."

"He's someone used to being obeyed, as well, maybe used to having his name and background pave over any potholes for him."

"Exactly. That threat about Jessica was a sort of ultimatum—drop what you're doing or suffer the consequences. He had control for a while, too, until I heard Jess's voice. Then I took control back by hanging up on him. It's all shrink stuff I've read about a thousand times, the ceding and taking of power. We're not dealing with Joe Blow Average Guy here, Court. We're dealing with a man used to being in the catbird seat his entire life, giving all the orders and getting what he wants. Which again leads right back to Joshua Brainard. He fits the bill, right down to his poor opinion of women. He cheated on his wife, remember?"

"So that's what, bottom line, you think these phone calls have been about? The man is trying to control you? *You?*" Now Court smiled, but it was a self-mocking smile. "Lots of luck with that. I'm still living with the consequences of my own stab at offering you an ultimatum. And no, we probably don't want to go there right now, so I'll shut up."

"Who says men aren't intuitive?" she quipped, trying to smile. This was no time for ancient history. But the time was coming, and they both knew that. In some strange way, Teddy's death, the old cases, Brainard's imminent arrest for murder, they were all preludes to the main event. At some point, she and Court had to talk about the past. Only then could they consider a future.

He leaned in and kissed her cheek. "You'll be all right? We have an agreement here? No ditching me and sneaking down the back staircase and out into the foggy, early-morning darkness, swirling your cape as you head off to confront Joshua Brainard on your own?"

"Last time I had to do a pinky-swear was with Jess, when she was eleven. Yes, I promise."

"I'd ask what a pinky-swear is, but it's probably a girl thing, right?"

"Pretty much. And I haven't been entirely honest with you. I checked on the Internet, and Brainard isn't scheduled to appear in public until seven-thirty tonight. We have all day to get through before anybody swirls any capes."

"So Matt and Jess will most probably be back by then. And you made me go through all that business about warning you not to try anything on your own?"

Jade nodded, feeling almost childish. "Yeah. You're cute when you're concerned. I mean, I could have done without that 'I forbid it' part, but the rest was pretty nice. I, uh, I like when you care. It's nice."

"No, Jade. It's love," Court said quietly. He was silent for a moment while she felt herself longing to melt into his arms. "Okay, then. I'll see you downstairs at seven."

"If Mrs. Archer isn't up yet, I'll make us some

bacon and eggs," Jade promised as she lifted her hand in a halfhearted wave. Once Court was gone, she grabbed clean underclothes from a drawer and half ran for the bathroom, feeling the need to wash away the fear she'd felt when she'd thought Jessica might be in danger. She shouldn't have let Brainard be the one in control, not even for a moment.

"Always be the one pulling the strings, Jade, honey, never the one dancing to someone else's tune at the end of them," Teddy had told her more than once when he'd explained the balance of power as it applied to the way he'd worked suspects during his years on the police force. She had the strings now, nearly all of them, Jade believed, and it was time to make Joshua Brainard dance to her tune.

Daylight couldn't come soon enough for her, and the all-day wait until Brainard's first public appearance at his seven-thirty rally seemed light-years in the future. Still, she had to prepare, as well as find a way to fill the hours. She'd read those damn files so often she knew most of them by heart. She'd give them one more shot, but she couldn't face another day of doing nothing but reading them again.

She had a command of the facts now. She'd

filled in any blanks with supposition and intuition. She'd practiced a killer opening line for when she confronted Brainard, sure, but after that she was prepared to simply wing it, go where Brainard took her for a while and then lead him where she needed him to go.

She'd save the Baby in the Dumpster for her coup de grâce, hit him right where he lived. No quarter, as Teddy would crow, no mercy.

So maybe, to kill some time, she'd do a little more work on the Scholar Athlete case, the one she'd chosen when she and Jess and Jolie had first divided up the cold cases. Jermayne Johnson haunted her, the sad, lost little boy still residing deep inside that huge, mostly grown-up body. If she needed closure about Teddy's death, how Jermayne must have been longing for the same thing in his brother's case this past decade and more.

Yes, that was what she'd do. She'd take another run at Jermayne, press him to remember more about the friends his brother, Terrell, had run with before he was killed, things like that. People knew, remembered, more than they thought they did. It was just a matter of coming at them from the right angle. You could ask the same question a dozen times and not be happy with the answer, and then, the thirteenth time, trying yet another approach, you could hit pay dirt.

Court could go with her, since he was feeling so protective of her. She had a feeling he'd be like gum on the bottom of her shoe until Joshua Brainard was arrested.

Then again, Court Becket, rich and powerful, also liked being in control. That was why they'd fought. That was why they'd both won their last argument, just as they'd both also lost it.

Jade had already begun stripping out of her pajamas when she caught a glimpse of herself in the mirror over the sink and stopped, approached the glass.

Who was this woman? Her hair long and straight, with no hint of curl because the curling iron had broken and she hadn't bothered to buy a new one. When was that? A year ago?

Jade touched a hand to her cheek, her too-thin cheek. She unbuttoned her no-nonsense cotton pajamas and pushed back the material to see the hollows around her collar bone, actual concave scoops. Thin might be in, but not this thin. When was the last time she'd had an appetite?

Tipping her head to one side, Jade continued the inventory. Eyes, huge but dull. Her complexion almost muddy. She leaned in close to the mirror, tracing what looked to be fine lines forming between her nose and mouth. She didn't wear foundation or powder. She didn't even bother with face creams or sunscreen. And it showed.

She was only eleven months older than Jolie, and Jolie looked a good five years younger.

Where was the young, carefree Jade, the girl she had been? Where was the well-loved woman she'd seen in the mirror at Court's hotel the morning after their first night together? Where had that woman gone?

Was there any way to get her back? Any way to get back what she'd lost?

"It doesn't matter," she told her reflection. "Nothing matters now but proving Joshua Brainard murdered Teddy. Nothing and no one can matter. Not me, not Court, not the past and not the future. Just the *now*. You got that?"

Jade turned away from the mirror, unable to lie to herself face-to-face.

Changing her mind about the shower, she returned to the bedroom to pull on cotton-knit shorts and a sleeveless top, and headed down to Sam's exercise room, intent on running a couple of miles on the treadmill.

If only the treadmill was a time machine, and

the faster she ran, the more the calendar flipped backward, until she'd returned to those first days after she'd met Court. Then, this time, she could move forward without making all the same dumb mistakes.

SOMEWHERE ALONG
BOATHOUSE ROW

JADE'S RIGHT running shoe found a shallow, slushy puddle as she was forced to move to the edge of the trail by a quartet of joggers decked out in brand-new jogging gear and iPods, and carrying containers of take-out frou-frou coffees.

Joggerettes, Jade called them, not really here for the exercise, but just to see and be seen. The four women had fanned themselves out across the running trail of the east bank of the Schuyl-kill River, along historic Boathouse Row, paying more attention to the men jogging by in the opposite direction than on where they were going.

"Amateurs," Jade muttered under her breath as, avoiding any more puddles, she redirected her attention to the asphalt. She touched her gloved right hand to her left wrist to check her pulse, and picked up her pace.

It was cold this morning, typical Philadelphia winter weather, but the sky seemed higher than it had when she first got to Fairmont Park, so chances were that the snow the TV weatherman had warned of earlier wouldn't come.

She was good on time, her routine telling her that if she'd just passed the Vesper Rowing Club boathouse, she'd be able to get in at least most of her usual run before meeting Teddy at the diner to discuss how they were going to approach their latest insurance case.

Their client was convinced that their insured's employee, one Maude Landers, was faking the debilitating back injury that had them paying through the nose for the past two years. Insurance companies were like that, all of them believing that if a PI just hung out up a tree with a video camera at the ready, he'd be sure to discover the so-called injured party bench-pressing a Buick in their backyard.

Since Teddy was the glad hand part of the Sunshine Detective Agency, a little too old for scut-type field work, Jade was left to be the one hanging out in that tree.

Jade didn't realize it, but her feet were pounding the trail harder as her frustration made its way down her body and out through them. Not that she hated her job or hated working with her father. But at times it all seemed so... Stupid wasn't the right word, but it was close.

She knew she was good at her job. She simply didn't have the same drive Teddy had, feel the same joy at that *gotcha* moment when a straying husband was caught on tape, or a computer background check showed up an undisclosed DUI arrest, or a devastated mother had to be told that it was a beloved son who had copped her family-heirloom silver to feed his meth addiction.

There were exceptions. Serving Harvey What's-His Name the other night had been one of them. The guy had been ducking process servers for six weeks, leaving behind his house in the suburbs as he hopscotched from hotel to hotel all over the Delaware Valley. But she'd found him, she'd run him down, and the check would clear soon, making Teddy happy.

Or as happy as Teddy got during the slow times—now, and again in June—when business always slacked off and he went back to his cold cases from the time he was on the force and took another shot at cracking them. Nobody beat the Irish at being emotional, and Teddy was Irish to his marrow. He could joke better, laugh harder and then turn around and sulk with more dedication than anyone Jade knew.

She checked her pulse again as the last of the ten landmark boathouses were behind her, and was surprised to realize her heart was pounding as hard as it was.

"Don't think, just run. Run, so you don't think."

She repeated her mantra several times as she looked out over the river, noticed the thin skim of ice doing its best to build out from the Schuylkill's banks. She reached up to adjust her wool Eagles headband—the one with the famous football-team logo, the bald eagle, emblazoned on both earflaps—more firmly down around her ears, and nearly lost her footing when a patch of black ice on the asphalt seemed to sneak up on her.

"Got you," she was assured by someone who grabbed her elbow for a moment. "There you go. You're all right."

"Thanks, I…" She turned her head to look at her rescuer. "Court?"

He was dressed all in black, light green neon reflecting patches picking up the glint of early morning sun as he moved along beside her, easily matching her stride for stride. His dark hair was only moderately contained by the plain black headband he wore, and his dark eyes were hidden behind reflective wraparound sunglasses. "That's encouraging. You remember my name."

Jade concentrated on the ground ahead once more. "I said I'd call."

"That was three days ago, Jade. I have to leave town tonight, get back to Virginia. The staff are beginning to look at me funny, thinking I'm here to close the hotel or do mass firings or something."

"You're leaving?" She fought against the sudden, involuntary flip of her stomach. "Well, of course you are. You've got a…an empire to run, don't you?"

She could feel his gaze on her. "Are you going to tell me that bothers you?"

"No, of course not. I'm just saying, Philadelphia isn't your home base, or whatever you want to call it. That's in Virginia?"

"With the marvels of technology, my home base is anywhere I am at the moment. But Virginia is my home, yes. You'll love it there."

Jade shook her head. "You know, Court, you're beginning to sound like a stalker. Should I be worried?"

"Tell me to go away, Jade, and I'll go. I won't like it, but I'll go. What I couldn't seem to do was leave without seeing you again. You can pick up the pace if you want. I don't turn white and clutch at my chest for at least another five miles."

"Is that right?" She decided to test him. "Do you know how to get to the Art Museum from here? To the *Rocky* statue? Good. I'll meet you there."

"How about I *wait* for you there? Winner gets to pick where we go for breakfast," he shot back, even as he lengthened his stride, easily pulling away from her before she could mentally shift gears and take off after him.

She watched as his long, leanly muscled body effortlessly sliced through the cold morning air. He wasn't running at top speed, but pacing himself, probably so he could save something for an impressive sprint as they neared the statue.

She could live with that. If he ran up the steps

to the Art Museum, then danced around in a cheesy Rocky Balboa imitation as so many others did, however, she might have to pretend she didn't know him.

Which, she told herself, wincing inwardly, she didn't. She'd slept with him, but she didn't know him. She'd called Jolie out in California, but her sister had never met Sam's cousin, so that had been no help.

The Internet, however, had filled in a lot of blanks.

Court Becket was a man with his fingers deep in many profitable pies, not just the Becket Hotels. Age thirty-three, never married, graduated near the top of his class at one of Virginia's best universities, where he'd also played first base on the baseball team. Served on the board of directors of a hospital, a bank and a historical preservation not-for-profit organization.

Add a perfect example of *tall, dark and handsome* to that, along with those fantastic eyes, his sincere-looking smile and his expertise as a lover, and was it any wonder that Jade hadn't called him? He was so far out of her league, they didn't even exist in the same universe.

For a moment, as Court disappeared around a bend in the trail, Jade considered stopping, turning around and heading back the way she'd come. But that was the coward's way out. Besides, if he'd found her here, he could probably find her anywhere.

So now she knew he was tenacious. And competitive. Traits she admired in herself, but sometimes not in others. Court Becket liked to win. He might even expect to win.

"But not today, buddy," she gritted out from between clenched teeth as she put everything she had into catching Court before they got to the *Rocky* statue.

She would probably never know if she'd actually outrun him, or if he'd let her win, but she made it to the statue a good ten seconds before he did, to stand there, bent over, her palms on her knees, trying to regulate her breathing. "I'll have…I'll have orange juice and a…and a cinnamon raisin bagel from the cart at the other end of Boathouse Row. No cream cheese. Your treat."

The man didn't look as if he'd even broken a sweat. "That's not breakfast, Jade. That's not anything even remotely *like* breakfast. We still have to get back to where we started. By then, I expect nothing less than eggs, bacon, potatoes and two pieces of toast."

Jade lifted her head, her ponytail slapping around her neck, and smiled at him. "You run, and then you stuff yourself with all of that saturated fat and cholesterol?"

"I run so that I *can* stuff myself with all of that saturated fat and cholesterol," he told her as they began to jog back the way they'd come. "Did I mention that I'd really like some pancakes to go with the eggs and bacon and potatoes? I'll get some blueberries on top. Blueberries, you know, are very good for you. So the one pretty much cancels out the other, or at least enough to fool my conscience."

"I hate to say this, but that all is beginning to sound pretty good. All right, you've convinced me. Now you pick the restaurant."

"Food quality and service are the hallmarks of Becket Philadelphia. And I hear the room service is outstanding."

Jade shot him a quick look as they kept their pace measured, not too slow, but not fast enough to keep them from speaking to each other. "Nice try. No. Besides, I have to get to work."

"And I'm scheduled to fly out of here at three, so I'm not going to back off now, Jade. Besides, it's New Year's Eve. Nobody works on New Year's Eve."

"The Sunshine Detective Agency does. I'm wrapping up a job today."

"Then I'll help you. We need to talk, Jade. I could follow you home while you shower and change."

"Not really. Today, these are my working clothes. And thanks, but you wouldn't like the job. Hey, would you like a short history lesson on Boathouse Row as we pass the boating clubs? All ten buildings are on the National Historical Preservation list, or whatever it's called."

"Good for them. I want to kiss you."

She kept her eyes averted, concentrated on

the boathouses as they jogged past them, each with its own distinctive architecture. "Twenty-five years or so ago, the boathouses were getting pretty run-down, and there was talk that they should all be replaced."

"All over. The only question is, where to start?"

"But this guy, this architectural-lighting-designer guy—I forget his name—he came up with the idea of outlining all the boathouses with white lights. Lights around every pitched roof and dormer and window. At night, those lights reflect in the Schuylkill. You've seen it, right, how this whole area looks at night?"

"Why didn't you call me, Jade?"

"Of course, everyone went crazy over how terrific the boathouses looked, and the next thing you knew, they were getting repaired, and then came the National Historical Preservation thing, and now the lights are all that new LED type, and they can glow different colors depending on the time of year. You know, like red and green for Christmas and…and I didn't know what to say to you."

Court put his hand on her arm, gently slowing them both to a walk as they neared the line of cars parked along Kelly Drive. "'Hello' would have been good for starters."

Jade knew he was right. She'd been stupid. "Hello for starters," she said, trying to keep her voice light. "Remember me? I'm your one-night stand."

They'd reached her car, which Court seemed

to know, and he turned her around to face him. "Insult me if you feel the need, but don't do that to yourself."

"I'm sorry, Court. But you could have called, too, you know? The phone works both ways."

He let go of her arm. "I did call. Several times. Didn't the guy who answered give you my messages?"

Jade fumbled in her runner's wallet for her car key. The man who answered? There was only one man at the Sunshine Detective Agency; it was a father/daughter operation. "No…no, I guess he didn't. I…I've been out of the office a lot the past few days. So, uh, how did you track me down?"

Court grinned, and Jade's stomach did another one of those little flips. "Why, Ms. Sunshine, do you really expect me to divulge professional secrets?"

"You're not a private investigator."

"No, but you are. So how would you have done it?"

Jade rolled her eyes. "Sam. You asked Sam. He knows where I live. He knows I go running here three mornings a week."

Court held open the car door for her. "Very good. Now, where are we going for this power breakfast we're to have?"

"I've got a job in the Kensington area today, so it may as well be the Aramingo Diner. We can meet there."

"Sorry, you lost me. Where's the Aramingo Diner?"

Jade couldn't help teasing him. "Why, on Aramingo Avenue, of course."

"Not funny." He pointed down the street. "That's mine, the black SUV between the other two black SUVs. Give me a minute, and I'll follow you."

She watched him as he jogged along the street on the way to his vehicle. If she got in her car now and simply drove away...he'd simply come after her. Besides, she had a phone call to make.

Slipping behind the wheel, she opened the glove compartment and pulled out her cell phone, hit a number on her speed dial. "Teddy? Forget meeting for breakfast, okay? I've decided I'm going to head straight from Boathouse Row to Kensington. Oh, and while I've got you, do you want to tell me why you didn't give me Court Becket's messages?"

The voice on the other end of the line was bluff, affectionate and laced with guile. "*Court* Becket? Don't know the name, honey, sorry. I thought it was Sam Becket, Jolie's friend. I told him she wasn't here. So that wasn't Sam Becket? Ah, sweetheart, your Teddy's getting old. Soon I'll be walking around with one of those hearing-aid things and saying, 'Hey, what'd you say, sonny?' Like those mopheads said, will you still love me when I'm all of sixty-four?"

"Those mopheads were the Beatles, which you should know better than me, and close enough,"

Jade said, fitting the earpiece of the cell phone into her ear as she pulled out into morning traffic, having checked to see that Court was behind her now. "Don't do that again, Teddy. Don't screen my calls or make my decisions for me. I'm not Jolie. Don't try to pull things behind my back."

"Now I don't know what you're talking about, little girl," Teddy soothed back at her, "although another father might be crushed to think his favorite daughter was thinking bad things about him or his motives. I love my girls."

"I know you do, Teddy. I'm sorry. What are you doing?"

"Me? I've started a big pot of ham-and-cabbage soup for us to celebrate the New Year, sweetheart, so why don't you swing by Millie's on your way home and bring us some of her lovely crusty sour dough rolls. Millie's getting pretty sour herself in her advancing years, but those rolls are still calling to me. Still, give her my love. She'd be crushed if you didn't, and it might earn us a baker's dozen. Where did you say you're off to now?"

"The insurance claim in Kensington," Jade said, giving up the battle; clearly she wasn't going to get any more out of Teddy about the phone calls from Court. "I'm getting into some major traffic now, Teddy, so I'll check in with you later."

Jade glanced into her rearview mirror so that she could see if Court was still behind her—and so that she didn't have to think about her conversation with Teddy. His favorite daughter? No, she didn't believe that one.

Jolie thought the sun rose and set on Teddy. Teddy thought the sun rose and set on Jessica. And Jade? Jade knew where she fell into the mix.

She had been designated, not the talented dreamer or the delightful baby of the family, but the reliable one, the one who just kept putting one foot in front of the other no matter what. Water rolled off her back, Teddy always said. Nothing fazed her, nothing stopped her, she wasn't at all silly or sensitive. She knew her duty and she did it.

So far, Jade had been fine with that. She'd accepted her place in the Sunshine family after her mother ran off, even took secret pride in the idea that she was indispensable to all of them, Teddy most especially.

She checked the rearview mirror again to make sure Court Becket was still back there.

She didn't want to lose him.

MONDAY, 7:12 A.M.

"I DIDN'T KNOW you ate home fries, Jade, let alone knew how to cook them," Court said, aiming a loaded fork toward his mouth once more. "Eggs, over light, just the way I like them, bacon, home fries, wheat toast with blueberry jam. What's the occasion?"

Jade sat across from Court at a small table on the flagstone terrace, the morning sun already warning that the day would be unusually warm for late Junc. "It's going to be a long day. I thought we should fill up when we can," she told him, but she didn't look at him as she said it.

Court let it go. He remembered the last time they'd had a breakfast like this one, but he was smart enough not to go down memory lane with Jade this morning. So he'd push at her, yes, but in another way. "A long day spent cooling your heels, waiting for Brainard's campaign appearance tonight, I agree. Because we are waiting for that, and for Matt and Jessica, correct?"

"I can't just sit here and do nothing, Court. I thought we could go back to the car wash and talk to Jermayne one more time. You don't have to go with me. Oh, and Jess texted me at some point in the middle of the night, although I didn't see it until this morning. She wants us to pick up Ernesto and his luggage and bring him back here. I'm guessing Matt's afraid his protégé might find a way to get himself in trouble again if he stays home. Oh, and I'm to make sure Ernesto brings the pets with him. I guess Matt bought another fish to keep Mortimer company. So say goodbye to this empty house, because it's going to fill up again tonight. Jess, Matt, Ernesto, goldfish."

"I don't mind. I like Ernesto. Kids like him always have a hard time, no matter where they live. He's simply too smart to make his peers comfortable. I made some calls to a few friends the other day, by the way, and I've set up a tour of some FBI facilities in Virginia later this summer. After all, if Ernesto is going to run the place someday, he may as well learn where the men's room is, right?"

Jade smiled at him over the rim of her coffee cup. "That was very nice of you, Court. Ernesto will be over the moon."

Court finished his last strip of bacon. "I don't like that the kid got mixed up in what's going on here, and neither does Matt. That wasn't a fun ride we all took him on last week. I thought we should thank him in some way."

"I'd say you found the right gift," Jade said, picking up her plate and coffee cup. "I'll clean this up for Mrs. Archer and then meet you outside, all right? Five minutes?"

"Sounds good. Hang on," Court said as his cell phone vibrated in his pocket. He pulled it out and looked at the number. "Morgan Eastwood. I was wondering when we'd hear from her again. I wonder if she's back in England now."

"Find out," Jade said, turning for the door to the house. "And say hello for me."

Court watched Jade walk away, shaking his head at the sizzle and crackle of tension that surrounded his uptight ex-wife almost visibly, and then hit a button on the cell phone and put it to his ear. "Good morning, Morgan, or good afternoon, depending on where you are. Any luck with solving our ancestor's mystery? What was that? We've got a bad connect— Oh, from the plane? All right, certainly. No, no problem. We've nothing planned for the day and were looking for ways to kill time, so this is perfect. Give me the time again. Yes, I'm familiar with the terminal. We'll see you then."

He snapped the cell phone closed and slipped it back into his pocket before picking up his own dishes and heading for the kitchen.

This was going to be interesting.

"Jade? Morgan's landing here later this morning and would like us to visit with her between plane changes. Just for an hour or so. She's also somehow arranged for a private meeting area just outside the security check-in. I said we were fine with that."

Jade turned away from the sink, where Mrs. Archer was rinsing the dishes. "Excuse me? You told her what?"

Court smiled, knowing he'd just thrown down a gauntlet, knowing Jade knew that, as well. "I knew you'd like that. You did speak with her on the phone, and she has invited all of us to come to Becket Hall for this treasure-hunt idea of hers. And we do have the day to kill, right?"

Jade looked over her shoulder at Mrs. Archer, and then headed out of the kitchen. "You're half-right. I could kill *something,*" she muttered as she passed Court.

"You know, Jade, I don't understand why our marriage didn't work. We get along so well."

"Very funny," she said as they entered the living room, and then she looked down at her navy slacks and green-and-white-striped knit top. "I dressed for helping Ernesto with the fish and for the car wash. How the hell do I dress to meet your English cousin?"

She was so seldom flustered, or at least she usually didn't let her guard down enough to let anyone, most especially him, see that she was flustered. "Oh, nothing fancy, Jade. A... What do they call those sweaters they wear? I've got it, a twinset. A nice twinset and pearls, and maybe white gloves? And you don't shake hands, you curtsy."

Jade's eyes narrowed. "And maybe, if I ask her nicely, she'll agree to order one of her henchmen to chop off your head. Then I could carry it with me everywhere in a wicker basket, like Sir Walter Raleigh's widow did. Seriously, Court, I don't know that I'm up to...socializing right now. Actually, the timing couldn't be worse, and you know it."

"Not really, Jade. You were looking for a way to fill the hours, and now we've got one. Granted, I could have thought of another way, one that didn't include leaving this house, but since I know that isn't going to happen, why not go out to the airport and say hello to Cousin Morgan?"

"All right, I give up. But let's leave now, so

we have time to talk to Jermayne before we head out there."

"Now as in right now? You're not going to change first?"

"You said I looked fine the way I am," Jade said, putting a hand to her throat as if checking for the string of pearls that wasn't there.

"You do. It's just nice when you let the female side out once in a while."

Jade went over to the coffee table and picked up her shoulder bag. "Are you insinuating now that I try to act like a man?"

"A man? Never that, trust me. I know you're all woman. It's just that sometimes I think you try to forget that."

"And try to think I'm a man."

"No, sweetheart. And try to think you're a machine. All performance, with no feelings, no desires, no wants and needs of its own."

"Damn it, Court, I don't—"

He held up his hands in surrender. "You don't need this now. I remember. When will you need it, Jade? Wasn't that phone call last night enough for you? When will you admit to needing anything? Or anyone?"

"When this is over. I've told you that, Court," Jade said, blinking rapidly. "I'm not a machine.

When this is over, when Teddy's cleared and can rest in peace, I want my own life."

"Did you hear what you just said, sweetheart?"

She winced. "Back. I meant I want my own life *back*. Oh, hell, don't look at me like that. When you're ready, I'll be outside."

Court watched her head toward the foyer. "You're beginning to figure it out, Jade, sweetheart, aren't you?" he said quietly, shaking his head. "You're finally starting to see Jade, and not just the reflection of Teddy's vision of you, the Jade he tried so selfishly to build."

CLEARFIELD STREET, KENSINGTON

"SO TELL ME exactly what you hope to see here," Court said as he sat in the passenger seat of her three year-old compact. They were halfway down the street from the brick row house with the bright red *Go Phillies* flag hanging out front, over the sidewalk.

Jade had been wondering if she didn't smell like a person who had just run four miles, and why she'd agreed to allow Court to join her on the job. "What? Oh, what am I hoping to see? Maude Landers doing cartwheels down her front steps and on her way to the corner bar for a wake-up bourbon on the rocks, I suppose. That would be nice and easy. Unfortunately, that hasn't happened so far."

"So far?" He motioned to the camera resting in her lap. "How long have you been tailing this woman?"

"This is it, last day of the year, last day on this job. One more look-see and we report to the insurance company that Maude is just what she says she is. Permanently disabled. Teddy found out she's suing her employer for five million."

"Teddy. That would be your father, correct? Why do you call him Teddy, if I might ask?"

Jade shrugged. "My youngest sister started it when she was about three, I guess. Mom called Dad Teddy, so Jessica, who parroted anything anyone else said, started calling him Teddy, as well. Well, she called him Ted-Ted until she got it right, but then she wouldn't stop and he thought it was cute that his Little Princess was calling him Teddy. So we all did."

"And your mother didn't mind?"

"My mother? She called him simple-sh— No, she didn't mind. I don't know if she even noticed." Jade raised the camera as a screen door opened down the street, but then lowered it again. It wasn't Maude's screen door, but the one on the house next door. "This could take a while, you know. She leaves the house every day, but the time varies between nine and noon or so. And then I have to follow her. Didn't you say you have to fly back to Virginia today?"

"I'll get there when I get there. It's just a dinner party that happens to come with noisemakers, funny hats and some people who don't want to start the new year sober. Believe me, it wouldn't break my heart to miss most of it," Court answered. "I'd much rather talk about the weekend. May I send my plane for you? I'd like you to see my home."

Jade, panicked, latched on to the first thing he'd said. "Your plane? You own your own plane?"

"Technically, it's the Becket plane, as in Becket, Incorporated, as in available for use by any of the companies under the Becket umbrella, but I do end up using it more than anyone else. Sam owns his antique business outright, an inheritance from his father outside the company, and I hold the majority of shares in Becket Hotels. Everything else falls under the larger heading, which could prove difficult if there were more of us, but Sam and I are the only ones left, as far as we know. Only children, both of us."

"I didn't get to know Sam well enough to learn anything about his family, other than that his parents are deceased."

"Mine, as well. I understand the Beckets were a pretty large clan two hundred years ago when they arrived here from England. But there were some typical family falling-outs, at least typical during the Civil War—things nobody would talk about—and then some of them listened to Horace Greeley's advice to 'Go West, young man, and grow up with the country.'"

"And you're not curious? You don't want to find any of these relatives? You know, there are genealogy sites all over the Web these days. We've used some of them to help estate lawyers track down missing heirs, things like that."

Court looked at her, his brown eyes twinkling. "Is that right? So that means I could *hire* you?"

She leaned past him to get a better view of the street. "Yes, I suppose so. Okay, here she comes. Where are we going today, Maude? Grocery store at one end of the block, bar at the other. You have to love Philadelphia. Ah, she's got that telltale mesh shopping bag attached to the front of her walker. I guess she's out of the staples, cigarettes and Tastykake chocolate cupcakes. Are you bored enough yet, Court, or do you want to spend the next hour watching Maude Landers thump melons at the local market?"

They both watched as Maude Landers, a heavyset middle-aged woman in a flowered dress, carefully using the folded-up walker to balance herself, closed the screen door as she stood on her tiny porch. She looked left, she looked right and then left again, as if about to cross a busy intersection, and then carefully picked her way down the few cement steps to the sidewalk.

The walker sides clicked open, Maude took her purse from her shoulder and slipped it into the mesh bag, and she was ready, she was mobile.

"Bored? On the contrary, Jade. It all sounds fascinating. How long have you been doing this?"

"This particular job? Twice a week for the past month, sometimes mornings, sometimes evenings, and thank God today's the last day, even if I couldn't nail her and she gets to collect all the money that maybe isn't owed her. This job in total? One way or another, I've been working with Teddy since I graduated high school. And no, I'm not going to tell you how long ago that was, so don't ask me."

Court frowned.

"What? Something's bothering you. You're ready to leave?" Jade knew it was a stupid question. Of course he wanted to leave. When a person had to choose between a private jet and all this…glamour, who would stick around?

"No, I'm just thinking. You're telling me that you've been watching this woman for a month, and she's never done any backflips, gone dancing, climbed a ladder to wash her windows—nothing? Did it ever occur to you that the woman isn't faking, that she's really disabled?"

"It is possible, yes. But Maude had a falling-out with her sister, it seems, and the sister tipped off the insurance company that good old Maude is faking it. It's either sour grapes or it's true."

"What do you think?"

"I think it's true. I think Maude was lording it over her sister about how she was going to be rich and move to the suburbs, and take a cruise to Alaska or whatever, while her loser of a sister had to stick it out here in Philly through another hot, humid summer, neener-neener and all that. That's what I'm thinking. I just can't prove it."

"All right, then, let's find out. Let's go. Bring the camera."

"Court?" Jade fumbled with the door handle, one hand grabbing the camera and her purse, and ran around the car to meet Court on the curb. "What the *hell* are you doing?" she asked him in a fierce whisper. "I know this isn't exactly high-level covert operations, but I really don't want to be out here where she can see me. Court? Hey, don't you *shush* me."

He had held up his hand as if commanding her to silence. Not only that, but he was grinning. She didn't know which made her more angry.

"Get that camera ready."

He slipped on the mirrored, wraparound sunglasses and zipped his black jacket up all the way, so that the roll-down collar was now almost covering his mouth. "How do I look? The new breed of physically fit mugger?"

Then, before she could answer him, he grabbed her shoulders and ground his mouth against hers in a brief, fierce kiss.

"Oh, one more thing, sweetheart," he said, holding her slightly away from him as she tried to catch her breath, "we'd better pray that your hunch is right, and that there aren't any of Philadelphia's finest around. Maybe you'd better keep the motor running."

"I don't believe this," Jade said as she watched Court turn and begin jogging down the sidewalk in the direction Maude Landers had taken. "I do not freaking *believe* this. The man is insane."

Still, she snapped off the lens cap, checked that the time and date stamps were correct and then raised the camera, ready to snap photographs of whatever happened next.

What happened next was that Court, keeping up his steady jogging pace, edged up beside Maude and her walker, deftly reached into the mesh bag and pulled out the shoulder purse.

"Hey! Stop! Stop, thief!" Maude Landers screeched in that timeworn cliché of victims everywhere. "*Somebody!* Stop that guy, he's got my purse! Damn it, somebody help me!"

In this particular neighborhood in the City of Brotherly Love, Maude should have known better. Or maybe she did.

She hesitated for all of about two seconds, and then tossed the walker to the sidewalk and took off after Court like Yogi Bear hot on the tail of an overflowing picnic basket.

Jade could barely stop laughing long enough to shoot frame after frame of Maude Landers chasing Court, who was hotfooting it down the sidewalk. Then he stopped, handed the purse to the pursuing Maude, appeared to say something to her, made a quick U-turn and headed back toward Jade, waving her back to the car as he ran.

She hopped in before he did and had the car already in gear by the time he had collapsed into the seat, laughing like a loon.

"Did you get it? Did you get her on film?"

"I got it, you idiot," Jade replied as she made two quick left turns, heading them out of Kensington as quickly as possible. "You said something to her, didn't you? What did you say to her?"

Court unzipped his jacket and removed his sunglasses. "I told her she might want to cancel that cruise to Alaska. Oh, and to have a happy New Year. I think my sense of direction is getting better. If we turn right here, it should be a pretty straight shot to the hotel, correct?"

"We're turning left. Your car is in a parking garage in the complete opposite direction, remember?"

"I've got the stub. I'll send somebody later to pick it up. Turn right."

The light turned green. Jade looked in the rearview mirror and saw that nobody was behind her. "I need a shower."

"I've got one."

"I need clean clothing. I ran in these, and I can't shower and then put them back on again."

"There's a terrific boutique on the mezzanine level. Give me a list of your sizes, and someone will send up whatever you need. Next objection? We're two stubborn people, Jade. I can keep going as long as you can. But at the end of it, we both know what we want. Don't we?"

A horn honked behind her.

Jade turned right.

MONDAY, 8:34 A.M.

"Turn right at the next corner," Jade said, and then sighed in relief as she saw that the car wash was already open for business. "I suppose we may as well get Sam's car washed while we're here. You stay with the car, and I'll go hunt for Jermayne. Just pray he's here."

But instead of pulling onto the lot of the car wash, Court pulled over to the curb half a block away. "You want to try that again, Jade? From the top?"

She sighed, almost like Jolie would sigh as a teenager when asked to actually make it home before her curfew. Almost theatrically. "Jermayne's shy, and nervous. I don't want to scare him by showing up with you next to me."

"Let's review. Jermayne Johnson, as I remember him from the last time we were here, stands well over six feet tall, and he's built like an All-Pro tackle. He could probably snap me like a twig if he wanted to, shy or not, so I think he can handle being a little scared."

"Jermayne is mine, Court. I get to handle him. You understand that and you won't try to take over?"

"When have I ever done that?" He grinned like a child. "Tried to take over, I mean. That part of your two-part question."

Jade laughed softly. "Right. Silly me. What could I have been thinking? All right, but just in case you're wondering, this isn't a good-cop, bad-cop situation."

"You're right," Court said, putting the transmission into Drive once more and then parking the car in the Valet Service area of the car wash. "It's a *no*-cop situation. Not to mention a no-win situation, since you've met with Jermayne a couple of times now, Teddy stuck close to him all these years, and nobody's gotten any new information out of either little Jermayne or big Jermayne."

"I love working with optimists," Jade muttered, opening the car door as she spotted Jermayne, dressed in bright yellow coveralls that could have doubled as prison garb, which seemed reasonable, as half the car-wash employees were probably on work-release programs. At the moment, Jermayne was wiping down the hubcaps on a car parked over in the shade. "Okay, let's go."

Jermayne saw them, or sensed them, and his entire body stiffened, as if an adrenaline surge had him caught between fright and flight.

"Jermayne, hi," Jade said quickly, hoping to make up his mind for him. "We were out this way and I thought I'd stop and see if you've filled out those forms I gave you last time. School starts soon, and you don't want to be too last minute, right?"

"I tol' you, Ms. Sunshine, I ain't goin'." Jermayne spoke softly, with a touch of velvet in his voice that belied his size. "I tol' Teddy the same thing I tol' you. It's too late. I messed up in high school, I messed up bad, so there ain't no way I can cut it in no trade school. Besides, Teddy, he done enough for me and my gran, so there ain't no need to do no more, you know?"

"Teddy wanted you to go to school, learn a trade, Jermayne," Jade reminded him, suddenly weary of hearing the same excuse yet again. "He did everything but hold a gun to your head to get you to sign the papers. He wanted what's best for you. He made that promise at Terrell's funeral, and if he can't keep it, then I will."

Jermayne seemed to reel where he stood, and Jade suddenly realized what she'd said.

Terrell Johnson had been shot in the head all those years ago. Just like Teddy. Talk about your dumb choice of words.

"Look, Jermayne, I'm sorry," Jade said quickly, reaching out a hand to him. But Jermayne shook off the gesture as he stepped back, again looking as if he might turn rabbit on her and take off. "Jermayne? What's going on here? What's wrong? What are you afraid of?"

"I ain't afraid of nothin', Ms. Sunshine. I just want you to go away. I can't take this anymore. My head's all messed up. I can't sleep, I can't think, I… Just, please, Ms. Sunshine, don't come here no more."

"Driving you crazy, is she?" Court asked, smiling at Jermayne. "I'm her ex, by the way, so I know the feeling. Look, Jermayne, how about you and I go grab a soda or something and talk this over some more."

Jermayne looked at Court, but not like a drowning man who's just seen the Coast Guard cutter pulling up beside him. It was more like Court had maybe just thrown him an anchor. "Why do you all keep comin' after me? I know what you want. You want to talk about Terrell, about who mighta killed him. I don't know. I tol' Teddy a million times. *I don't know.*"

Jade and Court exchanged glances, and Jade shrugged, telling him without words that she'd run out of ideas, because she had. Jermayne wasn't just built like a brick wall. Sometimes trying to get to him was like *talking* to a brick wall.

"My friend, that cop you saw here with us the other day," Court said, "he thinks you do know something. What about that, Jermayne?"

Jade lowered her head, rolled her eyes. Brilliant. Court had to mention Matt. If the kid was scared before, he had to be near to wetting his pants now.

"So what? Cops always think we know somethin' we don't," Jermayne said, and his voice was harder now, changed enough to have Jade raising her head to look at him, see the panic— yes, it was, it was panic—that had crept into Jermayne's soft brown eyes.

She was about to ask him why he was so upset when Court did it for her, just not in the way she would have done it.

"Terrell was a bright kid, right? In school, on the basketball court. He was getting ready to leave town, wasn't he? Go off to that big Division I school, leaving the neighborhood. Getting *out*. You know, Jermayne, I know this kid, Ernesto. He's also pretty smart, and he's getting out, too, just like Terrell was going to do."

"Yeah, so?" Jermayne was looking a little more confident now. "Good for him."

"Yes," Court said, "good for him. But you know what? Not everyone Ernesto knows in the neighborhood is all that happy for him. In fact, they pretty much beat him up on a regular basis. Took his books, chased him down the street, called him names. You know."

Jermayne grinned, a huge white slash in his huge face. "Ain't nobody tried that with Terrell. He broke some heads, let me tell you that. Ain't nobody messed with Terrell. Ain't nobody that dumb. You shoulda seen him."

"Big guy, huh?" Court was gaining Jermayne's confidence, how, Jade didn't understand. It must be some man thing. "Big as you?"

"Bigger," Jermayne said, his smile turning wistful. "Taller, I mean. Kinda skinny, but strong, too, and smart. Kinda like Kobe, you know?"

"Kobe Bryant," Court said, nodding. "He came from the Philly area, too, didn't he? Hell of a basketball player, Bryant. Are you telling me Terrell was that good?"

"He coulda been," Jermayne said defensively.

"If he hadn't been shot," Court said, and Jade winced again. The tough-guy angle hadn't worked for her. Why did Court think it would work for him?

"Yeah," Jermayne said, hanging his head. "That."

"Teddy asked you all about Terrell, didn't he? Did he run with any of the neighborhood gangs, did he have a problem with anybody, did he try hitting on somebody else's girl, all that. But you were only a kid, weren't you? What, seven years old? How would you know, right?"

Jermayne pointed at Jade. "So tell *her.* Tell her I was just a kid. All I remember is that Terrell, he tol' me he was goin' away, sure, but he'd be back for me and our gran, and we'd have a big house and a whole big garage full of fancy cars and... and a swimmin' pool in the backyard. Damn, I didn't even know what a backyard was, you know? He'd laugh, Terrell would, and he'd grab me around the neck and rub his knuckles on top of my head, and he'd tell me we was gettin' *out.*"

He looked at Jade, blinked. "We was gettin' out, like that Ernesto kid. All I had to do was behave myself, go to school and wait, you know? That's all I had to do."

"Jermayne, I'm so sorry," Jade said, but she was talking to the air that rushed in to fill the spot Jermayne had just vacated, throwing his chamois rag on the ground as he took off across the parking lot, headed away from the car wash. "Oh, Court, now look what I've done. They'll fire him for leaving his job. I keep trying to make things better for him, and I've only made things worse."

Court put his arm around her. He gave her a comforting hug that didn't quite make the grade, and she was sure he knew it. "I'll go speak to the manager, explain that Jermayne had a family emergency. I'll talk him around, don't worry about it."

"And if you can't, as you said, talk the guy around? Then what, Court? You going to buy the place so Jermayne can keep his job?"

"It's a thought. I don't think we own any car washes."

"You don't think you do? You don't *know?*"

THE PENTHOUSE

"I DIDN'T KNOW I was talking to your father when I called," Court said when Jade entered the large living and dining area of the penthouse. There was even a baby grand piano in the suite, and it looked small in the expanse. A very intimidating room for a girl who lived in a small brick house on a Philadelphia side street.

"Uh-huh," Jade said, still looking around the large room.

After a hot shower, she was wrapped in a soft white terry robe with the Beckct Hotels logo stitched on the breast pocket in navy blue and gold thread. Her hair was still damp and she wasn't wearing a bit of makeup. Her skin was flawless, her bone structure delicate, yet only a fool would think she was fragile.

"But now I've had some time to think about those phone calls, and I'm wondering why he wouldn't have passed any of my messages on to you."

Jade padded over to the couch, strewn with bags and boxes bearing the name of the hotel's boutique. "He gets forgetful sometimes. What are all these bags? I need something to wear, not an entire new wardrobe."

"I just had them send up a variety, so you'd have something to choose from, that's all. Clothes, some makeup if you want it—because you don't need it—and some shoes. A pair of boots, too, I think. The manager threw in a few size twos with the size fours. She said designer clothing tends to run a little larger."

"I wouldn't know," Jade said, opening one of the boxes. "I wonder how she knew I didn't know, though. Unless the hotel grapevine works at warp speed, and they saw us coming up here."

"Does it matter?" Court asked as he sat back on the comfortable chair and crossed an ankle over his knee. "I called my pilot and told him I'd meet him at five. So, where do you want to go for lunch?"

"You're hungry again already?" Jade picked up bright fuchsia silk slacks and a white sweater top embroidered all over with small fuchsia flamingos. "I'll say this much—you wouldn't lose me in a crowd."

"I don't plan on losing you, period, and you'd

look good in a paper sack. But I will say I'm not crazy about the flamingos," Court admitted, grinning. "Try another box."

"Gladly," Jade said, replacing the flamingos and putting the lid firmly back on the box. "I'm guessing that outfit would be considered cruise wear or for vacationing in Florida." She opened another box. "Oh, these are lovely. Look, Court— real suede."

"There's artificial suede?" he asked, admiring the chocolate-brown slacks as Jade held them against her waist. "Comes from artificial cows, I guess."

Jade was inspecting the slacks. "They're completely lined, too. Real silk. I love the color, and the suede is so soft." She suddenly folded the slacks and put them back in the box. "Okay, playtime's over."

"Jade? What's wrong?"

"You don't know? I saw the price tag, Court. Before I let you send downstairs for anything, I made you promise that I would pay you back. I just didn't think I'd have to break it to Teddy that we needed to take out a second mortgage in order for me to do that."

She pulled open a bag and withdrew something lacy before shoving it back in the bag and holding it to her waist. "Okay, the underwear I'll take. That couldn't amount to more than a month's salary, but everything else? No way."

Court got to his feet and put his hand on her arm before she could retreat to the bathroom. "I want you to have those slacks, Jade, and whatever goes with them. You obviously like them, and I can't wait to see you in them. Consider them a late Christmas present. Consider all of it late Christmas presents. Anything in there that you like. Okay, not the flamingos. You want those and you're on your own."

"I'm not for sale, you know, Court," Jade said quietly, her damp hair falling around her face as she dipped her head to avoid his eyes. "And I resent your thinking that I am."

He put his bent index finger beneath her chin and gently raised her head so that she had to look at him. "And I resent that you think I'd try to buy you. We've got something here, Jade. I don't think either of us knows for certain yet exactly what that is, but can you look me in the eye and tell me you don't feel it, too?"

He watched as her eyelids fluttered closed for a second, but then she opened them again and looked him straight in the eye. Straight into his soul, or so it seemed.

"I…I was…unhappy when you didn't call,"

she said quietly, so that he had to lean in closer to hear her. "I, uh, I think I missed you."

"You think you missed me."

She sighed and he could smell the fresh scent of mint toothpaste on her expelled breath. "Oh, all right. I *know* I missed you. Which is stupid, because I barely know you."

Court rested his hands lightly on her shoulders. "But you know there's something there. Here, between us. I don't want to lose this feeling, Jade, this sense that I hadn't really been alive until I saw you the other night. I don't want to lose you. I've played my share of games, Jade, I won't lie and say I haven't. But I'm not playing games now."

"I never play games," Jade told him, slipping her hands onto his hips, the bag of lingerie sliding, unnoticed, to the floor. "I don't know how. You could hurt me very badly, Court."

He nuzzled the side of her throat, took in the clean, soapy scent of her. "Then I'd have to kill myself, because I couldn't live with the knowledge that I'd ever hurt you. And," he continued, stepping back from her, "I'm not going to rush you. Not again. Take the slacks, Jade. Please. We won't stay here, we'll go somewhere else for lunch, and then we'll just see where it goes from there. Do we have a deal?"

MONDAY, 10:03 A.M.

"JERMAYNE'S MANAGER and I made a little deal. He agreed to look the other way if Jermayne shows up for work tomorrow, and I agreed the manager needed new, LED-lit wheels with chrome spinners for his piece-of-crap red truck parked over there under that tree," Court told her as they got back in the car.

"It must be nice, having all that disposable wealth lying around in case you need to bribe somebody," Jade said, strapping on her seat belt.

"Don't knock it if you haven't tried it," Court joked, and then winced when he realized what he'd said. "Scratch that. You tried it, you didn't like it. Are you ready to go to the airport? How do I get to I-95 from here?"

Jade told him and then asked him what he'd thought they might have accomplished with Jermayne, other than almost costing him his job.

"Truth? Much as I wish I didn't have to say it,

I do think Jermayne knows more than he's saying about what happened to his brother all those years ago. I don't know what either of us said today that touched a nerve, but something did, that's for sure. We're going to have to take another run at him, and I think the next time we're going to actually break through. Let's just give him a couple of days. Long enough to calm down, but not too long, or he'll have his defenses completely built back up again."

"We? As in you and me?" Jade shook her head. "When did we become partners?"

Court eased the Mercedes onto I-95 and merged with the considerable traffic. "When did you decide to change the rules? It's how we started this whole thing, remember? Jolie and Sam got the Vanishing Bride, Jess and Matt the Fishtown Strangler. And we got Terrell Johnson, the Scholar Athlete. The way I see it, our case is still open."

"You're going to have to go back to Virginia at some point," Jade said. "Or wherever else in the world your business takes you next time. Have you thought about that?"

Court shook his head slightly. "Right now, I'm thinking about what comes next. Right now, we're on our way to see Morgan. After that, we're waiting for Jessica and Matt, and then the four of us are going to confront Joshua Brainard. After that? After that, Jade, it's you and me, with no interruptions."

"Are you sure we still have something to talk about, Court?" Jade asked quietly. "I don't know about you, but I'm not looking forward to being a two-time loser."

He reached over and touched her hand. "We're older now, Jade. Hopefully wiser." And minus the complication of Teddy Sunshine and his seeming death grip on Jade's highly developed sense of family responsibility, although Court was much too intelligent to say so out loud. "We let our hormones do most of the thinking for us the first time around."

Jade turned her hand so that their palms were touching and squeezed his fingers. "They were some pretty powerful hormones, weren't they? They still are, not that I should tell you that. But we still don't have very much in common outside of those hormones, do we?"

Court returned his hand to the steering wheel as he got ready to shoot across two lanes to the airport exit ramp. "So you're saying that if I took a vow of celibacy, you'd turn and walk away without any problem? And expect me to do the same if you took a similar vow?"

Jade rolled her eyes. "That's hypothetical, Court, not to mention idiotic. I won't dignify that with an answer."

"Maybe it is, but it's no more idiotic than saying that all we have in common is that we're good together in bed. I know where to go to get sex, Jade. I want a life partner. I want someone to have children with, grow old with, mourn me when I'm gone. I want you because I love you, and I've convinced myself that you love me, too. Where the hell do I park?"

He sneaked a peek at Jade, who was sitting with her mouth fallen open, staring at him. "I cannot believe you just said that."

"Why? I've said variations of the same thing since the day I met you."

"No. I can't believe you said all of that *now*. At the airport, with us running late, so we're probably going to have to run to meet your cousin. With no way for me to possibly answer you or argue with you or…or…you don't play fair."

Court pulled into a short-term parking space and cut the engine. He turned on the seat to look at Jade. "I know. I'm trying something new here, the blunt, head-on approach. Is it working?"

Jade just sighed, shook her head, gathered her purse and got out of the car.

HOME OF TEDDY SUNSHINE

COURT HELD the driver's-side door of the compact car for her as Jade swung her long, chocolate-suede-clad legs toward him and, with obvious reluctance, exited onto the slushy street in front of the Sunshine home.

"I could have just phoned to tell him I'd be home later," she said, not for the first time.

She'd suggested it the first time over lunch in the hotel dining room, when Court voiced his desire to meet Teddy Sunshine. She'd tried it again as she gave him directions to the house, in case he lost her in traffic as he followed her in his own vehicle. Perhaps she thought the third time would be the charm.

"We're here now," Court reminded her as they walked to the sidewalk and then to the narrow cement path leading up to the door of the only slightly shabby, midcentury brick house. "Why do you look so worried? Does he bite?"

"No, of course not," Jade said as Court put his arm around her shoulders, tucking her in close to his side. He couldn't seem to keep his hands off her and kept finding ways to touch her, even casually.

She selected one of the keys from the ring that held her car key and inserted it in the front-door lock. "I don't know why I bother," she grumbled as they both realized she had just locked the door, not unlocked it. "He never locks the door. He never puts on the alarm. Life is just one big welcome mat for Teddy."

"Good to hear. That gives me hope."

"Then cling to that hope, because I'm pretty sure it won't last," Jade said, smiling for the first time in a while.

As they stepped into the small foyer area, Court immediately came up against a mix of smells, none of them unpleasant, that reminded him of years of pot roast cooking in the oven, and of his maternal grandmother's lifelong affection for pine-oil cleaners. "It looked to me like this is a pretty quiet neighborhood."

"It is," Jade said as she stripped off her jacket and tossed it, and his, onto the back of a worn, overstuffed chair the color of overcooked spinach. "But we sometimes come up against disgruntled husbands who don't like that we've provided their wives with photographs showing them coming out of motel rooms with young blonds on their arms. Uh-oh, brace yourself."

Court looked across the living room to see a large Irish setter bounding across the carpet after entering the room through a doorway at the far side. "Nice dog" was all he got out before the animal stood on its hind legs, put his front paws on Court's chest and began trying to lick his face. "Watchdog, I take it?"

"Rockne! You know you're not allowed to do that. Come on, boy, get down. *Now,* Rockne."

"Obedient, too," Court said as he rubbed the ecstatic dog behind its floppy ears until Rockne, probably knocked off balance by his wildly wagging tail, finally backed down.

"I'm sorry about that. My sister Jessica trained him, which explains a lot if you met Jessica. Come on, let's get this over with. Teddy's in his office, and obviously knows we're here."

Court followed Jade across the carpet as Rockne led the way back the way he'd come, allowing Jade to enter the room—office? den?—ahead of him. He was suddenly just the slightest bit nervous, as the last time he'd met a date's father had been his high-school senior prom. After that, it was college girls, and then the parade of beautiful, independent, interchangeable women he met along the way. How did that Frank Sinatra song go? *At thirty-five, it was a very good year…*

He wasn't quite thirty-five, but it had been a long time since a doting father had stared him down, sized him up.

"Teddy? Sorry to bother you if you're busy, but I've brought a friend home to meet you." Court stepped forward and put out his hand. "Teddy, this is Court Becket. Court, my father, Teddy Sunshine."

"We spoke on the phone, sir, I believe," Court said, his hand not only taken by Teddy Sunshine, but nearly crushed in the man's ridiculously tight grip. "It's good to meet you."

"Nonsense, *my* pleasure," Teddy replied with a broad wink. "I like when my girls bring their little friends home."

"Teddy..." Jade said wearily, but Teddy Sunshine's booming laugh took any sting out of his words. His warning?

Teddy Sunshine wasn't exactly as Court had pictured the man. He wasn't as tall, for one thing, probably not much taller than Jade, and he didn't think anyone would recognize them as father and daughter. Teddy's coloring was ruddy, his nose and cheeks flushed red with either long exposure to the outdoors or some sort of skin condition. He had the look of a once rather handsome, muscular man going slightly to fat around the middle, while still imposing enough to make anyone think twice before attacking him physically.

The thick shock of hair was a mix of silver and fading red, the eyes were Irish green, keenly intelligent, belying the loud Hawaiian print shirt that could otherwise trick a person into thinking him an affable, slightly silly middle-aged man interested in his dinner and his football games and the cold glass of beer at his elbow as he sat in his overcooked-spinach-colored chair.

"Becket, you said?" Teddy asked, taking another shot at forcing the bones in Court's right hand to cross over one another before he finally let go. "Any relation to Sam Becket?"

"My cousin, sir," Court said with a smile, resisting the urge to rub his abused hand. "But I'm hoping you won't hold that against me. We can't pick our relatives, Mr. Sunshine, can we?"

"Well, now, that's God's truth," Teddy agreed. "A few of mine come to mind that I could toss away and not miss." He waved Court to one of the pair of straight-back wooden chairs on the far side of the old desk that was one of the few pieces of furniture in the long, narrow room. "Where'd you meet my Jade?"

"Sam introduced us when I saw them the other day, Teddy," Jade said quickly. "Court really can't stay, but how about I get you both something to drink? Some coffee?"

"Shame on me," Teddy said with a self-deprecating chuckle, retaking the old leather swivel chair he'd risen from as they'd entered the room. "What a poor host I am. You do that, my angel, get us something to drink. Yes, coffee, I think, a fresh pot, and a plate of those sugar cookies you made the other night and think I don't know are hidden in the flour canister. I'll do my miserable best to make your new friend feel at home." He winked at Court. "Just slice and then bake, that's the best she can do, but still better than store-bought, right?"

Jade looked at Court as if suddenly sorry she'd made the suggestion, but then turned to quit the room, Rockne behind her, tail still wagging madly, as if he knew she was heading for the kitchen.

Having remained standing as long as Jade was in the room, Court now watched her leave and then turned his attention to the knotty-pine paneling, a wood he hadn't known still existed, frankly, before pointing to the wall behind Teddy's desk and asking, "May I?"

"That's why they're there," Teddy said affably. "Shameless promotion, but Jade thinks they add a little something to the room, so I humored her."

Court quickly scanned the framed certificates. "Jade didn't tell me you were a policeman, Mr. Sunshine. I'm very impressed. These are very impressive commendations."

"It's Teddy, and what the hell are you doing here? Most people would have figured she didn't want to see them again."

The friendly tone was gone. So was the wide smile that made the man look like a cross between a cherub and a Saturday-night drunk.

"I beg your pardon?" Court said as he returned to his chair. This time he sat down.

"No, you don't. You don't look like the kind that begs for anything. I tried to warn you off, but you're like Sam. You Beckets don't take hints well, not too swift on the uptake or something. So what do you want? Jade? Of course you do, or you wouldn't be here."

Court didn't bother to dissemble. "I think I'm falling in love with your daughter, yes. In fact, I've already told her I want to marry her. She may have thought I was joking, but I wasn't. I'm not joking now."

"Is that so? Too bad for you. Forget it. That's not happening. I told Sam the same thing when he came to see me."

Court sat back in the chair, his elbows on the wooden arms, his right hand pressed across his mouth, and looked at Teddy Sunshine. Just looked at him. Then he sat forward again, his fingers interlaced in front of him, and he smiled. "I think my cousin and I need to have a small talk. He's still laboring under the mistaken impression that you were trying to *help* him with Jolie."

Teddy shrugged, the hard edge leaving his tone, the affable smile back in place, although Court was fairly certain both changes were temporary.

"Who said I wasn't? I put my girls first, Court. I knew what Jolie needed. I knew what she wanted and I knew her dreams. Lord knows we all lived with them day and night since she was old enough to walk and talk. A genuine drama queen, my Jolie. I want only her happiness and set out to get it for her. Making your cousin Sam happy didn't interest me. Still doesn't."

Court decided to give the man a small push. "So you decide what makes your daughters happy? Do they know that?"

Teddy's green eyes narrowed behind his slyly lowered lids. "How many daughters do you have, Court? How many motherless daughters have you had to raise alone in this cold, dangerous, nasty world?"

Court nodded. "Point taken. That said, though, Jade's a grown woman."

"In some ways. In many ways, she's the brightest of the bunch. In other ways, she's the only child who still keeps me up nights worrying about her," Teddy said, and then sighed. "I did some checking up on you since you called, you know. You live in Virginia. That's a long way away from Philadelphia."

Court was beginning to sense where this was going. He was after Teddy's chick, and had been cast in the role of fox in the henhouse. "If you were walking, yes, or traveling by ox cart. Not that long driving or flying."

The leather chair creaked as Teddy tipped it back on its sturdy legs. "You've got money, too, I'll say that for you. Just like Sam. That doesn't mean anything to my girls, to their credit. Or to me, either."

Court had negotiated with some tough customers, but in business, most people danced, feinted, worked the edges, avoided going head-on with the other side of the bargaining table. Teddy Sunshine didn't seem to think he needed to do that. He just stepped right up and used his best weapon at the start, the loving-father routine, to flog his opponent—in this case, Court. He must have been a barrel of laughs in the interrogation room.

When Teddy didn't say anything else, Court obligingly filled the silence. "If you're waiting for me to respond to that, I don't have an answer for you. I'm certainly not going to apologize for having money, nor am I going to attempt to use that money as a weapon—the way you obviously use your influence over your daughters."

Teddy's smile was wide and unashamed. "Noticed that, did you? They're good girls, the three of them. Jade made certain of that, more than I did, I'm ashamed to say. Nobody knows better where her responsibility lies than my Jade, maybe too much. So I'm not warning you off, the way you think I am, Court. I'm saving you some heartache by telling you—Jade's going nowhere. Any bending will have to come from you, and I don't think you bend too easy, do you? You don't look the type."

Court got to his feet and looked down at Teddy Sunshine, still sitting at his ease behind the desk. "So let me get this straight. It's not me, it's Virginia. It's that I'd be taking Jade away from here. From you. Am I straight on this?"

"That's only me warning you. I know my daughter."

"Yet Jolie's in California, and Jessica is it? Where's she?"

"You said it, Court, you don't have daughters of your own. They're all different, my girls. Jolie never fit here, a real duck out of water. She fits now, where she is. It may not be where I wanted her to fit, but it's where she wants to be, so that's fine. And Jessica?" Teddy smiled again, looking all cherub once more. "Nobody has ever been able to steer that one anywhere she didn't want to go, or stop her once she figured out where that anywhere was. I'll say this to you in all honesty, Court, I'd rather try to hold up my hands to stop a train barreling at me down the tracks. You see? I know my girls."

"So you say."

"So I know. I'd let Jade go if I thought that would make her happy. But she's stuck to me like gum on the bottom of my shoe, my boy. That responsibility thing she's got firm in her head. Can't shake her from it. My fault, a lot of it, after her mother up and left, but here she is and here she'll stay, thinking her dear old dad can't wipe his nose on his own. I can be ready to let go, but until she is, here we are, and there's nothing you can do to change that."

"You seem so very sure of that."

"Only because I am. Now, I'm guessing you'll take this as a personal challenge, and I thought of that. Don't do it, son. It's not that I'll win, because

I'm not out to win. I'm just saying that you'll lose. And Jade will get hurt. I won't forgive you if she gets hurt, and I make a bad enemy."

"I'll be sure to keep that in mind," Court said, and then turned as Jade reentered, carrying a tray holding a coffeepot, three cups and a plate piled high with sugar cookies. She looked pale and painfully nervous.

He gave her a reassuring smile as he took the tray from her and said, "So soon? Teddy and I were just getting to know each other."

MONDAY, 11:25 A.M.

"LET'S TRY TO KEEP moving. I don't know Morgan all that well," Court said, taking Jade's hand as they negotiated the considerable foot traffic heading toward the security checkpoint of the departures area of the terminal, "but I'm guessing a woman like her isn't used to being kept waiting."

"We're not that late, Court," Jade told him, glancing up at one of the many clocks scattered along the walls. "Anyone would think you're afraid of her."

"Not afraid of her, no," Court said, edging them past a woman pushing a stroller while also trying to hang on to a crying toddler. "I just have a busy person's dislike of being late. It's a failing I try to fight."

"Obviously a losing battle for you so far," Jade complained, narrowly missing having her shin banged by a wobbly-wheeled carry-on. "Where did you say we're meeting her?"

"Morgan arranged for a private room somewhere near the security checkpoint and— Wait,
there she is now."

Jade looked down the seemingly endless
terminal, saw the well-dressed young woman
waving at them and couldn't help herself. She
said, in some awe, "Wow."

She wasn't the only person in the terminal who
had noticed the raven-haired woman in the trim,
apricot two-piece suit. Both men and women were
turning their heads, slyly or openly, to catch a
glimpse of Morgan Eastwood as they passed by
on either side of her.

The Englishwoman was petite, perfectly formed
from her short, sleek cap of curls to the refined flare
of her hips, to the very tips of her beige designer
pumps. Her waist couldn't be any larger than Vivian
Leigh's Scarlett in *Gone with the Wind*. As they
drew closer, Jade marveled at Morgan's flawless
English complexion, a lovely peaches and cream
that was only accentuated by those dark curls and
the moist, apricot-colored lip gloss, which reminded
Jade that she hadn't retouched her own makeup.

Morgan's eyes, Jade noticed as Court em-
braced the woman in greeting, were beyond blue,
very nearly violet, and if those long eyelashes
were fake, they were fantastic fakes.

But nobody could fake the easy confidence Morgan exuded from every pore, or the glow of life that shone from those violet eyes. In a word, Morgan Eastwood was elegant. In more than a word, she was gorgeous, refined, a walking advertisement for whatever path in life it was that she had chosen.

Jade looked down at her own clothing, a reflection of the life path she had chosen, and suddenly felt as if she should go hide behind a pole or something.

"Morgan," Court said, stepping away from his cousin, "I'd like you to meet Jade Sunshine. Jade, my cousin, Morgan Eastwood."

"Sunshine?" Morgan said, extending her right hand. "You kept your name for professional reasons? I hear that's done frequently these days. I think it's wonderful. How good to meet you, Jade."

Jade felt the cool, firm touch of Morgan's hand and returned the slight pressure. "And good to meet you. I'm sorry we were late. I'm afraid I asked Court to help me with something before we drove out here."

Morgan shook her head. "No problem. As it turns out, the room I was promised never materialized, so I decided to brave the security queue and meet you in a public area. I have my ticket to Atlanta, and I've been assured that is enough to take me back through Security, although I was warned I'd need to plan time for that entire embarrassing procedure, so we have only an hour at the most."

"Atlanta? I thought you were flying back to England today."

"I did, as well, Court, but I made the mistake of telling an old friend that I would be traveling here in the States, and she shamelessly guilted me into stopping off with her for a few days. Actually, I think she wants to introduce me to her brother, who is, I understand, very *nice* and has a *wonderful personality.* I'm looking forward to an uncomfortable interlude, but as I said, Clarice is an old school chum. Is there somewhere quiet we can go to talk?"

Jade looked left and right, and spied a small bar crowded with those seeking liquid courage before flying the increasingly unfriendly skies. "Over there?"

"I see a table you two can grab," Court said, "but I doubt we'll be served, so I'll go to the bar. Your orders, ladies?"

"A glass of white wine, Court, if possible," Morgan said in her precise English accent, and

Jade only nodded that she'd have the same. She didn't want wine, she wanted ginger ale, but she already felt underbred and underdressed. Being presented with a glass of ginger ale with a red-and-white-striped straw in it just wasn't in her plans.

"Court has told me so much about you, Jade," Morgan said as they took up tall chairs at a high round table, Morgan having to sort of boost herself into hers. "But I see even his kind words fail to describe your stunning good looks. There's such a quiet elegance and air of confidence about you. What I wouldn't give to be tall. People can smile and prattle on about 'pocket Venus' all they want. I'm still short. It's difficult to appear elegant when you sit down and your feet don't touch the floor."

"I never thought of that," Jade said, deciding she had to be very shallow, because she felt flattered. She was also liking this Morgan Eastwood more and more by the moment; she wasn't so dense that she didn't realize that the other woman was very deftly trying to put her at her ease. "And, uh, thank you."

Morgan's smile faded. "Oh, I'm so sorry. As I said, Court has told me about you, including the recent tragedy involving your father. Please allow me to extend my sincere condolences. To you, your sisters, your mother."

"I'll be certain to tell my sisters, thank you. My mother, however, is in Hawaii with her second husband, who also happens to be my father's brother, so I'll pass on that if you don't mind." Jade closed her eyes for a moment. "I'm sorry, Morgan. I have no idea where that came from, why I said that."

Morgan reached over and put her hand on top of Jade's. "Life is never easy, is it? And I've found, in the small research I've done, the larger the family, the greater the chances for heartache, the Beckets being no exception, I'm afraid. Of course, they've had two hundred years to fall out with each other over silliness, haven't they? Ainsley would have straightened them all out quickly enough, I'm sure—he was a very powerful man who brooked no nonsense. But time, distance…we are who we are, not what we want to be, yes?"

Jade nodded, and then thanked Court as he placed a glass of white wine in front of her. "Court's told me about your family, Morgan, and that the house you live in has been in your family for about two hundred years. I find that amazing."

"You should see it," Court said. "It's more than amazing. Becket Hall is extraordinary. A home, a fortress, a legacy."

"A prison," Morgan said quietly, and then

shook her head. "No, that's not entirely fair. Becket Hall is my home and I love it. Still, there's a difference between wanting to be somewhere and being constrained by your ancestor's whim."

"Ainsley Becket," Court said, "our mutual ancestor. I thought the letter you spoke of was a request, not an order. That Becket Hall should remain in the family, I mean."

"Not only remain in the family, as property, you understand, but also be inhabited by members of the family," Morgan said. "Generation after generation after generation. Which ends with me, I suppose, as there are no more male Eastwoods. When I marry and leave, as I cannot imagine any man I marry wishing to be so isolated on the marsh, Becket Hall will stand for the most part empty until it falls into the sea. Unless…"

Jade put her elbows on the table and leaned forward. "Yes, unless. Court told me there's some sort of curse, correct?"

Morgan's laugh was a delight. "A curse? I don't think I've ever heard it called that before, Jade. But I suppose it's all in how you look at the thing. And now we move into the area of family legend, don't we?"

"And the Empress," Court said. "It's all about the Empress."

Jade didn't want to rain on Court's and Morgan's little parade, but she didn't put a lot of credence in the story as she'd heard it. "Let's see if I've got this straight, okay? Ainsley Becket was a privateer, probably also a pirate—"

"Most definitely also a pirate," Morgan interrupted, her eyes shining. "And, from old records I've discovered, hanged as a smuggler after being found out as the Black Ghost, the head of a large smuggling gang that used Romney Marsh as their base during the last war with Napoleon. Of course, he didn't hang. Someone did, but not Ainsley. Do you know that story, Court?"

"Not yet, but I certainly want to hear it, along with all the other stories. The piracy, the smuggling." He turned to Jade. "Morgan told me the story is that Ainsley wore a black cape and mask when he led the smugglers over Romney Marsh. I get this mental picture of Zorro because, supposedly, he was on the side of good, helping the local residents supplement their meager earnings."

"Zorro," Jade said facetiously, "or Robin Hood. It would seem the man was a saint."

"Everything becomes more romantic the more the story is passed down the generations, I think. As for the supposed hanging, my grandfather didn't feel it to be a story fit for a proper young female. But we do have the proof that Ainsley didn't stretch at the end of a rope, as you say in your American westerns. From what I have been told as a proper young female, a portrait of Ainsley's first wife—the one you're descended from by blood, Court—was taken to America when Ainsley left, but then later replaced at Becket Hall by one of Ainsley Becket himself. It still hangs most prominently over the fireplace in the main drawing room, as if guarding us. Or daring us to disobey him. A quite lovely white plantation house is featured in the background of the portrait."

"Our house, Jade," Court said, and Jade didn't bother to correct him. "I've seen the portrait."

"A devilishly handsome man, our ancestor," Morgan said, smiling rather sheepishly. "I had a horrible schoolgirl crush on him for many years. So tall and straight, his black hair silvering slightly at the temples, so obviously a man comfortable in his own skin, I guess you'd say. And unless the artist was being fanciful, he had the most marvelous green eyes. I can easily imagine him striding the deck of the *Black Ghost,* which was also the name of his ship, his black cape swirling in the breeze, his eyes narrowed as he surveyed the horizon for fat prize ships sailing to Spain and France."

She put her hands to her chest. "You can have your movie stars, thank you very much. I'll take Ainsley Becket. You look a little like him, Court."

"I'll have to dig up a black cape and mask for you," Jade teased him. "You'd be a real hit at parties." Then she sobered. "I know you don't have much time before your plane, Morgan. Was there something in particular you wanted to tell us?"

"Oh, yes, of course. Excuse me," Morgan said, reaching into the rather large purse she'd carried with her to check on her airline ticket. "Oh, dear, I shouldn't be wasting time just nattering on and on. I have to go soon. My only excuse is that I was distracted by the two of you, I believe. You look so very good together. I'd very much like to paint you. Without the black cape for you, Court, sadly. On the beach, I should think, with Becket Hall in the background."

Jade tipped her head toward Court, waiting for him to explain.

"I didn't tell you? Morgan's an artist, Jade," he said, his voice colored with cousinly pride. "Seascapes, haunting panoramas of the Romney Marsh in every season, in every light. And then Becket Hall itself. I've already commissioned oils for the Becket Hotel penthouses, as well as a few for the house in Virginia. They're…the word I'd have to use is *powerful*."

Jade looked at Morgan, who was blushing prettily. Such a petite little thing, all sweetness and milk and honey, and her paintings were *powerful?* Obviously there was passion there, deeply hidden. Interesting. "I'd really like to see some of your work."

"I certainly hope you do, Jade. Which is another reason I asked you to meet me here today," Morgan said, leaning forward, her elbows on the tabletop. "I wanted to issue a personal invitation to you, Jade, and to your sisters, as well. Come to Becket Hall, please. Walk the shingle beach at dawn and again at twilight, ride across the Marsh on horseback if you're so inclined. There's peace there, Jade, real peace. I can't think of a better place for you and your sisters to heal at least the worst of the wounds caused by your father's tragic passing. I also want very much to meet Sam, of course, my other cousin."

"And to enlist our help in solving the mystery of the Empress," Jade said, shaking her head, her smile taking the edge from her words. "I'll say one thing for the Beckets. You all seem to find ways to get what you want."

Morgan sat back and clapped her hands together.

"Then you'll come? Oh, that's just brilliant! Ever since Grandfather died, I've been rattling around in that old pile all by myself. Granted, I've been madly busy." She looked at Court. "I'm having a gallery showing in London in October."

Morgan seemed so happy, Jade hated to rain on her parade. "I can't leave here until I've cleared Teddy's name. None of us can. I'm sorry."

Morgan looked at Jade, then Court and back to Jade once more. "Court tells me you've made real progress. I sincerely hope you solve everything to your satisfaction. I so admire you and your sisters, and Court and Sam, as well, for your loyalty and determination."

"Thank you," Jade said, and then pulled a sheaf of folded papers out of her purse, feeling the need to make her refusal less rude. "When Court and I were…" She stopped, rephrased what she had been about to say. "A few years ago, when Court mentioned his family history to me, I did some checking online."

"You did?"

"Yes, Court, I did. I'm a private detective, remember? I was curious when you told me the little bit you did about Ainsley Becket and all his adopted children." She unfolded the printed-out pages. "You were right. You're the only one who can be traced directly back to Ainsley Becket and his first wife, Isabella. They had one child, Cassandra, who married Court Becket. An adopted son," Jade clarified, looking at Morgan, who smiled and nodded.

"I can imagine the furor that must have raised," Morgan said, her eyes twinkling. "But really, they weren't related by blood, were they? When Ainsley married again, it was later in life, to an American—Marianna, correct? And they, of course, had no children, leaving Court here two centuries later as the last true blood descendant of Ainsley Becket."

Jade spread out the pages. "Here you are, Morgan. Ainsley adopted not formally, I suppose—a child named Eleanor, who eventually married a man named Jack Eastwood. Their descendants have lived at Becket Hall ever since. Over two hundred years. The rest, the other five? Scattered to the four winds pretty much, I'd say. I barely found anything I could call definite about any Beckets in America after about 1920s or so. And then I—" she looked at Court "—well, I stopped investigating. I should check census records. There's a census taken about seventy years ago that was amazingly detailed."

"What brilliant detecting skills, Jade. And yes,

I've seen that census online," Morgan said, nodding. "That's why I'm here, traveling about, introducing myself to long-lost relatives. Explaining to them that we're not really related, yet we're more related than most families because the original Beckets had *chosen* to be a family. I've had some rather strange reactions, but that's for another time. And just because I think I should be honest with you, Jade, I do have an ulterior motive for inviting you to Becket Hall."

Now Jade laughed, probably her first real laugh in weeks. "No, really? Don't say that you hope my 'brilliant detecting skills' will help you locate this supposedly priceless emerald?"

"I'm *so* subtle, aren't I?" Morgan pulled a face, making her look like a very pretty but very naughty child. "And I don't want to frighten you away, but I feel that, as we're being honest now, I should tell you something. My grandfather told me that years ago, *his* grandfather had hired someone to hunt for the Empress, and the man ended up losing a hand to, well, to some sort of booby trap. My grandfather said that was because Ainsley meant for only a Becket to find the Empress. So you see, anxious as I am to find the stone and to fulfill whatever destiny Ainsley expected of us, I'm not about to launch a search on my own. No one has searched, frankly, not in more than one hundred years. The legend of the Empress and its bad luck were too daunting."

Before Jade could answer—and really, what was there to say after that?—Morgan checked the slim gold-and-diamond watch on her wrist and hopped to her feet. "Blast! Must run, and I only pray I don't mean that literally, not in these heels. Quickly, promise me you'll all come to Becket Hall just as soon as you can. You can't deny me now that we've met and become friends. I'm no longer just a voice at the other end of the phone."

Jade heard herself saying yes to the visit a heartbeat before being enveloped by the scent of Morgan's perfume as the smaller woman hugged her fiercely. Then it was Court's turn, as Morgan stood on tiptoe to kiss his cheek, and then the woman was gone, an apricot blur racing deeper into the terminal.

"Well, that was different," Jade said, sitting down. "But, much as I hate to admit it, I am intrigued, far more than I was prior to meeting your cousin. The man lost a hand to a booby trap? That's bizarre."

"Not when you know that Ainsley lived by his wits as privateer, pirate and smuggler. Not when you know that he lived for many years somewhere on the coast of Haiti and that he actually brought a voodoo high priestess to Romney Marsh with him to act as nanny to his daughter Cassandra. Can you even imagine that? We're talking about a whole other age here, Jade, and people we can't easily understand."

Jade got to her feet. "Okay, now you've lost me. Voodoo, Court? And don't tell me you believe in that nonsense."

"So says the hardheaded realist. I'm not so sure. There are a lot of things in this world that defy explanation, Jade."

But Jade wasn't listening anymore. She had suddenly clamped her hand on Court's arm and pulled him away from the bar's entrance and back into the dimly lit interior. She'd seen the bright lights come on smack in the center of the wide corridor, seen the camera, the reporter holding a microphone and calling to someone approaching from the area of the gates.

"Brainard," she said quietly, looking at the tall, blond, handsome, extremely confident candidate in his two-thousand-dollar suit. "Father and son. They must have just landed."

Court peered around a large pillar. "That's them, back from their ranch or wherever they went so that Daddy Brainard could recover from his *spell* last week. So I guess we were right, Jade.

Even the front-runner can't stay away from the action too long. Now we know he'll definitely make his scheduled appearance tonight."

"Look, they're going to stop."

"There was no question that they wouldn't," Court said. "What's that old saying? If you want a politician to appear, just hold out a camera or a microphone and you'll be beating them off with a stick in less than sixty seconds. Come on, let's go, unless you want to watch?"

Jade squeezed her hands into tight fists, her fingertips biting into her palms. "You don't know how badly I want to go out there and confront him right now."

"Oh, I think I do, which is why I suggested we leave now. You promised to wait for Jessica and Matt," Court said quietly. "You've got lights, camera, action here, sure, but the middle of Philadelphia International Airport probably isn't the best place to play *Gotcha* with Joshua Brainard."

"No," she agreed reluctantly as she watched people on their way into the terminal having to skirt around Joshua and his father as the candidate spoke for the cameras. Still, this was a golden opportunity. She visually searched the crowded terminal as if for answers. There had to be something, some way she could… "Come with me."

Taking Court's hand, she kept her head averted as the two of them threaded their way across the sea of pedestrians and carry-ons, straight to a line of courtesy phones on the far wall.

"Should I ask what you're doing?" Court said as she picked up one of the receivers.

"Shh," she warned, keeping her back to the terminal and the ongoing interview. "Hello?" she said as an operator came on the line. "Hello, yes. Could you please page someone for me? It's *very* important. Yes, yes, thank you. The name is Tarin White. T-a-r-i-n, yes. Uh…to right here, Terminal B, is it? Oh, good, that works. How long will it take until— Immediately? Thank you so much."

She replaced the receiver and turned to smile at Court. "Let's see Joshua's reaction when he hears the page. What are you doing?"

"Hey, anything you can do," Court said, grinning at her as he lifted the receiver and paged Dr. Norman Myster.

"Tarin's *dentist?*" Jade repeated Morgan's earlier action and kissed Court on the cheek. "It's a two-fer. You're brilliant."

"Yes, hold that thought until the next time I try to get you alone to make mad, passionate love to you. I'm a real keeper, Jade."

"You're impossible," Jade countered, but she

was more amused than put off by his teasing, by the way he had managed to slide his arm around her back and pull her close as they turned to watch the action. "Now just pray the interview isn't over before the page comes over the public-address system."

Jade didn't have to worry for more than another ten seconds before the operator's voice could be heard loudly and clearly: "Tarin White? Tarin White, your party is waiting for you at the yellow courtesy phone bank in Terminal B. Tarin White, please meet your party in Terminal B."

Joshua Brainard's head snapped back hard enough to give him whiplash, and he quickly looked left, then right...which was when Jade lifted a hand and waggled her fingers at him in a mocking greeting.

"Gotcha," she mouthed quietly. "Don't try to tell me later that you don't know who Tarin White was, buddy boy."

The public-address system squeaked again. "Norman Myster, Dr. Norman Myster, please come to the yellow courtesy phones in Terminal B. Norman Myster, Dr. Norman Myster."

Joshua Brainard was still staring at Jade and Court, although his eyes shifted upward momentarily, as if he could see the dentist's name scrolling by on the tiled ceiling above his head. *Why?* he then mouthed silently to Jade, his expression tortured as his father kept a smile on his face, attempting to redirect his son's attention to the local television-news reporters who were still standing there, cameras and microphones at the ready.

But Jade wasn't buying the man's sincere act. "He plays the innocent so well, doesn't he? Well, see you later, Josh, baby. And you're going down. You're going *down* tonight."

"Yeah, yeah, Rocky, we got that. Come on, before this gets ugly. You made your point."

"He responded, Court. You saw it, one mention of Tarin's name and, bam, his head went up like a setter going on point," Jade said, almost dancing beside Court as he quickly led her to the end of the terminal and into the larger mass of people all moving like lemmings toward the exits. "Now, to get him to agree to talk to me tonight, which won't be easy. No, I don't think the man likes me very much."

BETWEEN HERE AND THERE

"I DON'T THINK I HAVE much chance of hitting your father's list of his top ten people," Court said as he climbed into the driver's side of his car after the awkward *interview* with Teddy Sunshine. "On the other hand, I think I like him. He's nothing if not honest."

Jade rolled her eyes. "What did Teddy do? He did something. He wouldn't be Teddy if he didn't do something. I told you I didn't see any reason for us to stop here. Warned you, actually, if you'll remember. The man was a cop, Court. He lives to interrogate."

Court headed for the highway and the drive back to his hotel. "Wrong, he lives to intimidate. And he's quite good at it, by the way. A lesser man may have packed his bags and headed for the hills." He turned to smile at Jade. "I am not, by the way, a lesser man."

"Yes, I've already sensed that," Jade said with a sigh, and then smiled. "I have the rest of the day off, you know. When did you say you were leaving for Virginia and your New Year's Eve party?"

"As soon as we find you a suitcase and pack up the rest of the clothing back at my hotel. Remember, Jade, tomorrow is Saturday. Nobody works New Year's Day, unless they have to. We leave in an hour, will be in Virginia before I can ply you with too much champagne on the plane, and won't be more than an hour late for the party. Or did you think I only asked you to come back to the hotel with me for some quick goodbye sex? This isn't a game I'm playing here, Jade."

"Court, I—"

"You can't go, you can't leave Teddy. He'd be helpless without you," he said quickly, pretty sure he was pushing the right button.

"Don't be ridiculous. Teddy's a grown man. But I can't go with you, Court. It's…that's not something I do."

"A new year, trying something new—you're not afraid of me, Jade, are you?"

"I'm here, aren't I? I took you home to meet Teddy. Under protest, but I did take you. But Virginia? For an entire weekend? I don't know…"

Court slowed at seeing the stoplight ahead turn yellow when he could easily have made it through, and caught the red light. Which made it possible for him to keep his foot on the brake as he reached over to cup the back of Jade's neck and slowly pull her toward him.

He put everything he had into their kiss, he knew that, and Jade melted against him in a very satisfying way until they both seemed to hear the sound of a honking horn at the same time and Court moved his foot to the gas, the car passing beneath the very green traffic light. "So?" he asked quietly.

"You don't play fair, Court Becket." Jade slipped her hand onto his thigh. "I won't need much. We can probably make do with just your suitcase...."

MONDAY, 2:23 P.M.

"REMIND ME AGAIN how you roped me into agreeing to this?" Court said as they parked the car in the lot adjoining Lieutenant Matt Denby's apartment building.

Jade grinned at him, still pretty much on a high after spooking Joshua Brainard at the airport. "Hey, I went with you, now you come with me. It's fair."

"Sunshine fair, not Other People fair, but we're here," Court said as he joined her on the faded and cracked macadam. "What will you do if Ernesto isn't ready to leave yet?"

"You know the trouble he's been having with some of the neighborhood tough guys, Court. He had a black eye, for God's sake, when Matt and Jessica brought him to Sam's house. I'm sure Matt will feel a lot better if he sees Ernesto when they get back tonight. He's leaving for Penn State in a couple of days, anyway. Besides, I like him. And Rockne misses him."

"Uh-huh," Court said, holding open the heavy steel door to the building. "If I say all right, will you stop now, or do you have more arguments for me?"

"I've got plenty, but we're here, so the whole thing is moot, anyway, right?" Then Jade softened her words by going up on her toes to give him a quick, hard kiss. "And no, I don't know why I just did that."

"I'd like to think I do," Court said, and gave her a playful pat on the rump as they walked into the dark foyer that smelled of taco salad. It smelled pretty good, actually, reminding him that they'd made do with a few bites of some pretty bad hot dogs at the airport. "Jess told me that Matt's place is on the third floor, but Ernesto and his mother live down here. Let me check the mailboxes."

Ernesto opened the door to his apartment a minute later, immediately breaking into a grin when he saw Court. "Hey, man," he said, holding up his hand to give a high-five, "what are you doing here? Come to see where the little Spanish kid lives? I should have told my butler to answer the door."

Then he frowned, looked over his shoulder back into the interior of the apartment and stepped into the hallway, closing the door behind him.

"Miss Sunshine, hi. You guys hear anything from my amigo? He ran out of here yesterday like a cat with its tail on fire."

Jade had tried to peek inside the apartment before Ernesto closed the door. She'd thought she heard someone calling the boy's name. "Matt and Jessica are together, visiting his parents. Did someone just call you?"

"Me? Nah, not me," Ernesto said, shifting from one foot to the other. "You here for Sunny? Matt didn't give him a name, but he has to answer to something, right? So I named him Sunny. You know, for Sunshine? He's upstairs. I mean, I wanted to keep him down here but... Let's go upstairs. He probably needs to go out, anyway."

Court and Jade exchanged puzzled glances, and then Court shrugged and motioned for Jade to precede him as they followed Ernesto up the three flights.

As Jade climbed the stairs, she thought about how Ernesto had come into their lives. A brilliant scholar, he had been targeted by bullies—thanks to his slight size and his large brain—and Matt had appointed himself Ernesto's bodyguard. Jess had seen Ernesto, seen the kid's black eye, and that was all Jessica had needed to get Ernesto moved to Sam's house until he left for summer classes at Penn State and his full scholarship in logistics.

Matt had moved back to his apartment only yesterday after he and Jessica solved the Fishtown Strangler case—when Matt had run scared, fearing his attraction to Jessica—and he'd taken Ernesto with him.

But now Matt was with Jessica, and Jess had texted her earlier that she'd really appreciate it if she and Court brought Ernesto back to Sam's. She hadn't mentioned a Sunny—but that was Jess; details were for other people.

Jade had gone over all this again with Court on their way here from the airport, but nobody could explain Sunny to her. She did get the idea that Jessica had *done something,* because Jessica had a lifelong reputation for *doing something.*

When they all got to the landing, Ernesto fished in his pocket for a set of keys and opened the door to Matt's apartment, only to be immediately greeted by a small, round, yipping bunch of brightly colored fur that had launched itself at his knees.

"Sunny, no. What did I tell you about the slobbering, huh?" Ernesto admonished, picking up the Irish setter puppy, which immediately began licking his face. "Cut that out or I'll give you to Mrs. Chen in 2-B. She told me that back home in China, you're a delicacy, you dumb mutt. Okay, she was only teasing—but I don't like dog kisses, you hear me?"

Jade turned to Court once more, her eyebrows raised, her tongue rubbing back and forth across the bottom of her top teeth as she thought this one over. Then she smiled. "She had a plan, she said, Court. She left us yesterday to go see Matt— whom she'd let fly free because he couldn't seem to commit, if you'll remember—and she said she had a plan. A couple of hours later, she and Matt are back together and *planning* a wedding. A dog? A dog was her *plan?*" And then, because her baby sister had amazed her yet again, Jade laughed. "Ernesto, let's go inside, and then you can tell us all about Sunny."

While Ernesto carefully picked up a few soiled puppy puddle pads with a pair of ice tongs he brought in from the kitchen and dropped them into a plastic garbage bag, he told Court and Jade what had happened the previous day.

"Matt brought me home and told me to start packing for school, and then he went upstairs and then he went shopping for some food—he brought me bread and milk and spiced ham because he keeps forgetting I don't like spiced ham—and then he stayed up here, and then Miss

Jessica showed up with Mortimer and the puppy
and asked me to help her."

"Mortimer, right. Matt's ugly black goldfish.
He'd forgotten him *again*. All right. So Jess
showed up, and you helped her with *what?*" Jade
asked, sitting on the floor now, Sunny in her lap.
Sunny looked just like Rockne had more than a
dozen years ago, when Jessica had brought him
home, hoping Teddy would take to him and forget
his wife had just taken a permanent hike with his
own brother. The girl did have a thing for dogs—
and simple ideas.

"I'm still not sure about that part, the *what* part,
Miss Sunshine. Miss Jessica can be a little *loco,*
so I just did what she said, you know? I carried
Sunny and the puppy stuff up here for her, and she
carried Mortimer."

From there, Ernesto went on to explain the
look on Matt's face when he opened the door to
see Jessica standing there with Mortimer, and his
reaction to having Sunny pushed into his arms.

"Miss Jessica, she said he had to learn to
commit sometime, or something like that. First
Mortimer, then the dog and then, someday, maybe
he'd be ready to commit to a person. Like that. And
then she left my amigo standing there with his
mouth opening and closing, just like Mortimer."

The next thing Ernesto knew he was being handed the dog and Matt had grabbed his car keys and was running out of the apartment while mumbling "stupid, stupid" to himself—and that was the last Ernesto had seen of Matt or Jessica.

"So they're getting married?" he asked when he was done, looking hopefully at Court. "That's cool. That way Miss Jessica still gets to keep Sunny."

"The way to a man's heart is through an Irish setter?" Court asked, smiling. "All right, I'll swallow that. But I don't think Sam or I are ready yet to concede that your sister isn't a witch."

"Uh-oh," Jade said, looking around Matt's very clean, yet very sad and empty-looking apartment. "Matt was just existing, wasn't he, Court? I really like him, and I think he and Jessica will be good together. Come on, let's grab Mortimer, too, and get back to Sam's. Ernesto, please tell me you're packed and ready to go."

Jade had barely finished speaking when the door to Matt's apartment slammed open so hard it hit the wall.

"There you are, you ungrateful little bastard. I told you I want those fancy calculator things you've got hidden in your room. *Now,* Ernesto, or I'll rip the room apart."

Jade quickly put down the puppy and got to her feet, startled by the appearance of what had to be Ernesto's mother.

The woman was taller than Ernesto, with long, frizzed hair colored a hideous orange-red, matching the bright slash of lipstick smeared around her mouth. She wore a pair of denim cutoffs above too-thin bare legs, and a bright pink halter top studded with matching sequins. If the woman ever ate anything, it didn't show.

Her eyes were deeply brown, the pupils dilated, and as she stood there, bracing her outstretched arms against the doorjamb, the smell of her— cheap perfume and sweat—threatened to over-power the room.

"Mama, no," Ernesto said, quickly moving toward the door. "They gave me those calculators for college, I told you that. You aren't going to sell them." He looked quickly to Court and Jade and then added quietly, "You've been using all day, Mama. You don't need more."

"Don't you tell me what I need! Don't you ever tell me what I need!" the woman shouted, already raising one hand as if to slap him, and Ernesto flinched reflexively. But Court was too fast for her, grabbing her wrist and turning her around, right arm now pinned behind her, heading her back out to the landing. "Take your grimy paws off me! Let me go! Who are you to... *Oh.*" The tone changed from maddened screech to come-hither nauseating. "You want some of this, pretty boy?"

Jade watched, embarrassed for Ernesto, as his mother shook off Court's hand and ran her own hands down her body, then cupped her breasts, pushing them at Court as she made an *O* of her lipstick-smeared lips.

"Mama—"

"Ten for a quick blow, twenty if you want to touch me, you know, in my girly places. Fifty, and I'll bark like that damn dog while you poke me any way you like if that's what gets you off. Come on, handsome, you know you want what I got."

Court's answer was to grab her by the elbow and half push her down the steps with him.

Jade was already in the kitchen, her hands shaking almost uncontrollably, opening drawers to find the plastic wrap so she could seal the top of Mortimer's bowl. "Get Sunny and his things, Ernesto, sweetie," she called over her shoulder. "We're out of here."

But Ernesto only stood where he was, tears standing in his eyes, his hands drawn up into impotent fists.

"Ernesto," Jade said quietly, depositing Mortimer's bowl on a table and taking the boy's chin in her hand. She looked deeply into his eyes as she took a tissue from her slacks pocket and dabbed at his cheeks. "We understand, honey. We do. And don't be ashamed. We're not judging. But you can't fix some things that are broken, especially if they don't want to be fixed. It's time for you to go, sweetheart, start your new life. It really is."

By the time they were back on the ground floor, Court was walking out of Ernesto's apartment with a small canvas bag in one hand, Ernesto's pair of new calculators in the other. "Okay, buddy. Anything else you need, we buy, all right?"

"But…but Mama?"

"I think she's going to lie down for a while. She sends you her love, Ernesto," Court said, looking at Jade. "I think you need your own cell phone before you go away. You can call her from college in a few days."

"I, uh…" Ernesto looked once more toward the closed door behind Court. "Okay. I mean, I guess so…"

"How much did that cost you?" Jade whispered to Court as they followed Ernesto toward the car.

"Enough to keep her high for a while, I'm sorry to say. I'm also sorry to say that the best thing that could happen to Ernesto might be if she used it all at one time and overdosed. I need a shower. While I was searching Ernesto's room, she kept throwing herself at me, trying to kiss me, grabbing at my crotch, throwing out prices for each of her different *talents*. I thought I knew a lot, but she came up with things I've never even heard about, and never want to hear about again."

Jade tried to ease the moment. "She couldn't help herself. You're irresistible."

"Thanks for the compliment, but that woman would hump a mailbox for a nickel bag," Court gritted out from between clenched teeth. "Ernesto never comes back here, Jade. Never."

"You're adopting him?" Jade asked, longing to hug him for his fierce protectiveness of a defenseless boy.

"I don't know what I'm doing, but he doesn't come back here. He has school breaks, he comes to me, in Virginia. I don't care who or what I have to take on to make that happen, but that's what's going to happen."

Jade watched Ernesto climb into the back seat with Sunny, then pick up Mortimer's bowl from the macadam and clumsily climb into the car himself with the small menagerie.

She turned to Court and stepped even closer to

him, slid her arms up and around his neck. Just before she kissed him, she whispered, "There are times I really could love you, Court Becket..."

FLYING HIGH

HE COULD BE in love with her. After only a few days. Hell, from the moment he'd first seen her walk into the hotel bar. And Teddy Sunshine and his opinions be damned.

She approached his private jet with the air of someone walking the gangplank over a tank filled with alligators, her long hair blowing away from her face, giving him a clear look at her widened eyes.

"It's, um, it's really not all the *big,* is it?" she said as he reached for her hand and squeezed it in his own. "In fact, it's...I think you could say it's pretty *small.* Like, um, like a toy plane."

Court squeezed her hand again as he coaxed her into walking close to the jet. "It's a fifteen-seater, which isn't huge, no, but it's a lot more than a puddle-jumper. Do you want to interview the pilot? Ask to see his license?"

Jade lowered her chin into the faux-fur collar of her new, deeply emerald down jacket, courtesy of the boutique in the hotel lobby. "I, uh, I've never flown before," she admitted quietly. "I know, edging up on thirty years old, and I've never traveled farther than the Jersey Shore. I mean, I've thought about flying somewhere, but there's never been anyplace to go. Teddy flies to Ireland once a year with Father Muskie, and he's asked me to go with them a couple of times, but...common sense says airplanes shouldn't be able to get off the ground, okay?"

"All right, so you're telling me that you've never flown before."

Jade's smile was tremulous. "No, I think I'm saying I don't want to fly *now*. In *that*. I'm sorry, Court, I know I'm being stupid, and don't try to *kiss* me out of this one, because this time it's not going to work the way it did back at the hotel."

Court let go of her hand and slipped his arm around her waist. "A lot of things worked out very nicely back at the hotel," he told her quietly, recalling how they'd made love before she'd finally agreed to come with him to Virginia. Quick, and passionately hot. He was looking forward to the long weekend and more leisurely lovemaking.

He kept edging her toward the short flight of steps that led up to the plane. "Would it help at all to tell you we've got parachutes on board?"

"Not if I'm more afraid to jump out of a plane than I am to fly in a plane, no," Jade said, but he could feel her tense body beginning to relax. "This is stupid. People fly every day, every second of every day. The chances of crashing are about a million times less than getting run over by a semi on the expressway, and I drive on that all the time."

She took a deep breath, let it out slowly, her warm breath making a small cloud in the increasingly cold air. "All right. Let's do this."

"Should I be humming snatches of the 'Battle Hymn of the Republic' as we march arm in arm toward the stairs?"

"Funny man," Jade said as they reached the plane. "Everybody loves a comedian. Except maybe me."

He grinned and waved for her to ascend the portable stairs first and then motioned for the attendant to quickly close the door behind him—before Jade changed her mind.

"Champagne for the lady, please, George," he said quietly to his employee. "I think we've got a nervous flier here."

"Yes, sir, Mr. Becket," the attendant said. "But we'll be cleared for takeoff in just a few moments, so if it can wait…?"

"It can. Go strap yourself in, George, and I'll do my best to keep her from trying to open a window and leap to safety."

"Yes, sir, Mr. Becket," George answered, grinning. "I'm guessing you'll think of something."

"What were you whispering about?" Jade asked as Court sat down in the comfortable leather seat beside hers and helped her with her seat belt. "Did you tell him not to worry if he heard screaming back here?"

"Pretty much, yes." Then he laughed as she grabbed his forearm in a death grip.

"We're moving. Court? We're moving. *Backward.*"

"Yes, the pilot finds that easer than making a U-turn through the terminal. Come here, Jade," he said, putting his arm around her again. "Let me introduce you to the joys of takeoff."

"I'm being an idiot. I'm sorry, Court." Again she took a deep breath and let it out slowly. "Okay, tell me about the joys of takeoff."

Court felt the plane begin to taxi forward and, from previous experience at PHL, knew they'd be taking off very shortly. He eased Jade closer to him and slid both arms around her. With his mouth close to her ear, he told her, "There's this thing called thrust. Well, maybe not, but for the sake of this conversation, I'm going to call it thrust."

"Thrust, huh? You would," Jade said, her laugh shaky. "Go on."

The pilot announced that they would be taking off in one minute.

"Oh, God…"

"Shh," he told her quietly. "Just close your eyes and concentrate. Runways look smooth enough, but we'll be rolling over strips in the concrete, and you'll feel them rumble, vibrate up through the belly of the plane."

"Thrust. And now vibrate. You're going somewhere with this, Court, aren't you?" Jade's voice was even smaller now.

"Yes, and it's starting. Feel it? Feel the rumble?" His arms tightened around her—he had forgone his seat belt in order to be close to her. "Now close your eyes and feel it build as we accelerate. Hear the engines? It's time, Jade. There you go, feel that? Feel the throbbing power of the engines as we build speed? Feel the *pull* on your body as your heart beats faster, as we rocket down the runway, trying to defy gravity, to escape it. Up, up into the air, that's where we want to be. Masters of the universe, Jade, soaring like a sleek, powerful eagle, our wings spread wide as we… There. There it is, liftoff. Now we climb. Here we go. Let the speed take you. Faster. Faster…"

He lifted her chin and crushed his mouth into hers as the engines lifted the jet from the tarmac and they were climbing steeply into the air, their bodies melded more closely together by the pull of that thrust.

Jade clung to him as the plane continued its rapid climb up and over the city of Philadelphia that was now no more than bright lights rapidly disappearing behind them. He imagined that he could taste her fear, even as he could imagine that fear dissolving and a new feeling taking its place. She held on now, but it was because she'd been caught in the exhilaration of the takeoff, the breaking free of the earth and taking wing.

She pushed him back against his seat, leaning over him as she pinched at his chin and held him as she kissed him almost fiercely. Evidently the woman was taking to the notion of flight.

"Cleared, sir. I'll have the champagne for the young lady in a…well, maybe not," George said, retreating to his seat on the other side of the curtain.

Jade let go of Court and settled back in her seat, her head flung back against the headrest, her breasts rising and falling rapidly. "*Wow.* That was incredible!"

"Should I take that as a personal compliment, or do you want to go meet the pilot?" Court asked her, tickled by the beatific expression on her face, the shine in her eyes.

"No, I meant the *wow* for you. Although you almost lost me with that 'masters of the universe' line."

"Too over the top?"

"Trust me. *Way* too over the top. But I'll say this, I'm up here. And I think I like it. Sort of, anyway." She looked out the porthole window at the night sky—although Court noticed her hands were white-knuckled as she held tight to both armrests, as if she might otherwise fall out of the plane—and then turned to him. "Thank you. You're a nice man."

She then immediately went back to looking out the window, leaving Court to lightly place his hand over hers and watch her as she watched the faraway ground below.

Did she know why she was so excited? He doubted it. But she was escaping, leaving Teddy and her responsibilities behind, lost in the lights below them, most probably for the first time in her life. This beautiful, unique, fascinating, accomplished woman, who looked so sophisticated, yet was still in many ways little more than a child, this beautiful creature who seemed to have been waiting in her safe, snug cocoon, waiting for him to find her, to sweep her up, fly her away, show her a whole new world.

Not a rescue. An awakening.

One that included him.

"I'M GLAD YOU DIDN'T try to come here on your own after Jess asked you to pick up Ernesto," Court said as he checked the busy cross street at the stop sign. "I like being included when you're in areas like this."

His innocent statement raised her hackles. Damn it, and just when they'd been doing so well

"This is nowhere near the place where I was shot at, Court. And, to be precise, it was *almost* shot at."

"Let's be even more precise, all right?" he said quietly, just as stubborn as Jade and not ready to concede his point, not yet. "It's nowhere near the place where you could have been shot and killed by a cheating husband with a jammed Saturday Night Special and a dislike of being tailed by the female private investigator he did manage to knock around a little—using her own camera on her, instead of his fists—before help arrived. It's nowhere near the several circles of living hell I was dropped into when I heard about your injuries from Teddy while I was stuck in Athens and couldn't get to you for almost one full day. Not that I'm delving into ancient history here or anything."

"You already have. And Ernesto is sitting right behind us, remember?" Jade put her hand on Court's arm as he readied to turn left. "Wait, go straight here."

He did as she asked and then looked to her for an explanation. "You know this neighborhood?"

She shook her head. "No, not really. But if you go another two, no, another three blocks, I think you can turn left and we'll see the playground where Terrell died."

"Jade…" Court said warningly, not as surprised as maybe he should be, because Jade had always been like a dog with a bone about her assigned Scholar Athlete case. "I know you don't want to give this up, and I don't blame you. But we've already got a busy evening ahead of us. What good is there in looking at a crime scene over a dozen years old?"

"Yes, Court, but you've never seen it, and Ernesto had some pretty good thoughts on the trajectory of the bullet and all that when we all discussed the case the other night. So why not go there just one last time?"

"I don't know. Because we're driving a Mercedes and not wearing flak jackets?" Court said under his breath, and then gave it up. Jade was a bundle of nerves and he knew it. They had to find something to fill the hours before Joshua Brainard's public appearance that night. "Tell me where to turn."

Five minutes and one wrong turn quickly corrected by Ernesto later, Court eased the Mercedes close to a crumbling, weed-choked cement curb and they got out of the car, Ernesto carrying Sunny after attaching his leash.

Court slowly turned in a full circle, taking in the four-story, block-long warehouse with all its windows broken out, the row of narrow homes across the street, most of them sprayed with graffiti, many of them with boarded-up windows and doors. The playground next to the warehouse was a stretch of weed-choked macadam behind a sagging chain-link fence, the basketball hoops made out of rusted rims and chain nets.

"Not exactly a testimony to urban renewal, is it?" he said, shaking his head as Sunny did his bit for weed control by lifting his short leg against a thistle that had been left to grow almost three feet high. "I know every neighborhood can't be perfect, but getting rid of that warehouse would make a good start."

Even as he made the comment, two strong and not-so-friendly young men stepped out of the dented steel doors to the building. They stopped, folded their muscular arms across their straining chests and stared at Court and the others.

"We've been noticed," Jade said quietly. "My bet is that's a crack warehouse now, and we've just stepped on their turf. Come on, let's go look at the playground."

"Using the term loosely," Court muttered, for there were no swings, no slides, no jungle gyms. Just the weeds poking through the macadam and the two basketball hoops. "Ernesto? You don't come here, do you?"

"Me? What, I look stupid to you? This is gang turf. Tell me again why we're here? I think I should know that before I die, which will be soon, if we don't get out of here. Poor Sunny, he's so young to die."

"Don't do that, Ernesto," Jade warned him, "don't look frightened. They can smell fear. Come on, we're just going to go inside the fence and take a look around. Then we'll leave."

"She's not going to quit, Ernesto," Court said, and then led the way to the opening in the fence.

He walked to the center of the court that might once have had foul lines painted at either end, although he doubted that, and waited for Jade and Ernesto to join him. "About here, Jade?"

She nodded. "Terrell's body was found in the middle of the court, that's what Teddy wrote in his notes. So, Ernesto? You said it couldn't have been a drive-by, even though the street's right there, right? Tell me why."

Ernesto stood very close to Court, his eyes directed at the ground, his knees knocking almost audibly. "I told you, Miss Sunshine. Fence is all around, see, three sides of fence, one of the brick wall of the warehouse. No way could any gang member I know aim one shot to the head from a moving car through one of the openings of the chain link. This isn't the movies, Miss Sunshine, you know? And nobody'd be dumb enough to get close to Terrell one on one by coming inside the fence. You read it in the report, Miss Sunshine, Terrell was one big dude."

"The shooter wouldn't necessarily have acted on his own," Court pointed out reasonably. "Maybe it was the shooter and a bunch of his pals. You know, courage in numbers?"

Ernesto shook his head, still keeping his gaze directed toward his feet. "That's not the way it works. One pops, they all pop. *Pop-pop-pop.* That way, nobody flips on the other guys. If there was more than one of them, Terrell would have been full of bullets, not just the one."

"Not to keep trying to shoot holes in your reasoning, Ernest—pardon the pun—but maybe it was several gang members and one gun."

Ernesto shrugged. "Same thing. You got a clip, you empty the clip. That way your buddies don't see that you can't shoot worth crap, because one of the bullets is sure to make it. That's why so many little kids sitting on porches minding their own business and old ladies watching some soap opera inside their own houses get shot when gangs fight. Lousy aim, but lots of bullets."

Court ran this information through his head until he thought he'd translated it correctly. "All right, so it was one shooter. One lucky shooter, inside the fence. Which, it would seem to me, would be someone Terrell knew?"

Ernesto sighed, at last lifted his head as he sighed in exasperation. "People, people, we can't know that for sure. But we can say that the cops got it wrong all those years ago, and that's *all* I'm saying. Okay, that, and nobody looked too hard because gang shootings are hardly ever solved and the cops know they'd just be busting their rumps for nothing.

Besides, back then? It's not like there wouldn't have been another gang shooting the next day to keep them busy. This was no drive-by, and I don't think it was a gang thing, either. But what do I know? I only grew up here. Not that I come here, I mean, not right *here*. Not that I want to be here right now."

Court looked at Jade, who sighed and nodded her head.

"Just one more thing," she said, taking Court's hand. "Something maybe Ernesto has seen, but you haven't."

"Me? I told you, Miss Sunshine, I don't come here. You stay on your own blocks, that's the way it is. Maybe the guys on your own blocks beat you up once in a while, but they're at least your own guys, on your own blocks. They don't beat you up so bad you don't get better so they can beat you up again, you see what I'm saying?"

"Sort of like fraternity hazing," Court said, "that goes on forever. All right, Jade, what did you really bring us here to see?"

"That," she said, pointing toward the warehouse wall. And then she dropped her hand and jogged toward the wall. "Damn it! What's the *matter* with people?" she asked as she dug in her purse for a tissue.

Court and Ernesto exchanged looks, Ernesto

shrugging his ignorance, and the two of them, after checking to make sure they weren't soon about to get company, walked over to the wall to watch as Jade tried to clean something off a bronze plaque attached to it.

"I never saw that," Ernesto said, impressed. "That gum on there, Miss Sunshine?"

"Yes, that's gum on here," Jade grumbled as the tissue she'd tried to use to pluck the gum from the bronze-relief face of Terrell Johnson just made things worse, the warmth of the day keeping the gum soft enough that the tissue only stuck to it. "If Teddy could see this..."

"Teddy put up this plaque?" Court shook his head. Teddy Sunshine had been the most complicated man he'd ever known, and just when you wanted to hate him, he pulled a stunt like this.

Court read the inscription—Terrell's name, the fact that he'd been All-State first term the year he'd died. "The gum is lousy, Jade, but with the price of brass these days, and people actually taking apart rest-room toilets to steal the brass fittings, I'm just surprised this plaque is still here. And that makes me a cynic, right?"

She wasn't listening. She'd managed to pull off the worst of the large pink wad of bubble gum, but had dropped the tissue. Reaching down into the collected leaves, candy wrappers and God knew what else that had been blown up against the building, she came up holding a small bouquet of dead roses tied with a blue bow. "Who…?"

It was rapidly becoming a day of surprises. Court shoved his hands into his pockets. "Jermayne?" he suggested. "The grandmother is dead. I can't think of anyone else who'd still bring flowers after all these years. Hell. I don't mind saying, Jade, that gets to me. The plaque, the flowers, the good kid dead and the young brother left to fend for himself—I can see why Teddy kept pushing for answers all these years."

She dropped the flowers, dragged a fresh tissue out of her purse and wiped at her eyes. "I've tried so hard, Court. But Jermayne keeps insisting he doesn't want our help. Sometimes I think I'm getting close, you know, and then he pulls away again."

"I know, sweetheart. Ernesto, what are you doing?"

The teenager was dancing on one foot, or so it seemed, and making faces at Court. "You know those two guys we saw standing in front of the warehouse?"

"Yes," Court answered, realizing he'd forgotten them, which had been stupid of him.

"Well, they're not standing in front of the warehouse anymore. Can we, like, *get out of here?*" Without waiting for an answer, he scooped up Sunny and took off for the Mercedes with enough speed to make Court wonder if he couldn't have gotten a track scholarship to Penn State if the logistics thing hadn't worked out for him.

"Come on, Jade, time to go. Unless you want to stick around and talk to our new friends, that is."

"I don't think so, no," Jade said, looking at the two, who had stopped just outside the open gate in the fence and were staring at them like local ex-heavyweight champion Joe Frazier staring down Muhammad Ali before their famous Thriller in Manila. She looked around the playground one last time. "Poor Terrell. What a horrible place to die. Oh, damn, there goes my cell phone."

"Walk and talk, Jade, walk and talk," Court said, taking her by the elbow as she opened her cell, waving to the two tough guys as he steered her back toward the car.

"Yes, this is she," Jade said, and a moment later she was squeezing Court's arm. "Yes…yes, I can do that. Of course." She grinned up at Court as he opened the passenger door for her. "I agree, it is important. When? I'll see you then, and you can save that for when we meet. Goodbye, Mr. Brainard."

Court heard her last words as she climbed into the passenger seat and looked at her quizzically. "Mr. Brainard? Which one, father or son?"

"Son," Jade said, looking rather smug. She waited until he was behind the wheel before adding, "He wants me to come to the rally tonight, about a half hour early, so we can talk about what happened at the airport."

"Oh, he does, does he?" Court checked the rearview mirror and saw Ernesto heaving a sigh of relief as they pulled away from the curb. But then he caught a glimpse of orange-red hair and long, too-thin legs, and watched as Ernesto's mother crossed the narrow street behind them, hurrying toward the warehouse. The two goons went to stop her, but she held up several bills and they let her go inside.

Great. Now he'd aided and abetted an addict. *Life in the fast lane,* Court thought with an inner grimace he'd about had enough of it, thank you.

Court quickly turned at the next corner. Ernesto didn't need to see what had happened. "I wonder," he said, saying the first thing that came to mind, "how do you suppose our friendly neighborhood mayoral candidate happened to know your new cell number?"

"All right, I called his office a couple of times,

trying to convince him to see me. So sue me. I didn't try to go there without you, did I?"

"Yet," Court reminded her. "You didn't try to go there without me *yet*. And you won't. When and where do we meet him?"

"He invited me, not you, you know," Jade said, but then sighed. "But I want you there. And Jess. And Matt. I'm not stupid. The man's a murderer. He sounded so sincere, like always, telling me that Philadelphia needs him. That he's not perfect and he knows now that I know that, but that he's no murderer. Yeah, right."

"But you'll admit he sounded sincere."

"Oh, big deal, Court," Jade said, pushing at her hair, which had tangled around her face in the breeze that might be carrying a thunderstorm with it later that night. "He sounds sincere when he says he's going to fix all the bridges and give the police and fire and EMS departments raises and better health care—all without raising taxes. Not that he ever says *how* he's going to do any of that. He's a politician, Court. I don't think any of them know how to tell the truth, but some of them sure can lie convincingly."

"That's how they get elected," Court agreed. "Where to now, since I seem to be cast in the role of chauffeur today."

"Back to Sam's, I guess. We meet with Joshua Brainard at seven, by the way. I need some time to prepare. But first," she said as she turned in the seat, to look back at Ernesto, "are you hungry, Ernesto? I am. I always eat when I'm nervous."

Court hid a smile. Yes, he'd noticed that.

THE COUNTRY CLUB

As she took another bite of grilled salmon, Jade watched the other woman eat. Or watched the other woman *pretend* to eat, because Savannah Harper might be doing a pretty impressive job of pushing food around her plate, but she wasn't really eating anything. Jade was pretty sure the woman, who had already complained that the selection of "decent couture gowns in size zero was always so limited," rarely ate at all.

While Jade couldn't seem to *stop* eating. Probably—definitely—because she felt more like a fish out of water in this country-club setting than did the salmon on her plate. When Savannah had asked her who designed her gown, Jade hadn't been able to answer her, because she didn't know. She hadn't seen any reason to look at the label, because she probably wouldn't have recognized the name, anyway. Savannah had spent a good five minutes marveling over that lack of interest, pointing out other women in the dining room and the designer labels they wore.

Jade had taken refuge in what was on her

plate, only smiling when she thought it was time to smile, and nodding when she couldn't smile. Now she felt so full she was afraid she might burst out of her simple black silk gown, which probably cost more than she earned in a year—the extra clothing Court had ordered sent up to the penthouse had all arrived minus price tags.

She deliberately put down her fork and folded her hands in her lap and pretended an interest in the New Year's Eve decorations hanging from the chandelier above their table.

"How are you doing?" Court asked her, leaning close to whisper the words in her ear. "I'm sorry I was ignoring you. Buzz and I had some catching up to do about business matters I promise not to bore you with. Is she getting to you? Don't worry. As you can see, Savannah doesn't bite. *Anything.*"

Jade bit back a nervous giggle. Court had told her about their dinner partners on the way to the country club: Buzz, CFO of Becket Hotels, and Savannah, the trophy wife, younger than Buzz by nearly thirty years, and as "sharp as a sack of doorknobs."

"At least she talks, which is more than I'm doing. I'm sorry, Court. I'm still having trouble figuring out how I even *got* here."

He reached over and squeezed her hand. "We flew, we changed in borrowed rooms at the airport, and then we drove, and we arrived just before the fruit cocktail at our place settings got too warm. Remember now?"

While Savannah prattled on to a similarly young, emaciated woman who had stopped at their table, and the plump, balding Buzz wrestled with the lobster on his plate—it looked like he might be losing—Jade took the chance to say, "No, I remember the *how*. It's the *why* I'm still working on. The plane, this gown, this *place*. What am I doing here?"

"Being spontaneous?" Court suggested, a gleam in his eye she probably didn't want to ask him about at the moment. "We're about to begin a new year, Jade. I wanted to begin mine with you. I might have rethought dropping in here at the club, but we can leave soon. I've seen these parties before, too many times. In another hour they'll all be drinking so much no one will notice we've left."

Maybe not, but Savannah Hunter was noticing her again now, both her and her pretty blond friend, who kept looking across the large round table at Jade, whispering to Savannah, looking at Jade again.

"Here it comes. They want to know who I am," Jade said. "Where we met. All that."

"So? Tell them," Court said, oblivious, it would seem, to the pointed glances that had been heading her way ever since they'd walked into the country-club dining room.

"Yes, that would be good. I'm a private investigator and we met when I was playing a high-priced hooker in order to serve a man with a subpoena—oh, but only after I had body-slammed the guy. That should go over big."

"You're ashamed of what you do? Then don't tell them. Be a woman of mystery."

"No." She shot him a dirty look. "And don't do that. Don't use reverse psychology on me so I say what you want me to say."

"Was I doing that? What is it you think I want you to say?"

She shrugged. "I don't know, Court. I don't know you that well. Can't we just leave? Please? I just want to be with you."

He looked at her for a long moment, long enough for her toes to curl against the bottoms of her strappy silver heels, and then recited a number to her, repeated it slowly. "My cell phone number. Should I say it again?"

"No, I've got it. But—"

"You have your cell phone?"

"Yes, in my purse. It's about the only thing that fits in there. What are you thinking?"

"Excuse yourself, go to the women's room—it's just through those doors behind us—and then you'll see a flight of stairs down the hall on the right, I think. Call me, wait until I pick up, then close your phone and come back here. We'll be out of here in five minutes, and at my house in twenty. Any longer than that, and I may suffer permanent damage after hearing you say you just want to be with me."

Jade smiled, slowly, enjoying the hungry look in his eyes. "You're an evil man, Court Becket. No wonder I like you."

Five minutes and thirty seconds later, to be precise, the excuse of an emergency at the Becket Hampton Roads Hotel behind them—invented by Court as he spoke into a dead cell phone—they were on their way to his family home.

Court had untied the black tuxedo bow tie and opened the collar of his starched white shirt as he drove, and the full moon of the crisp winter night made it easy for Jade to watch his profile as he steered along a winding strip of asphalt in the otherwise dark night. He was so achingly good-looking.

And he wanted her.

Did he have any idea how that made her feel?

This perfect man. Handsome. Intelligent. Successful, accomplished.

Wanted *her.*

Why?

"Court…?" Jade said as he slowed the car and turned in between two thick fieldstone pillars onto another curving roadway, this one constructed of brick pavers she could see outlined in the headlights.

"Almost there," he said, turning to smile at her.

She didn't know what to say. "Do…do, um…do you live alone?"

He smiled at her again. "Yes, I do. I sent the wife and kiddies to Florida for the holidays."

"That isn't what I meant. Let me rephrase that. Does anyone else live in your house with you? How's that?"

"My housekeeper, but she has her own quarters over the garages. I am one lonely man rattling around in a house built to contain a family. A large family." He took one hand off the wheel and laid it on Jade's thigh. "So, how soon do you want to start filling some of those bedrooms?"

"You keep doing that, Court. Teasing me like that, scaring me like that. Please don't. We're already moving much too quickly. Your life is so different from mine. We've got nothing in common except..."

Court stopped the car and put the transmission into Park. "Wild animal attraction?" he suggested as he opened the door, and Jade turned her face away from the illumination of the dome light. "Don't knock it, Jade. It's working so far."

It was useless, trying to talk to him. Hadn't he seen how out of place she was just a few minutes ago at the country club? She had no conversation for people like that, and they might as well have all been speaking another language. Stocks and bonds and pork futures? Margin calls? Botox injections and minilifts? Doggy day care and couture showings in someplace called Bryant Park?

The only *real* conversation she'd had in the two hours they'd been there had been with the Woman's locker-room attendant, who had helped her find her way back downstairs to the dining room.

So why was she here? She had to be out of her mind!

The passenger door opened and Jade could do nothing but allow Court to help her out of the car. She looked up at the immense porch that stretched from one end of the house to the other—from one horizon to the other, it seemed—its Greek Revival roof held up by at least ten round white columns, each at least four feet in diameter. Huge, black, wrought-iron carriage lights hung from chains all along the porch, so that the facade of the house, also white, made her feel as if she was stepping from night into day.

"It's…it's a plantation house," she said, still holding Court's hand as they ascended the wide, shallow steps to the porch and the fan-lit front door. "I've seen pictures, and they're all really beautiful, but the reality is so much *more.*"

"My ancestor had a flair, I guess you could say. Personally, I think that since he was the new kid on the block, as it were, here in old Virginny, Ainsley Becket wanted to make a statement. You know. I'm here, I'm staying, and there's nothing you can do about it but smile and get with the program," Court told her as he fished in his pocket for a key and opened the door, motioning for her to precede him into the well-lit foyer.

"I doubt anyone missed the point. Is the White House this big?"

"I don't think so, no, at least not as originally built. We've installed more plumbing, electricity, moved the kitchen inside. But for the most part, this is the same house Ainsley Becket built when he and his second wife purchased this land in 1816, although his wife's family resided in Virginia for a long time before Ainsley showed up. We talk about our roots a lot, here in Virginia. I've got the added cachet of having an honest-to-God pirate as the first-generation Becket in Hampton Roads. Take a look around while I go get our suitcases."

Jade was barely listening to him. The foyer had been grand enough, with its black and white marble tiles, the crystal chandelier that had to weigh at least half a ton, the freestanding curved staircase to an open balcony, the bits and pieces of grandeur that all looked worthy of a museum. Her entire family home could probably have fit inside that foyer, with room to spare for Rockne's doghouse.

Straight ahead, the wide hallway ran beneath the curving staircase, and Jade could see what looked to be a wall of French doors a million miles away, leading out into the night. From somewhere in her head she pulled the information that plantation houses were built this way for cross-ventilation in the warm summer months.

Not that she'd ever see this house again, winter or summer.

But the room Court found her in a minute later had made her forget that unnerving thought. It was *huge,* and filled with so many treasures Jade didn't know where to look first. "You *live* like this? Where do you *sit?* You don't sit on any of these beautiful chairs or couches, do you? It would be…it would be sacrilege."

Court's laugh made her realize what she'd said, and she took a deep breath, trying to collect herself.

"I'm sorry. I'm just thinking about Teddy's favorite chair and what it would look like in here."

He came over to her and took hold of her upper arms, looking deeply into her eyes. "It's a house, Jade. I didn't build it, I didn't furnish it. I had nothing to do with it, so I can't take credit for it. Do you think that this house is me?"

"Well, it's certainly not *me,*" Jade said, trying to smile. "So where do you really live? Because if you tell me that portrait of the beautiful woman in the striped gown slides back to uncover a humungous flat-screen TV and you spend Sundays stretched out on one of these couches, drinking beer and wiping potato-chip grease on the upholstery while you watch the game, I'm not going to believe you."

"That's quite an image. You're right. Nobody uses these rooms anymore, except for large events. They did once, but that was another time, another century." He took her hand. "Come on, it's been a long day. Let's grab the luggage and go upstairs. You can take the grand tour tomorrow."

Jade was nervous the entire way up the curving staircase. She had been nervous from the moment Court asked to meet Teddy and every moment since.

But then she stepped into Court's suite of rooms, and suddenly there was nothing to be nervous about anymore.

The room was large—she had a feeling there was no such thing as a small room in this house—but a section of it had been designed as a sitting area, and someone had started a fire in the grate. The room was warm, welcoming.

And it looked like Court. Masculine, solid. Bookcases flanked the marble fireplace, and the books looked jumbled on the shelves, as if someone used those shelves often. She saw one book, open and turned on its pages, lying on a small table next to one of the leather chairs that also flanked the fireplace. The large antique mantel clock chimed once and she realized that it was already eleven-thirty, just a scant half hour from midnight and the new year.

She walked over and picked up the book to read its title. "You read thrillers?" she asked, seeing Lee Child's name on the spine. "Not one of Donald Trump's how-I-did-it-so-there books?"

"No, sorry. I can't seem to get past the hairstyle, for some reason. You read thrillers? Not mysteries?"

"Mysteries are full of private investigators. Been there, done that, know how boring ninety-nine percent of the job is," she said, putting down the book. "You shouldn't open your books like that, you know, it breaks the spine."

"I know. I like my books to feel lived-in." He lifted one of the suitcases and put it on a low table and then unzipped it. "Yours. Where do you want it?"

Jade looked around the room as she realized something she hadn't thought about earlier. "Does it matter? I can change after I shower tomorrow, but I don't think there's a nightgown. And here I'll bet you thought you'd thought of everything."

"Who says I didn't?" Court said as he joined her in front of the fireplace. He'd stripped off his tuxedo jacket, but the opened bow tie was still hanging from beneath the collar of his shirt. He looked like an ad in *GQ*. Better. He was close to her now, but he didn't touch her. "Jade? Still nervous? Still wondering what the hell you're doing here?"

"Not when you look at me that way, no," she said honestly. She couldn't seem to find a lie when she was with him or even a convenient evasion. "I like being with you."

He put his hand against her cheek, lightly cupping her face, so that she closed her eyes and went with the sensation his touch sent through her. "Just the two of us," he said softly, intimately. "We make sense, don't we, when it's just the two of us."

She bit her bottom lip, nodded. "I don't understand it. I've never felt like this before. I don't know what to do about it. I'm not impulsive, Court. I'm not...reckless."

She opened her eyes and looked up at him, her eyes openly imploring him to help her. "But then you look at me and the next thing I know I'm...I don't know. Where am I, Court? Where are we?"

"We're where we belong, Jade, you and I," he told her quietly as he lowered his head toward her. "We're together."

She moved into him with a sigh, knowing he was right. For tonight, if not forever. For as long as they could keep the world away—that would be the romantic way to look at it. But as she closed her eyes and waited for his kiss, she knew she should be thinking: for as long as she could keep common sense away.

His kisses were slow, drugging. Hypnotizing. She was caught up in the spell of him, the taste, touch and smell of him. She reached for the ends of his bow tie and held on, making sure he didn't leave her, anchoring herself before she floated away.

He was smiling against her mouth, she could feel the curve of his lips, and when she smiled back it was as if she'd learned another secret button to push, for her arousal immediately went up another notch.

This was a fairy tale. He was Prince Charming and she, while not exactly Cinderella, was certainly no fantasy princess. She didn't need a glass slipper; she didn't want one. She could live without a prince or a castle.

But she didn't know if she could live without Court.

Her arms slid around his back and clung tighter to him, as if she could hold the fantasy, draw it and him inside her and keep both with her forever.

"Court," she breathed in aid of nothing as he slipped one arm around her back, bent down to slide his other arm behind her knees, lifted her high against his chest. She simply liked saying his name.

He carried her over to his bed and gently laid her down, then followed her to cover her body with his own. His kisses trailed across her cheek, down the side of her neck and onto her bare shoulder, even as he slid the single strap of the gown down her arm.

"Court…"

She lifted herself against him, so that the soft whisper of the zipper sliding free brought an answering whisper from her.

"Yes…please…"

The night air could do nothing to cool her body as he exposed each inch, kissed each inch, possessed each inch of her. His passion, his want, was so amazing to her. That he seemed to believe she was precious, even somehow fragile. Feminine. And eminently desirable.

She was more than ready for him when he came to her, when he lowered himself onto her, into her. She sighed as she felt the now familiar fullness of him, bit back a small cry when his low moan of pleasure ripped at her very core.

He took her high. Then he took her higher. What she thought she knew about pleasure paled beneath his measured movements, and then shattered when she knew he had lost control, that she had excited him past his Southern gentlemen perception of himself.

"Yes." She breathed the word into his ear even as she nipped at his lobe, tongued the remarkably soft flesh. "Yes, Court…yes."

When the mantel clock struck midnight, Cinderella never even heard the chimes.

JADE DIDN'T LOOK UP from the file folder she was reading as Court entered the living room back at Sam Becket's house. "What time is it?"

Court sat down on the facing couch, resisting the urge to grab the folder from her and tell her, *Enough, Jade, enough!* "Time to begin planning alternative ways to explain to Sam why he's going to need new fringe on his dining-room carpet, I guess. Sunny must be teething."

"Oh, no," Jade said, closing the folder on her own and sitting back against the cushions. "There's not a stick of furniture or a carpet in this place that's not some kind of antique. Please tell me you're joking."

"All right, I'm joking," Court said affably. "But we're still going to have to find a way to explain the chewed fringe to him."

Jade ran her fingers through her hair, lifting her hair away from her face, not realizing that

Court had always considered the gesture a turn-on, as it highlighted her magnificent bone structure.

Unfortunately, today it seemed to highlight the fact that she'd been losing weight, as well as the faint blue bruises of weariness beneath her eyes. "Sweetheart, why don't you go take a nap? We've got a long night ahead of us."

But either she didn't hear him or she was ignoring him. "Jessica will be back soon," she said, seeming to relax a little. "Her dog, let her handle it. There, one problem solved. Although I hope Ernesto is keeping Sunny outside."

"He is. Rockne is initiating Sunny in the fine art of digging for gold in Sam's flower beds. Would you like something to drink?" Court pushed his hands down on the couch on either side of him, prepared to stand up, when he thought he felt some resistance beneath his left hand. "What's this—music?" he asked, reaching between the cushions and pulling out a CD in a clear plastic case.

Jade held out her hand and he passed the case to her. She opened it and turned the case slightly to read something written on the disk itself. "Not a CD, Court, a DVD, I think. And I think it's probably news clips from Jessica's station. Video from the Fishtown Strangler case, Terrell's case. Oh—and Teddy's funeral. That's on here, too. I didn't know she had all this." She closed the case and got to her feet.

"Hold on, Jade," Court said, also rising. "You want to watch it, don't you? Don't do that, sweetheart. What good is that going to do?"

"Well, Court, I won't know that until I watch it, will I?" she said, not as good at sarcasm as some people, but she did a good imitation. Then she shook her head. "I'm sorry, that was uncalled-for. I don't know what's wrong with me. My mind keeps jumping from here to there and back again. One minute I'm living in the moment and the next I'm back a dozen or more years to these cold cases, and then I'm partway in between, thinking about…"

"Yes? Go on, Jade," Court said as they headed for Sam's private den—and the DVD player that was sure to be there. "Sometimes you're where, thinking about what?"

She surprised him by stopping in the middle of the hallway and turning to confront him. "Us, okay? I keep thinking about us. About where we were, about what happened to us that we ended up like this, neither here nor there or knowing where we go from… Let it go, Court. Please, just let it go. I can't deal with this right now."

He put his hands on her shoulders before she could turn away, flee up the nearby stairs to her bedroom or whatever.

"Jade," he said quietly. "I'm not trying to press you, sweetheart, I'm really not. I'd like to, I admit that. But I'm here because you're hurting and I want to help. And yes, I'm also thinking about us a lot right now, about what happened to us. What happens tomorrow? I don't know, neither of us knows that. And that's all right. I just don't want you to fight me now. I don't want you to fight yourself. I only want you to take whatever strength I can give you, no strings attached."

"Oh, Court," she breathed, stepping closer to him, her body against his, her cheek against his chest. "I don't know how you put up with me, I really don't. I'm…I'm so confused right now. I don't know if I can trust my own emotions."

He leaned down and kissed the top of her head. "You just lost your father, Jade. Your anchor for a lot of years. You have to feel like you're drifting. It's only natural."

"You never liked him," Jade said, sniffing, and then she pushed back slightly to look up in his face. "Did you?"

"I liked Teddy well enough, Jade. He was a

likable man. I didn't like that he was my competition."

"He wasn't. You make that sound almost inces-
tuous, Court, do you know that?"

Great. Once again, he'd put his foot in it. Sometimes he found it hard to believe he could actually
walk and chew gum at the same time, let alone run
a pretty good-size business empire. "You know
what I meant, Jade. He needed you, I didn't.
That's how you saw it."

"You'd *agreed,* remember? You traveled for
business nearly every week. What was I supposed
to do when you were gone—turn into one of those
insipid ladies who lunch? So Teddy needed help
a couple of days a week, background checks,
clerical help, and couldn't really afford to hire
anyone to replace me. So what? And I can't
believe we're having this conversation."

"Neither can I," Court said, mentally kicking
himself for his lousy timing. "Let's go look at
this DVD. But you know, Jade, if Jessica had
found anything important on it, she would have
told us."

"Always the dreamer, Court," Jade said, and
even smiled. "You're really cute when you're
gullible."

"Ha. Ha," he said, watching as she once more

headed for Sam's private den, relieved that the awkward moment was behind them. He really had to start rehearsing what he was going to say to Jade when this thing was over, if it was ever over. She was experienced enough now not to give in to their intense physical attraction and then simply pretend that was the answer to all their problems. She wanted and needed more. Deserved more.

Come to think of it, so did he.

Court returned to the living room to grab two cold sodas from behind the bar and then joined Jade in the large, darkly paneled room that not only could have been taken from an English gentlemen's club, but actually had been, board by board, by Sam's great-great grandfather.

The room smelled comfortably of leather polish and the occasional cigar Sam indulged in, but was kept from being oppressively proper by the collection of Phillies and Eagles paraphernalia scattered throughout the bookcases. Yachting trophies and the like were reserved for men who didn't like chowing down on spicy French fries and drinking cold beer from plastic cups in the cheap seats.

Jade was sitting on one of the leather couches and the DVD was already playing on the enormous flat screen, usually hidden behind an oil painting by some long-dead Dutch artist.

"Anything yet?" Court asked as he handed her one of the soda cans and sat down beside her.

"Not really, no. *Oh,*" she said quietly.

Court looked at the screen. Jade had stopped the action on Teddy's face. He was at a funeral, standing in the rain, and he looked like he'd just lost his best friend. "That was a few years ago, don't you think? Teddy looks…younger." Really, what else was there to say?

"Tarin White's funeral, or so it says on the disk. He doesn't look so good, does he? I mean, I'm not sure I ever really *noticed,* you know? I guess kids don't. We just see what we want to see. He was so handsome. I think some of my friends in junior high had secret crushes on him. When did it all change? He was sad, that I knew—we all always tried to make him smile, make him laugh. But he was also a troubled man, wasn't he?"

"He was a complicated man," Court said, resting his hand on Jade's thigh, the move meant to comfort. "Teddy didn't have an easy life."

"And he had a harder death," Jade said quietly, hitting the play button on the remote once more. "I think Jess was trying to protect me. That's why she didn't let me know about this DVD. I sort of wish she was better at hiding things."

"Then let's turn it off," Court suggested, giving her thigh a gentle squeeze. "I'll go tell Mrs. Archer that we'll need an early dinner, definitely for three, hopefully for five if Jess and Matt show up in time, and then we can go see Joshua Brainard. And then—" he wished he didn't sound so pathetically hopeful "—maybe this will all finally be over. Jade?"

She sat forward, stopping the DVD and then reversing it. She scanned forward, frame by frame, and then stopped the action again. "This is film of Teddy's funeral. Look beyond the priest's head, Court. Way back, all the way to the line of trees. Do you see him?"

"I see something," Court said cautiously, getting to his feet and walking close to the TV screen. "Okay, all right. There's somebody standing there. But he's all in shadow from the trees. Tell me what you think you see."

She was beside him now, her head pushed forward on her shoulders as she squinted at the large screen. "Look at how tall he is, Court. His head is all the way up to the first split of the branches."

She touched a fingertip to the screen. "And

look at those wide, hunched shoulders. Look at the way he's standing there, his hands in his pockets, sort of leaning on one leg. Come on, Court, when was the last time you saw shoulders like that, somebody who stands like that? Like he wishes he was smaller than he is, more able to hide."

"This morning, at the car wash. That's Jermayne," Court said, knowing that his life had just gotten more complicated again. "You said you didn't see him at the funeral. You said he'd told you he had to work and couldn't come. But he was there."

"There, but not there. Hiding," Jade said, still staring at the dark outline of Jermayne Johnson's distinctively tall, muscular body. "Why? Why wasn't he at the church? Why did he hide? Why didn't he join us at the grave? Why did he lie and say he wasn't there?" She stepped back, turned to Court. "There has to be a reason, there's always a reason. So why, Court?"

"Much as I really don't want to say this, Jade, I don't have the answers to those questions. You'd have to ask Jermayne. Which," he said, watching as she fished her cell phone out of her slacks pocket and flipped it open, "seems to have already occurred to you."

Jade held up one finger to silence him and then turned away, walking to the far end of the room as she waited for Jermayne Johnson to answer.

Court ejected the disk and turned off the DVD player, privately hoping the disk wouldn't one day be labeled Exhibit A in Jermayne's murder trial. He wondered if Jade had considered that and decided she hadn't.

"He didn't answer," she said, joining Court again. "I left a message and gave him Sam's address. I told him I had something for him, something of Teddy's I wanted him to have to remember Teddy by—a gold pocket watch—and asked him to come here as soon as he could."

"Dangling bait?"

"No, not really," Jade said as they walked to the foyer and she turned for the stairs. "All right, maybe. I also told him I wouldn't go at him anymore about going to school, that I respect his decision, and that I'm leaving town at six o'clock tonight for a job, driving down to Florida for the next month or so. I just wanted to meet with him one last time before I left. To give him the watch, to give us both closure."

"You packed a lot of lies into one short phone message. Have you been taking lessons from Jessica? Tell me, did Teddy even own a gold watch?" Court asked, following her up the stairs.

"He did once. His father's. Mom took it with her when she left, and either she or Teddy's brother probably hocked it. But Jermayne doesn't know that." She paused on the landing and sighed. "God, I hope he shows up. I really need to know why he lied to me. I mean, there was no reason to lie to me, right? Not unless Jermayne was hiding something, hiding *from* something. I might even let Matt flash his badge, question him."

"Don't do that, Jade," Court said, following her into her bedroom, following her like a puppy, damn it, like Sunny, eager for some attention.

"Don't do what? Bring Matt in on it? All right, maybe that's pushing it. But Jermayne never really answers me. He keeps avoiding any real answers."

"No, Jade, I don't mean about Matt. I mean, don't do this to yourself. Don't go building up your hopes again. Because that is what you're doing. Teddy wanted Jermayne to go to school, and you're going to keep trying to do what Teddy wanted. I think Jermayne should go to school. I agree with you that he's going nowhere fast as it is, and that his life would have been very different—better—if his brother had lived. But Teddy couldn't fix the world, sweetheart, and neither can you. You can only get hurt."

Jade looked at Court for a long time, her expression unreadable. "You think he did it, don't you? You think Jermayne killed Teddy."

"No. I think it's *possible* he killed Teddy. He was strong enough to wrestle the gun from Teddy, turn it on him."

"Teddy was drunk that night, maybe even passed-out drunk. Anybody could have taken advantage of him like that, not just Jermayne. Besides, where's Jermayne's motive?"

She turned away from him, rummaging in a chest of drawers and coming out with a silky nude-beige bra and matching panties.

"Motive? Come on, Jade. We live in a world where people kill other people for cutting them off on an exit ramp. We've gone from honking the horn to flipping the finger, to beating them to death with a baseball bat we keep under the front seat, all in the past ten or fifteen years. We're a violent society. I don't know why Jermayne might kill Teddy. You said the case Teddy kept his gun in was there, right on his desk. We don't know why it was on his desk, why Teddy had it out at all. But it was there and if Jermayne was there and Teddy pushed him one too many times about going to school, maybe the kid just snapped."

"But that would mean that Joshua Brainard

killed his wife, but never planned to frame Teddy for the murder. That the whole thing was coincidence. Two crimes, two killers, one night. No, Court, I don't think I can buy that one." She headed for the walk-in closet and emerged a few moments later with a thin, silvery blouse draped with a very interesting V-neckline, and black slacks hanging over her arm.

The bias cut of the blouse, the simple lines of the slacks—both were severely tailored, without frills, and could have had Jade's name written all over them, so suited were the pieces to her refined, sophisticated look. Court had seen the pieces and brought them home from Italy. He'd given the outfit to her for her birthday, two months before their breakup.

Another woman would have thrown the outfit away. He wondered if Jade had considered that, and then decided to be practical. He wondered if she remembered that he had given her the pieces.

He decided to give it a shot.

"I've always liked that outfit on you," he said when she looked at him, one eyebrow raised, as if to say, *I'm going to take a shower now, you know, so what are you still doing here?*

"It's very comfortable. Court? It's after four o'clock. I want to take a shower."

"You used to like baths. Bubble baths. You used to invite me to share the tub with you. I'd have to take a shower afterward to get the scent of your bubble bath off my skin, but it was worth it." He walked closer to her. "One night I didn't bother with the shower. We'd had…more important things to do…and we overslept the next morning, so I had to just dress and leave for the office. Do you remember that, Jade?"

"Court…"

"Do you remember Kristine, my secretary? She teased me all day about it. She said the last time she'd been around a man who smelled that good was when her cousin Billy May—just May to his friends—came to town to announce his sex-change operation."

"You told me," Jade said quietly. "I remember. Then you told me Kristine was making that up."

"She gave me a bottle of bubble bath as a gag gift for Christmas. An entire gift basket, as a matter of fact. I hadn't told anybody yet that you'd left me. You see, I was still so sure you'd come back."

"Court…I'm sorry. We were upset, under some considerable pressure. You said things…I said things." She laid the clothing on the bed and kept her back to him. But he could tell that she was rubbing her hands together, her posture more pro-tective than dismissive. "We…it just wasn't work-ing out."

"So like the horn honk that turned to flipping the finger that grew into the baseball bat kept under the front seat—the argument turned to stupid ultimatums and then, bam, the big bat came out. The lawyer. Who hired him, Jade? It was Teddy, wasn't it? And then the ball just kept on rolling."

Finally she turned on him. "Why? Why would you only ask that now, Court? Why did you just let it all happen?"

"Because I was hurting. Because I was jealous. Because I wanted to come first in your life, and I'd just realized I didn't, because I'd fought that war and I'd lost it, just as he'd warned me I would. Because I'm a goddamn idiot who let pride make me do things I regretted the moment I'd done them, but by then it was too late. I thought you knew that, Jade."

Jade's eyes were bright with tears. She pressed her hands against her mouth, but not before she moaned quietly, "Oh, God…oh, my God…"

"And now he's dead, and any chance I had of giving us both some time, and then maybe we could try again, might have died with him," Court said, wishing he could stop talking. But he couldn't.

Maybe it was seeing Teddy on that DVD, maybe it was seeing the plaque the man had put up for Terrell Johnson, maybe it was everything he'd been hearing about the enigma that had been Teddy Sunshine for the past two weeks all stirred in together with everything he'd known about the man that he'd never shared with Jade. The veiled threat, the way Teddy had set himself up as Court's competition.

"Yes, Court, and now he's dead. That much is certainly true."

"And the rest of it? Because now he's Saint Teddy, isn't he, Jade? I thought it was bad before, but it's even worse now. Saint Teddy? Tell me Jade. I love you. I always have and always will love you. But how in hell do I compete with *that?*"

Court turned to leave the room, to go somewhere and either get himself under control or figure out a way to beat himself up for his lousy timing and worse words.

"Court, wait! Damn it, Court Becket, you come back here!"

He kept his back to her as he shook his head. "No, it's all right, Jade. I didn't mean for us to have a postmortem right now on our dead marriage. I was out of line. Go take your shower. I'll meet you downstairs."

But before he could move again she was behind him, her fingertips digging into his left shoulder as she tried to turn him around to face her. "Don't you leave me like this, Court. Don't you dare leave me like this. Everybody…everybody always leaves."

Court turned, took hold of her arms as he watched the first tears run down Jade's too-pale cheeks. "Everybody, Jade?"

She lowered her head, avoiding his gaze. "Wow, where did that one come from?" She looked up at him again. "I…I don't know why I said that."

He led her over to the bed and they sat down next to each other. "Your mother left, Jade. She left your father."

"She left all of us," Jade said, wiping her cheeks with the back of her hand. "We weren't enough for her."

"And then your sisters left, right?"

She looked at him, her expression incredulous. "My sisters? What does that have to do with anything? They grew up, they went to live their own lives."

"After what you did for them, after everything you sacrificed for them. Jolie, off to Hollywood to chase her dream. Jessica, chasing her own dream. After you'd given up *your* dream for them. You gave, they took."

"They…nobody knew I wanted to go to medical school. I worked with Teddy, even while I was still in high school. They knew I would stay with him."

"Leaving them free to go."

"Their mother left them. Jessica was barely in her teens. Somebody had to take care of them."

"*Teddy* had to take care of them, Jade. Not you. You weren't that much older than Jolie. Yet she got a free pass, didn't she? You grew up, so she didn't have to. You gave her and Jess not only their childhood, but yours."

"It wasn't like that. I think Jolie missed our mother the most. I think Mom's leaving hit her harder than it did either Jess or me. I mean, if Mom had a favorite, it was Jolie. She encouraged her dream, made sure she had dance and voice lessons, that sort of thing. I don't think Jolie noticed when Mom began to look at her differently. As if she envied her, maybe even disliked her for being so beautiful, so talented. I really worried about Jolie, about the day she'd figure out that Mom had begun to hate her. Instead, Jolie cried for months after Mom left."

Court didn't think it was time to point out to

Jade that her mother hadn't just left *her* physically all those years ago, but she had left her emotionally years before that, in favor of her younger sister. In fact, it could almost be said that Jade had always been a motherless child.

Who sought approval, acceptance, more than a child looking for love? Jade had needed to be needed, and her sisters had needed her. Teddy had needed her.

Teddy had made her feel indispensable to him, and Jade had been more than happy to play the role that had been given her. He loved her, he loved all three of his daughters the best Court could tell, but he had also slotted them into convenient categories: Jessica, the baby; Jolie, the dreamer; and Jade, the responsible one who took care of everyone.

Which made Teddy's life so much easier, didn't it?

He could wallow in his misery over the wife who'd left him, the brother who'd betrayed him. He could continue to work long hours as a Philadelphia homicide detective and then, later, at the Sunshine Detective Agency. He could travel to Ireland with his friend Father Muskie, pretend he was still a cop by working his cold cases, and he could occasionally drop into a bottle—and Jade would *understand.* Because Jade knew what it was like to be rejected by someone you loved.

But all of that was for another time…

"Did you think I didn't need you, Jade?" he asked her quietly, holding her hand, stroking his thumb across her palm.

"No, don't be ridiculous, of course I…" She stopped, lowered her head again. "I knew you needed parts of me. We weren't married all that long, Court."

"No, we weren't, were we? And I was gone a lot, wasn't I? I should have taken you with me. That was stupid. But I thought I could work faster if you weren't with me and I could be home sooner. I, uh, I don't travel nearly as much as I did when we were married."

Jade simply nodded. "That's…that's probably smart. You were always on the move."

"I'd never had a reason to stay in one place, not until you. And I'll admit it, Jade. Every time I came home, it was like a honeymoon all over again. I really didn't think about what you were doing while I was gone. I think I just supposed you were happy doing what other wives did. You shocked the hell out of me when you said you wanted to work with Teddy again. I thought that part of your life was over."

"We should have had this talk a long time ago, Court," Jade said, wiping her hand across her damp cheeks again. "We probably should have had this talk before we got married."

He reached over to push a lock of hair behind her ears. "We're talking now."

"Yes, we are, aren't we." Jade turned to look at him, and he longed to believe it was with love in her eyes. "There hasn't been anyone since you, Court. I think you should know that."

"I didn't even need cold showers," Court told her with a small, self-deprecating smile. "I just wasn't interested. You're the only fantasy I've ever had, and if I couldn't have the reality anymore, I didn't want the fantasy."

Jade touched her fingers to the opened collar of his dress shirt. "We could…maybe if we were very careful, and if we didn't expect too much of each other too soon…you know…then maybe we could…we could maybe *try* to—"

He put his arms around her and gently took her mouth, even as a soft cry escaped her lips.

Did she feel it? Holding her, loving her, was like coming home. The passion was there, yes. That had been there since the beginning. Maybe it was only in this last year, spent apart from that passion, which had given them both the time to realize that even if they could live without the passion, they couldn't exist without the love.

The salty taste of her tears mingled in their kiss, bittersweet, and he felt an involuntary shudder rack him when she slipped her arms around his waist.

Yes. This was what they needed right now. Not the passion. The love.

"Hi, honey, I'm ho-ho-ho-home. Whoops— talk about your lousy timing. Sorry, guys."

Court swore under his breath as he and Jade looked at Jessica, who was now grinning like a...well, the way only Jessica could grin. "Hi, Jess. Matt downstairs?"

"Uh-huh," she said, still grinning. "Hey, look what I got," she then said, holding up her left hand, her fingers spread. "Wait, let me go stand over next to the window so the sun can catch the stone. Matt picked it out all by himself, and it's perfect. Jade, don't you think it's perfect?"

"Do you want to kill her or should I?" Court said quietly, barely moving his lips.

Jade squeezed his hand. "It's probably for the best right now. You go downstairs and tell Matt what we learned about Jermayne, how we're going to meet with Joshua Brainard in a couple of hours, and I'll let Jess gush at me. We, uh, we'll continue this later?"

"Yeah," Court said, seeing the mix of confusion and dawning realization in Jade's eyes. She didn't look defeated anymore, no longer the wounded bird she'd been since Teddy died. He believed, needed to believe, that she was at last beginning to look forward again, beyond the mistakes of the past, beyond solving her father's murder. "Let's do that. Let's very definitely schedule that really soon. In fact, why don't you just pencil me in for the rest of your life?"

The sun shining on Jessica's engagement ring could be no brighter than Jade's smile. "I think that could probably be arranged."

"Hey, people!" Jessica said, walking back over to them. "Doesn't anybody want to see my ring?"

THE SUNSHINE HOME

"Look, Teddy," Jade said, walking into his office holding the large crystal vase filled with three dozen long-stemmed yellow roses. "Look what Court just had delivered. Aren't they beautiful?"

"Beautiful, honey." Teddy barely looked up from the newspaper crossword puzzle he was working at his desk. "What's a seven-letter word for remuneration? Starts with P."

"Payment," Jade said as she put the vase down on the desktop and leaned over Teddy's shoulder to peer at the puzzle. "I don't see that clue there."

"There's clues everywhere, Jade, if you just look," Teddy said, and he was pointing his pencil at the roses as he spoke. "Court Becket must have enjoyed your company this weekend."

Jade felt her cheeks flush with embarrassed heat. "Now I see where you're going here. Subtle, Teddy, really subtle. Those flowers are not payment for services rendered, Teddy. That's cruel."

He pushed back his chair and swiveled the seat to look up at her. "Maybe you're right. But it's meant to wake you up, little girl. You went away for the weekend with a man you barely know. You went to his house, you slept in his bed. In my line of work, there's a name for women who do that. I told Father Muskie you'd be at Confession this Saturday."

"Oh, you did, did you? Well, you can just tell Father Muskie—"

"He's wrong for you, Jade," Teddy said, his tone now soothing, that hint of lilt he always came back with from his trips to Ireland softening his words. "No, no, don't look at me like that. I'm only thinking of what's best for my little girl."

That was Teddy's answer for everything he did: he was only doing what was best for his girls.

But today, for reasons she didn't understand, Jade wasn't buying it. Today, she had another theory.

"Are you, Teddy?" she asked him, walking around to stand on the other side of the desk. She braced her palms against the old wood as she looked at him. "Or are you thinking about how Court lives in Virginia? How maybe I might soon be living in Virginia if he asks me to marry him? About how, if he did ask me, maybe I'd say yes? Maybe even about how you'd manage here alone without me? Would you be that selfish, Teddy?"

Teddy's fists came down so hard on the wood that Jade involuntarily stepped backward. "Selfish, is it? You're calling me selfish? You've got a nerve, Jade Sunshine. I've been alive a damn sight lot longer than you have, little girl, and I know what

I'm talking about here. I see the stars in your eyes. You think it's enough to be all starry-eyed and your stomach doing flips when you see him?"

"Teddy, I—"

"You think kisses are enough? Looking at those flowers, I'm thinking he thinks the same way as you—with anything but his brain. You don't have a mother, so it's up to me to say these things. *Sex,* little girl, that's what you've got right now, since you're looking at me like you don't know what I'm saying here. There's a lot more to marriage than sex, Jade."

"So speaks the marriage expert," Jade muttered, a part of her wondering who could have said those words, because it certainly couldn't have been her. She never spoke like that; she wasn't a cruel person. What was wrong with her? "Ah, Teddy, I'm sorry."

He got to his feet and came around the desk to fold her in his big, comforting arms, to kiss the top of her head as he led her over to one of the chairs in front of the desk.

"It's all right, sweetie pie. You just said what you were thinking. I'm no expert, that's for sure. But that doesn't mean you can't learn from my mistakes. Come on, sit down here and let your sorry excuse for a father bare his battered old soul to you."

Before she sat down, Jade touched the vase, perhaps for courage, and then waited for Teddy to open the left bottom drawer of the desk and pull out the cloth bag that held his treasured bottle of Crown Royal and a shot glass. Reverently he lifted the squat bottle from its pouch and poured a measure into the glass.

He also kept a bottle of fine Irish whiskey in that same drawer, and she saw that emerge more often. The Crown Royal was held in reserve for either the best or the worst of times. She thought she had a pretty good idea which of the two this moment was for him.

"*Sláinte,* Jade," he said, holding up the glass, and then he sipped at it, not downing it quickly, as he did his nightly shot-and-a-beer, because, as he said, this was liquid gold he was drinking.

The problem was, he was drinking that liquid gold and those "medicinal" shots and beers more and more often as the years went by. As he grew lonelier?

"Where do I start, Jade?" he asked her, leaving the Crown Royal bottle on the desktop. "How about with this, all right? Opposites attract, sweetie pie, but they don't stick for long. You are who you are, and Court Becket is who he is. Opposites. Like me and your mother."

"Court isn't anything like—"

"Don't interrupt, Jade, this isn't easy for me. "Your mother was the most beautiful woman I'd ever seen. You look so much like her, my heart still sometimes has to remind itself to beat when I look at you and see her young again, mine again, looking at me like maybe I was something special, not just this dumb flatfoot street cop like my dad before me."

He took another sip from the shot glass.

"You showed up seven months after we were married, Jade, did you know that? You did, and I was that thrilled to have you, because you got my Claudia to the altar. I was so happy, I didn't see what I should have seen, what we both should have seen. Opposites attract, Jade, like I said. That doesn't mean they fit well together."

"Are you saying you and Mom might not have gotten married if she hadn't been pregnant with me?" Jade didn't know how that made her feel, not exactly. She did know the news didn't make her feel particularly good.

Teddy took yet another drink from his shot glass, this one more of a full swallow. "Back then, I don't think it would have made a difference, no. Now I wonder if maybe I wasn't already feeling her looking at me a little differently, wanting things I couldn't give her. So maybe we slipped up one night and maybe we didn't. Maybe it was just me. Does it matter? Your mother was so happy to be getting married and having her own house, her own babies. We just needed to be together. You were our first fight, though, I'll say that."

"Then she didn't want me," Jade said, nodding, because that explained a lot, answered many questions she'd had all her life.

"No, she wanted you," Teddy said quickly. "It

was the *Jade* I didn't want. Jade? What kind of a name is that, not that it didn't grow on me. But Claudia wanted fancy, had a big thing for fancy, and so you're Jade. When Jolie came along I didn't even fight it, because by then there were other battles. The big new house Claudia wanted, the trips she wanted to take, the cleaning lady she needed, the hairdresser up on Broad Street who cost twice as much as the shop that was good enough for every other wife we knew. The worst, though, was that I was never home. Hell, I was moonlighting three nights a week just to pay for the fancy car she said she had to have."

"And Hawaii?" Jade asked, looking at her father's colorful Hawaiian shirt, thinking of his closet filled with other colorful Hawaiian shirts.

"I told her we'd get there," Teddy said, and Jade got the feeling he wasn't really talking to her anymore, but only *at* her, as he relived years of unhappiness. "I needed to put in my thirty years, get my pension and then we'd go. Then…then, uh, there was Jessica. Claudia never forgave me for Jessica. By then maybe I didn't care so much. I was getting pretty tired of the big ideas, the big dreams, the *I want, I want, I have to have.*"

"That's when she started going away, wasn't it? After Jessica was born. Where did she go, Teddy, those times she left?"

Teddy finished off the contents of the shot glass and poured another measure. "You think I asked? If I asked, she might have told me. I was only glad that she came back. Until she didn't come back. Maybe a part of me was glad then, too."

He looked across the desk at Jade. "And that's what I'm telling you, sweetheart. Wanting isn't enough. That stars-in-the-eyes feeling isn't enough, not in the long run, not for the long haul. You and this Court Becket? You're from different worlds. Born different, raised different, with different hopes and dreams. I don't want you hurt, baby. I want you to look past the stars in your eyes and see that before you and that man do something you'll both regret."

"I, uh…" Jade said, getting to her feet, picking up the vase of fragrant roses. "I'll think about it, Teddy. I think you're wrong, but I'll think about it."

He picked up his glass, drained it in a single gulp. "You do that, little girl, you just do that."

She hesitated in the doorway. "Don't drink it all, Teddy, please."

"Don't you worry about me. I'll be fine," he said, pouring yet another measure. "Jade?"

She turned around one last time. "Yes, Teddy?"

"Margaret Mary," he said, his smile sad. "That's the name I wanted for you. Maybe all our lives would have been different if Claudia could have been content with just a husband who worshiped her and a sweet little baby girl we'd named Margaret Mary Sunshine…."

MONDAY, 5:18 P.M.

"TELL ME THE NAME again, Court, please. I want to get it right for my news exclusive when we bring good old Joshua down," Jessica said as she filled a plate with the small, crust-free sandwiches Mrs. Archer considered proper. "Carpenters' Hall? Where's that?"

"She was never great at history," Jade said, shaking her head, and thanked Court for passing the salt. "Jess, Carpenters' Hall is set back a little from Chestnut Street, and it has been around since the 1700s. The First Continental Congress met there for a while. Benjamin Franklin negotiated with a French spy there, he even kept some of the first Philadelphia library inventory stored there. The building's on the National Register. Tourists go there every day."

"Well, then, that explains it. I grew up here, I'm not a tourist," Jessica said smugly. "And Joshua

Brainard's got the place for his speech tonight? How'd he manage that one?"

"He doesn't *have* Carpenters' Hall," Jade explained patiently. "He does have the area *outside* Carpenters' Hall for this rally he's got planned for tonight. Maybe five hundred people, maybe a thousand. And he's holding it at night, as the sun starts going down, because he looks good with television lights on him, according to what you've told me before about politicians and good lighting. Plus, if the crowd is small, nobody will know. Understand now?"

"No, I don't, not completely. If this rally is outside, where is he meeting you?"

Jade looked from Court to Matt. "All together now?"

They said it all together: "At his campaign office downtown."

"Which is only a few blocks away," Jade added before her sister could ask another question.

"Oh. Well. That's all right, then. Do you know we're supposed to have thunderstorms tonight? They're even talking hail, high winds, power lines down, all the usual baloney that never happens. Still, I found out that we're already sending a crew, and I told them to keep their cells on, because we might need them for a big story."

She popped the last of her sandwich in her mouth as she and Matt both stood up. "Which is why we're heading to the studio now. I need makeup, some other gear. Jade? You wouldn't consider wearing a hidden microphone and camera, would you? Would you mind if I did?"

"Jessica Marie Sunshine," Jade said flatly. "Go. Don't talk anymore. Just go. We'll meet you outside Brainard's campaign headquarters at seven o'clock, all right?"

"Say good night, Gracie, it's time to leave," Matt said, grinning at Jade. "Don't worry, Jade. I've got Sunny's leash in my pocket. I'll keep her in line."

"Funny man," Jessica said, but she smiled at Matt adoringly as she said it. "Let's go. I want to show off my ring to everybody."

"I don't think I want her there," Jade said once Jessica and Matt were gone. "She's doing that dumb, spacey-blonde routine of hers, you know, which means she's already planning to go for Joshua Brainard's throat. Eight will get you ten, Court, that by the time we see her next, two more of those blouse buttons will be open and the girls will nearly be coming out to play. Hi, look at us, aren't we cute and sexy, aren't you the nicest man, and then…*bam.* So, Josh, baby, you strangled your wife and tossed her in the pool, right?"

"Embarrassing for you, I imagine," Court said, grinning. "But they're...I mean, *she's* pretty effective."

Jade gave him a dirty look. "You've been looking at Jessica's breasts, Court?"

"Can I plead the Fifth?" He smiled again. "Oh, come on, Jade, I'm only kidding. Besides, Matt carries a gun."

Jade bit back a smile of her own. "You're in a good mood."

"I am, yes. It's had its ups and downs, but today has been a pretty good day overall. And you look beautiful in that blouse. Joshua Brainard won't even notice the *girls*."

"*Everybody* notices the girls," Jade said, rolling her eyes. "According to Jessica, Chris Matthews shouts people down, Keith Olbermann uses his smart mouth, Wolf Blitzer goes more for the 'Help me out, please, I'm confused' question, and that other guy? Bill O'Reilly? Oh, right, he pushes the moral-outrage line. Jessica says everybody has to have a gimmick. The girls are hers. I think cable-television news has a lot to answer for, personally."

"Would I be inviting disaster to say that, from a male point of view, hands down Jessica's got the best gimmick? Oh, hi, Ernesto, you're just in time to save me from falling into the hole I just dug myself."

"I think you mean he's saving you from having me push you into that hole you've been digging yourself," Jade said quietly. Not that she was angry. Unbelievably she, too, was actually feeling pretty good, which was amazing, considering what she faced in the next few hours. "Are you hungry, Ernesto? We're just grabbing sandwiches tonight."

The teen didn't answer, didn't give Jade his usual smile. Instead, he pulled out a chair and poured his skinny body into it, sliding down onto the base of his spine in a boneless move that threatened to continue until his butt hit the floor. Except that teenagers must practice sitting like that, because he seemed able to anchor himself before disappearing under the edge of the table.

Jade and Court exchanged looks.

"What's up, Ernesto?" Court asked, and then sort of winced. "Sorry. Dumb question. It's about your mother, right?"

"I just left her there," Ernesto said, still avoiding their eyes. "I didn't even say goodbye." He finally looked up and straight into Jade's eyes. "Who's going to feed her, Miss Sunshine? She doesn't eat if I don't make her, you know? Who's going to take care of the apartment, wash her clothes and stuff like that? She's on disability, you know? She gets those checks once a month. But if I don't take some of the money and give it right to the landlord, then she won't pay him. She'll be out on the street."

Jade slipped her hand into Court's beneath the table, and he gave her fingers an encouraging squeeze.

Ernesto was quiet for a few moments. Then he sighed, a sigh that came from the depths of his young body, before he spoke again, his voice low and threatening to break. "Who am I kidding, Miss Sunshine? I can't go to school. I can't leave her. She can't make it without me."

"There're, uh, programs, Ernesto, places she could go," Jade said, knowing she didn't sound convincing. "You know, rehabilitation programs? We could try to arrange something like that for your mother. We could do that, right, Court?"

Ernesto shook his head. "She did those. Twice. After she got picked up for, you know, for soliciting? The judge sent her. They put me into the system and sent her away to get clean before she could get me back. She said she got better drugs in there than she ever did on the outside."

"They took you out of there and they let you go back to her?" Court asked, looking at Jade in disbelief. "What the hell?"

"Twice, Mr. Becket. They let me go back to her twice. They knew she needed me, right? Somebody's got to be responsible for her, and I'm her family. You don't just walk away from family because you don't want to do it anymore. That's not right."

Jade felt Court's gaze on her again, almost heard him: *Tell him. Responsibility has its limits. Go on, Jade, tell him.*

At the same time, Jade was having so many lightning flashes of her own childhood, her own decisions—her own mistakes, her lost dreams for her own future—that it was almost as if Jessica had burned them all onto a DVD that was playing before her eyes now.

"Ernesto," Jade said, getting up from her chair and going around the table to hold out her hand to him. "Come outside with me. Please, sweetheart. We'll take a walk down around the pool, maybe sit there awhile. You and I really need to talk."

COURT'S APPETITE disappeared sometime around the moment Ernesto had entered the room, and he gave up eating as a bad job, deciding instead to walk down to the gatehouse and tell Bear Man they might be expecting a guest.

If indeed he did show up, Jermayne Johnson

wasn't exactly the sort of guest the ex-profes-
sional wrestler was probably accustomed to
letting through the gates to Sam's house, so a
phone call to the gatehouse might not do it.

He checked his watch as he stepped outside. A
little more than two hours before they were to
confront Joshua Brainard. Had this been the
longest day of his life, or did it only feel that way?

A breeze had begun to kick up after the heat of
the day. Although it felt good, Court knew that
Jessica was right, and there would probably be a
storm later. His check of the weather channel had
shown heavy thunderstorms already moving east
toward Harrisburg. That usually meant about two
hours before Philly got hit, unless the storm went
north of them.

"But that's all right, Mr. Brainard," Court said
under his breath. "One way or the other, your little
parade is going to get rained on tonight."

Court continued down the curving drive, wondering how Jade and Ernesto were making out
with their heart-to-heart. Jade saw the similarities
between her story and his; Court knew that. No,
Teddy hadn't been an addict, but he'd been needy
in his own way. Jade had tried to be mother and
father to her sisters, and maybe wife and mother
to her own father while she was at it.

But that was Jade. If somebody dropped the ball, you could count on her to be the one who picked it up, ran with it. Court was pretty sure Jade now realized what she'd done, the decisions she'd made in her teens and then stuck to because nobody else stepped up to carry the ball—like Teddy, who just let himself get comfortable in the role of deserted husband, wounded cop, avenger of all those forgotten victims and protector of those the victims had left behind.

The guy had been half-martyr, half-saint.

But he hadn't been Jade's father in the ways she'd needed him to be, not for a long, long time.

When he had been mad at the man, which had been often, Court believed Teddy had consciously decided that Jade, as the oldest, saw the sense in being the spinster daughter, destined to play the role of the loyal child who stayed home and took care of her parents—in this case, Teddy.

When he was feeling more charitable, Court believed the man didn't realize what he was doing.

Except that Court had never felt all that much in charity with the guy, not when it came to Teddy's almost archaic treatment of Jade.

He felt his hands clench into fists at his sides. They had to solve Teddy's murder. It was time to put the man to rest. Jade's one last rescue of the man. Only then would she feel free to get on with her own life, pursue her own dreams, feel free to share that life with him.

And if that was selfish of him, then damn it, so what?

"Problem, Mr. B?"

Court looked ahead to see Carroll "Bear Man" Yablonski stepping out of the gatehouse, adjusting his pants, which had a tendency to hang beneath the man's waist by a good two inches.

"No, Bear Man, no problem, thank you," Court said. He realized that, although Bear Man wasn't very tall, he packed a lot of muscle into his square frame. "No more reporters camped outside the gates?"

Bear Man wiped a hand beneath his nose. "No. All gone. I think I kinda miss them. They used to bring me stuff. Doughnuts, those big pretzels you get at the ball games, cheese steaks. One of them tried to give me money. I told him where to get off, let me tell you. Food? That's okay. I mean, if I didn't eat it, then it would just go to waste. But money's a *real* bribe, an insult to my integrity and stuff, and I tossed those guys in a hurry, let me tell you! They all thought I'd tell them something they didn't know, or maybe let them sneak inside for a couple of pictures of Miss Jolie when she was here. I didn't."

He smiled, showing off a startlingly white set of dentures. "Ate well, though. I think I put on a good five pounds."

"You're a man among men, Bear Man," Court said, keeping a straight face. "I don't know what we would have done without you when the media was camped four deep on the other side of that gate."

"Hey, it's Sam, you know? You think I don't know what he did for me? Bringing me here, giving me a place to live, a real job to do? My brains got a little scrambled during my pro-wrestling days. Some from taking hits when I zigged, instead of zagged, or when some rookie forgot to pull his punch, and some of it from those 'roids we all used. I swore I didn't use them, but Sam knew I'd messed myself up. He didn't care. I was his friend and that was that. He took care of me. So now I take care of him. Just like I did on the football field back at old Temple U. You always got to protect your quarterback. That's just the way it is."

"I understand," Court said, not at all amazed that Sam had manufactured a job and living quarters for Carroll Yablonski, although he did think that was probably the longest speech the man had ever made, within his hearing, at least.

Bear Man put up his arms. "Hey, hey, I shouldn't have said that."

"It's all right. I already knew, Bear Man. Sam told me."

"No, no, not about Sam. That's good about Sam. I shouldn't have said that about the zigging and the zagging and pulling the punches. That wasn't true, okay? It's real. Pro wrestling's *real,* it really is."

"Now you're lying to me, Bear Man," Court said, laughing. "If pro wrestling is real, so are those teeth of yours that you already told me Sam bought for you, no insult intended."

The other man lowered his hands—hands the size of small pizzas, attached to forearms that could have doubled as tree trunks. He wouldn't have wanted to have faced Carroll Yablonski across the neutral zone back when he was playing college ball. "Okay, okay. I tried. Just don't tell nobody, all right? Kids and little old ladies especially. They believe the dream. Now, what can I do for you, Mr. B? You didn't just come down here to hear about my glory days. Is something up? I can get Chief Iron Claw back here to watch the gate, if you need me somewhere else."

"Chief...?" Sam had a sudden memory of the gates being opened one day by a tall, fierce-looking guy of about sixty wearing fringed buck-skins and a big feather war bonnet. "Oh, right, your wrestling friend. You know what, Bear Man? I came down here to tell you to look out for a visitor we hope is going to show up soon, but I think you just gave me an idea."

"I'll go call Claw," Carroll said, already heading back to the gatehouse.

"Whoa, Bear Man," Court called after him. "How about you let me tell you my idea first. You might not want to do it."

"If you say so, sure. Shoot."

"All right," Court said, wondering if he should consider someday writing his memoirs for his grandchildren. Bear Man would make a great entry. "We'll be leaving in a little while, Miss Sunshine and myself, for an appointment downtown. I don't anticipate any problems, but I do know that the man we're going to see isn't exactly happy with either of us at the moment, and that he travels with a bodyguard. A man named Leslie."

"Leslie?" Bear Man put a fist to his mouth that didn't quite cover his snort of laughter. "You want maybe I should send my grammy Yablonski, instead? She can beat him up with her walker."

Court laughed. "Names can be deceiving, *Carroll*."

Bear Man sobered quickly. "That's not funny."

"I know, I'm sorry. I've been having a strange day, Bear Man. Please forgive me. But you'll do it? Nothing overt, but I'd like to be able to point the man out to you so that you can watch him. He shouldn't bother us, but the guy seems to have a pretty quick temper."

"He makes a move, I'm on him like white on rice, whatever that means. Put him down, show him the Bear Man Mangle hold. No problem."

Court belatedly realized he might have wanted to choose another phrase besides *nothing overt*. "Our friend Leslie might be carrying a gun," he added, as he felt it necessary to point out that possibility to Bear Man.

Bear Man only shrugged. "Okay, so I'll do what I did when Chief Iron Claw and me turned bad guys for a while. I'll use the Bear Man Massacre. That means I'll come up on him from behind and dropkick him in the kidneys. For real."

"Sounds like a plan," Court said, knowing it was about all he could say. And then he heard the unmistakable sound of a motorcycle coming up the hill outside the gates and turned to watch as the motorcycle stopped.

"Don't look much like a reporter," Bear Man said, turning for the gate. "Hey, you! This look like one of them rest stops to you? Move it, buddy. Go pee somewheres else."

The rider and the bike were both pretty impressive. The bike was a Harley-Davidson, vintage, with a terrific paint job and chrome so shiny it reflected every ray of the sun. The rider, who was *big* even still straddling the bike, was dressed all in black. Black jeans, black boots, black leather jacket with silver studs, black leather gloves that went halfway up his forearms, shiny black helmet with a black visor. Darth Vader comes to suburban Philly.

"Bear Man, wait," Court said, watching as the rider reached for his helmet and pulled it off. "Son of a gun, she did it. She got him to show up. So now what?" he breathed quietly, and then shook his head, knowing the coming interview wasn't going to be easy. "Just when you thought it was safe to go back in the water— Bear Man, it's all right. This is the guest I told you about. Let him in."

"If you say so, Mr. B," Bear Man said, retreating into the gatehouse to push the button that opened the gates. "Hey, would you look at that— it's Sam and Miss Jolie. I didn't know they were coming back today."

Court watched as the gates opened and

Jermayne rolled his bike on through before pulling off to the side of the drive and letting the Town Car pull up and stop beside Court.

The rear side window rolled down, and there was his cousin Sam, grinning at him. "Hey, Court, it's nice of you to come down here to welcome us home. I didn't expect rose petals strewn in our path, but where's the confetti?"

"Hi, Court," Jolie said, leaning across Sam's lap to wave at him. "Hop in and we'll drive you up to the house."

Court looked at Jermayne, who was suddenly looking like the world's biggest, blackest rabbit, and about to run like one, too. "Uh, no, that's okay. You guys go ahead. Jade might still be down near the pool with Ernesto. You want to tell her Jermayne's here to see her? Just first tell me what you're doing here. We thought you were flying to Ireland in a couple of days."

"My co-star slipped on a blonde last night getting out of the bathtub and dislocated his shoulder," Jolie told him. "Shooting is postponed for six weeks, minimum, so we thought we'd fly back here and surprise you." She grinned. "Surprise!"

LAS VEGAS, NEVADA

"COURT BECKET in the flesh, this is a nice surprise," David Langsdowne said, his gaze on Jade even as he held out a hand to his boss. "And here I thought the negotiations were going pretty well."

"As far as I know, they are," Court said, shaking the man's hand. "Let me introduce you to my friend, Jade Sunshine. Jade, this happy, smiling man is David Langsdowne. He's about to make the Beckets casino-hotel owners, aren't you, David?"

"It's so nice to meet you, David," Jade said, forcing a smile as she simultaneously tried to take in the over-the-top decor of the hotel lobby. "This is the hotel you're buying, Court? It's, uh, very nice."

David, a tall, black man with a rather uncanny resemblance to Denzel Washington, gave a discreet snort. "Nice? Pul-*eeze*. This place is back-stage Hollywood 1930s Babylon on acid, Miss Sunshine. If the gods are kind and we get this deal done, the whole evil empire comes tumbling down like the walls of Jericho—keeping with the biblical analogies, not to say that Vegas isn't still Sin City." He winked at her. "Even if it is, the kiddie rides and all that family-fun nonsense to one side."

Jade didn't know what to say to the man, so she just looked at Court, who was laughing and shaking his head. "Did David just say you're going to buy this place and *then blow it up?*"

"That's the plan, yes. The hotel has a fairly small footprint compared to the newer casinos, so we need to devote the entire ground floor to the casino and then just go up, up, up. Still, it will be a relatively small hotel. We're going for quality, not quantity, and targeting high rollers—whales, as they're called. David, I'm assuming you've found room for us somewhere?"

David handed him a small folder with a key card inside. "I was on it, Court, the moment I heard you were here. Top floor. One of the high-roller suites, or so they tell me. I hope you don't mind pink bathtubs. I have a meeting in ten minutes with the owners, who are taking one last shot at playing coy. They'll stop that when I pull out the financial statements for their last three operating quarters. I'm in full shark mode today, especially now that our Fearless Leader is on-site. I hope to see you later, Miss Sunshine."

Once David melted back into the aimlessly milling crowds of tourists, Court offered her his arm and they walked toward the bank of eleva-tors. "Jade, you look so amazed."

"That's because I am," she said quietly. "When you said you were thinking about buying a hotel and did I want to go see it, I didn't think you meant you were going to buy a hotel and then blow it up." She looked at the two-story-high frieze she was pretty sure was meant to denote a sultan's harem room complete with concubines, and winced. "Although, on second thought, it might be a good idea, actually."

"Sorry you came?"

She shook her head. No, she wasn't sorry she came. She was sorry about the argument she'd left behind her, and the last words she'd said to Teddy: *I'm old enough to make my own decisions.*

And his answer: *Old enough to make your own mistakes, you mean. And this, my starry-eyed little fool, is a doozy. Your name might be Jade, but in your heart, you're Margaret Mary. Don't you forget that.*

Jade knew she shouldn't have been surprised by the argument. She and Teddy had only maintained an uneasy truce since the day she'd shown him the roses Court had sent her. In fact, it might have been the charged atmosphere in the Sunshine house that had her saying yes five days later when Court had called and asked if she wanted to fly to Las Vegas for the weekend.

They'd spoken every day on the phone, but Court had dropped her back in Philadelphia on his way to England and round-the-clock meetings on some project or another. She'd met him at the airport six hours ago, and after he'd kissed her hello he'd pretty much apologized for being so tired and then lain back in his seat after George handed him a blanket. He'd slept all the way to Las Vegas, trying to make up for so many changes of time zones.

She'd spent most of that time marveling at the scenery they passed over and watching him sleep, and she'd enjoyed every moment of her quiet vigil.

Now, in what seemed to be a blink of the eye, she once more had been transported from her rather ordinary life and plunked down in Court's world, one that couldn't be more alien if he had lived on Mars.

"You live in a whole different world than I do, don't you, Court?" she asked as they stepped into one of the elevators and he pushed the button for the top floor. When the other occupants got off on the seventh floor, she said, "Maybe even a whole different universe. My question is, what am I doing here with you?"

She imagined he thought the swift, hard kiss that had her clinging to him mindlessly was a good answer. Actually, it was. A very good answer.

The elevator doors opened and Court waved her out into the hallway, looking at the room number arrows before taking her hand and quickly leading her to their left. He fished the key card from his pocket and opened the door, once more waving her ahead of him.

"Oh…my…*God,*" she said as she stepped into the suite, and then put her hands to her mouth to hold back the giggles. "You're right, Court. You have to blow it up. Quick!"

The room was enormous, she'd give it that, but that only meant there was more space to fill with gilt and pink silk and faux-marble pillars and filmy, flowing sheer draperies and X-rated statues and… "Is that a fountain?"

"Watering hole for the camels, which are also probably pink," Court muttered, and then swore under his breath.

Jade turned to look at him. He seemed genuinely disgusted, not even slightly amused.

"Come on, we're leaving, right after I break David's neck for not checking out the suite before he gave me the key, short notice or not. I'm sure we can get a suite at another hotel."

"Court, no," Jade said, laughing. "It's all right. It's funny. Look. You can lie on that couch over there and I can peel grapes and feed them to you. Unless the ghost of Rudolph Valentino shows up to woo me away. Then, as we high rollers like to say here in Vegas, all bets are off."

"This isn't how I planned our weekend," Court said, still looking upset, even embarrassed. The big business tycoon, flustered, looking so very masculine in the middle of this cotton-candy-pink fantasy room. She liked that; it made him less intimidating, more human.

"No? How did you plan the weekend, Court?" she asked him, slipping her arms around him as she laid her cheek against his chest. "Tell me. Did it start with a seduction?"

He kissed the top of her head. "That would be in the way of a rhetorical question, I hope. God, Jade, I missed you. Phone calls aren't all they're cracked up to be, not when all I want to do is hold you, make love to you."

He kissed her then, and any doubts that had haunted her during the time he was gone, after the arguments with Teddy, disappeared in that instant, banished if not vanished as she returned his kiss, as they somehow made their way toward the trio of faux-marble stairs that led to the dais holding the ridiculously large, pink-silk-festooned bed.

The one with the rather unique ceiling above it.

Jade, lying on her back, with Court delightfully nibbling on her right earlobe, started to laugh. Silently, trying not to interrupt the moment. But since Court was sprawled half on top of her, he could feel her body shaking, probably sense that she was holding her breath for some reason.

"What?" he asked her, raising his head to look into her face. "You've got a ticklish earlobe?"

Jade couldn't hold back her laugh. "No! But... but you've somehow picked up a bit of string on your... Wait, I'll get it." She pulled the length of pink string from his rump and held it between them so he could see. "All gone."

He looked at the thread, looked at her. "How did you know there was a… Oh, for crying out loud." He grabbed on to her and rolled over onto his back, so that he could look up at the ceiling and their reflection in the large, gold-veined mirror.

"Let me up, Court," Jade said, not sure she was showing her best side at the moment. "You're right, we should go somewhere else. Someplace where the words *den of iniquity* aren't in their advertising slogans. Court? Court, let me up. What are doing?"

He had one hand on her waist as he eased down the long zipper on her simple green sheath dress. Slowly lowered the zipper. "Interesting. Sort of a do-it-yourself striptease. Nice bra. The black is a nice contrast to your creamy white skin."

"Which is a not-so-interesting-or-nice contrast to the embarrassed red in my cheeks," Jade said, trying to twist away from him. "We're not kids, Court. Cut that out."

She felt the snaps of her bra release.

"Court? You're not listening to me."

"Probably not, no. Long zipper. Ah, and now the black panties. Anyone would think you dressed for the occasion."

"I did, smart-ass. Just not *this* occasion." She closed her eyes, swallowing hard as he slipped his hands beneath the low-riding waistband of her panties to cup her buttocks, pull her more tightly against him. "This is turning you on, isn't it?"

"You noticed?" he asked, breathing the words into her ear. "You have the most incredible body." He moved one hand, trailing it up the length of her spine and then back down again, sending shivers through her. "How do we get rid of this dress?"

Jade had given up trying to fight him. He took his hands off her and she pushed herself up, straddling him as she slipped her arms out of the dress and her bra straps. He helped her push up her hem until she could get a good hold on the material she then lifted up and over her head, sending both the dress and the bra flying onto the floor.

She was about to slide off her panties when he stopped her. "No, not yet."

Jade felt an immediate tightening between her legs, a highly pleasant physical reaction not only to his words, but his tone.

"Take my hands," Court said, and when she did, he let her pull him up until, wearing only her black panties and her black heels, she was straddling his lap.

Jade dared a look upward to see herself, Court's hands on her breasts, her legs bent at the knee as their clothing still kept them from the most intimate contact.

She didn't need him to tell her what to do next. As he cupped her breasts, his fingers doing incredible things to her nipples, she unbuttoned his dress shirt and pushed it down over his shoulders. Bending her head, she began to kiss his chest as he fought his way out of the shirtsleeves, and then she attacked his belt and zipper.

She wrapped her arms around his neck and went fully to her knees so that he could push down his slacks and boxers, but was unwilling to let him go.

She settled onto his lap once more, and Court continued to arouse her with long, intimate, penetrating kisses until she thought she might explode. She actually whimpered when he gently pushed her from him, held on to her hands as he moved forward, so that she was slowly lowered back between his legs.

"Court…?"

He was on his knees now, levering her legs on either side of him, putting his hands on her upper thighs so that he could slip his thumbs beneath the crotch of her panties.

Her breath escaped on a silent sigh.

Then he was moving his hands again, charting a path over her hips, across her belly, skimming her breasts.

"Open your eyes, Jade," he said from somewhere far away, high above her. "See what I see when I look at you. The most beautiful, the most desirable, the most incredibly unique and precious woman a man could ever hope to have as his own. Watch me touch you…watch me love you. Because I love you, Jade. With everything I am or ever hope to be, I will love you for the rest of my life. Marry me. Marry me now."

Jade didn't know how she managed to be in his arms before he'd finished speaking, but she was. Holding on tight as together they fell back against the ridiculous pink satin bedspread, and it was only a matter of moments before Court was deep within her and, not just together, but now one person, they rode out wave after wave of passion intensified by love.

It wasn't the sort of deeply heartfelt scene they'd one day share with their children, or the intimate dinner and dancing and down-on-one-knee moonlight proposal Court had planned when he'd bought the three-carat diamond in London, but it was their romance, their way. Quick, impulsive, burning with passion.

They agreed they might at least show their children and grandchildren the photograph of the Elvis impersonator who married them later that same night in a chapel on the Strip.

They phoned Teddy early the next morning to tell him the news, Jade still so in love, cocooned in the merciful obliviousness love can use to fool the unwary, actually crying with happiness as her father gave Court his best wishes and his oldest daughter his blessing.

They'd honeymoon later, as soon as the deal in England was done, the negotiations currently at a point where Court never should have left the country, and wouldn't have if he could have concentrated on anything except needing to be with Jade.

Thirty-six hours after the Elvis impersonator had said, "You may kiss the bride, and leave the building!" Court was on his way back across the Atlantic and Jade was back at home, eager to see her father, eager to thank him for being so understanding, so nice to Court when they spoke on the phone.

She quickly put down her overnight bag, calling Teddy's name until she found him in his office, asleep or passed out, his head on his arms at his desk. She could see that he had at least a two-day growth of beard shadowing his cheeks.

There was an empty bottle of Irish whiskey next to his elbow, as if he had hung up the phone after her call from Vegas and crawled directly into a bottle.

Where, although she'd never told Court or her sisters, he'd pretty much stayed for the next seven months, not coming out again until Jade came home one last time, bringing all of her luggage with her....

JADE WAS WAITING at the front door when Court and Jermayne got there, Jermayne with his hands on the handlebars of a large motorcycle he was pushing along with him.

She was shocked by his appearance. He looked so big, and maybe even bad in his black leather with his intimidating motorcycle. But when he looked up into her eyes as she stood at the threshold, he might have been that seven-year-old boy huddling against his grandmother's skirts at his brother's graveside.

"Let's go into Sam's office," she said, "where we can talk. Court?"

"How's Ernesto?" he asked her.

Jade gave a small smile. "We swapped a couple of horror stories, and we've agreed we're probably charter members of Enablers Anonymous, but I think he's going to be all right. He's in the dining room having a sandwich with Jolie and Sam, so at least he got his appetite back. These things take time." She looked at Court, hoping he understood what she was saying. "You know—time heals all wounds?"

"And wounds all heels, as we hope to prove with Joshua Brainard in less than two hours," Court told her quietly as Jermayne worked his way out of his leather jacket, revealing a green camouflage muscle shirt that stripped away any thoughts that he was still seven years old. He was standing just where he'd stood when he entered the large foyer, as if afraid just being in the house might mean he'd break something. "You haven't had much time to come up with a game plan for our friend here."

"It's all right, we'll have to wing it. I'm just so glad he's here. Come with me?"

Court squeezed her hand and pointed Jermayne down the hallway toward Sam's office. "What about Sam and Jolie?"

"Jolie said she thought too many people might scare him off." She slipped past Jermayne and into the office, telling Jermayne to take a seat and asking him if he'd like a soda or a sandwich, or anything at all.

"No, Miss Sunshine, I'm not hungry," Jermayne said. His jacket folded over his clasped hands, he slowly made his way around the length of the bookcases, looking at the contents of the shelves. "Wow, a Mike Schmidt rookie card. And it's even signed." He looked at Court. "This yours?"

"No, Jermayne, this is my cousin's house," Court said. "I live in Virginia, and I'm a Washington Nationals fan, I'm afraid. Don't hold it against me."

Jermayne's pained smile showed a mouthful of beautiful, straight teeth. "Better than the Mets," he said, and then he took a deep breath and looked at Jade. "I don't want you to think I came here just, you know, just for the watch? I don't want the watch, you should have it. I wanted to say thank you for talking to my boss after I ran away like that. I mean, I really need the job."

Jade had a sudden thought and dropped into one of the leather chairs. "Oh, Jermayne, I'm so sorry. I didn't realize— How could I not have realized? Of course you need the job. So how can you give it up to go to school, right?"

Jermayne put his head down, again looking like the scared little boy. "No, it's not like that. Teddy took care of that, too. Gave my gran money every month to put away for me, and that's just what she did." He looked at Jade again, blinking, as if his eyes burned. "I won't touch it. I can't do that. It wouldn't be right. My gran taught me what was right, and that ain't right. There ain't nothing been right for a long time. I kept telling Teddy that, like I keep telling you, but he wouldn't listen. He just kept coming after me, you know? He said he wouldn't ever give up on me, wouldn't let me alone. I told him that night that I couldn't…"

He turned his back on Jade and Court, dropping the jacket and putting his hands to his temples, almost violently pounding his fists against the sides of his head.

Court took a step forward, but Jade motioned for him to sit down. Her heart was beating so fast she had to take a deep breath to try to settle herself.

"Jermayne," she said, her tone deliberately changed from congenial to demanding. "What are you not telling us? I'm tired, Jermayne. My father's dead, somebody tried to burn down my house, they're calling my father a murderer and a coward who took his own life rather than go to prison. We loved Teddy, Jermayne, you and I. We know he was a good man, a caring man. I know you've got answers for me, I know you want to help me. For Teddy. So if you know something, if you know anything at all—"

"I killed him," Jermayne said, his voice so low Jade wasn't immediately sure he'd said anything. He dropped his arms to his sides and turned to look at her, his face streaked with tears. He took a breath, his massive chest rising and falling rapidly, and raised his voice. "I killed him, all right. I killed him, and you can't fix that. Nothing can fix that."

Oh, my God. This was a nightmare. A nightmare.

Court got up and went over to close the door before Jermayne said anything else, probably hoping Jolie and Sam hadn't heard anything. "Sit down, Jermayne," he then said, leading the now sobbing boy to one of the couches.

Jade immediately left her own chair to sit down beside him. She looked up at Court and mouthed, "Now what?"

Court put out his arms in a hugging gesture and Jade, wondering if her arms would even fit around Jermayne, reached out and tried to pull him close to her.

Jermayne's genuine grief broke her heart, loud, racking sobs that shook his massive, muscular frame. "It's all right, Jermayne," she crooned, trying to keep her own balance and not fall sideways on the couch with him. "It's all right, sweetheart, it's okay. Teddy forgives you. I know he does…"

Jermayne sat up and lifted the hem of his muscle shirt to wipe at his nose and eyes. "I know. He said he did, and he said he'd help me, but then I came back and he was dead and I didn't know what to do—"

"He what? Teddy *forgave* you for…" Jade looked up at Court again, her own eyes wet now. "You didn't mean Teddy, did you, Jermayne?" she said, still looking at Court, trying to borrow strength from him. "No, of course not. You meant Terrell. You meant your brother. You're telling us you killed Terrell? The night…the night Teddy died, you'd told him *about* what happened to your brother?"

Jermayne's sobs took control of him again, but this time Court waved Jade off the couch and took her place, pulling the little boy who looked like a man into his own embrace and holding him, holding him, the two of them rocking back and forth.

"Keep him here, just let him cry, okay?" Jade said quietly. "I'll go get a box of tissues from the kitchen and be right back."

She closed the door quietly behind her, and then turned and ran for the dining room, her heart beating like a trip-hammer, but Sam and Jolie weren't there. Only Ernesto, who was busily feeding pieces of the leftover sandwiches to Sunny and Rockne.

"Hey, what's up, Miss Sunshine? You don't look too good," he said, getting to his feet. "Did I do that to you, dumping all over you like that? I'm sorry."

Jade waved off his apology. "No, no, nothing like that. I'm fine, really. Ernesto, where are Sam and Jolie?"

"They went upstairs. Something about changing their clothes, I think. You want me to go get them? Maybe Mr. Becket, too? I mean, you really don't look too good."

"I know where Court is, thank you. And no, I don't want you to go get them. I want you to tell me again about how you think Terrell Johnson was shot. Will you do that? Not your theories, your *conclusions*. I know you've read the file again. And the condensed version, Ernesto, please, I'm sort of in a hurry."

"I can tell," Ernesto said slowly, clearly gathering his thoughts. "My *conclusion* is that it wasn't a drive-by. Whoever did the trajectory tests really screwed up. The shot had to be closer than that, and it had to come from below Terrell. Not a ricochet, or like Terrell was standing with his head up—you know, like at the foul line, looking up at the basket? Like that? Except it could be like that. Mostly, though, I think whoever shot him did it from down low. Why?"

"No reason. Thanks," Jade said. "Take the dogs outside for me, please, sweetheart, and then stay out there until somebody comes to get you, all right? I've got to…I've got to do something."

She went through the kitchen, past Mrs. Archer and up the back stairs, because Sam's bedroom was located nearer the back of the house. She pounded on the door with the side of her fist and then opened it, to see Jolie stepping into a cream-colored skirt.

"Jolie!"

Her sister nearly fell, grabbing at the bedpost to steady herself. "Don't *do* that! Jade? What's wrong? Oh, God, something's wrong. Sam!"

Sam came out of the bathroom, wiping the remnants of shaving cream from his face. "What's up? Jade? Oh, hell, honey, are you all right?"

"Not really, no, but I've got to get back. Two things, quick. Jolie, call Father Muskie and get him over here right now. I don't have time to explain, just tell him we need him here for one of Teddy's friends. And I do mean right now. And

Sam? Call the Brainard campaign headquarters and have them tell Joshua we have a change of plans and need to meet him…I don't know, at his house," she said as she decided. "Yes, we'll meet him at his house, right after the rally is over. Don't take no for an answer, Sam. He has to see us tonight. Oh, and call Jess and tell her about the change of plans. Gotta go."

"Gee, and to think I thought I sometimes missed getting orders from you," Jolie said, and then held up her hands. "We're doing it, we're doing it. But you'd better have some answers for us soon, because I know I've got lots of questions."

Jade turned away and then stopped, taking a shaky breath, before she raced over to pick up the box of tissues on the table next to the bed, and then gave her sister a quick hug. Tears threatened again, but Jermayne needed her; she could fall apart later. "I love you. I love you both very much. Stay up here, please, and Court or I will come get you soon to explain. Jermayne's downstairs with Court now. It's bad, Jolie, but it's going to be okay."

"Jade, wait," Jolie called after her, but Jade kept moving, this time down the front stairs, hoping Court was working some sort of man-to-man magic on Jermayne.

She was back in Sam's den only three minutes after she'd left, closing the door and handing Jermayne the box of tissues as she sat down cross-legged in front of him on the patterned carpet, doing her best to catch her breath. "How are you doing, Jermayne?"

"Not so good, Miss Sunshine," he said, pulling half-a-dozen tissues from the box and rubbing at his eyes and nose again. "I'm sorry. It's like it was before I told Teddy. You know, all bottled up inside, tying me up in knots? Then I told him and it was a little better for a couple of minutes. Except then…and then it all came back and it was even worse, because now he wasn't here to help me."

"Then let me help you, Jermayne, let us all help you," Jade said softly, taking his large hand in both of hers. "You went to Teddy and told him what happened that night, didn't you? The night Teddy died? Why don't we start with that? Tell me what happened, Jermayne. Let me help you."

Jermayne's huge frame shuddered as he sighed yet again. For a moment Jade was afraid he'd break down again, but then he said, "He was going to leave us, you know? Go away, be the big star. What if he forgot us? What if he never came back to get us like he kept saying he would? He said we were going to have a swimming pool and a big house, but why would he want a kid in that big house? And he was so mad at me. He told me I was already in trouble once, and this time they'd take me away from Gran and put me somewhere and when was I gonna learn."

"I don't understand. Maybe you can help me out, Jermayne. Why was Terrell so mad at you?"

"The gun," Jermayne said. "Terrell was mad about the gun."

Jade's stomach turned to stone in her belly. She glanced up at Court, who was slowly shaking his head.

"What about the gun, Jermayne?"

"They gave it to me, like before. I got caught the first time, with the drugs, you know? But they said if I was smart that wouldn't happen again. All I had to do was hold it for them until they asked for it. They don't do nothing to kids who hold stuff for the gangs, not bad stuff, anyway." He sniffed, blew his nose. "It was a big gun, really big."

He looked at Jade. "Teddy always thought I knew who'd done it, who'd shot Terrell. He moved Gran and me away, to show me, see, you're safe now, Jermayne, you can tell me now, Jermayne, tell me who shot your brother. That I wouldn't feel really safe, or really good again, until I told him.

But how could I tell him what I did? How was that going to make anything *right* again? Gran would hate me, and so would Teddy, and they'd put me somewhere, put me in some jail. I couldn't tell anyone, they told me I couldn't tell anyone. Even after Teddy moved us out, I knew I couldn't tell or else they'd come after Gran and me both. Besides, I'm the one who killed him."

"Tell us how it happened, Jermayne," Court said, pulling one of the leather side chairs over and sitting down next to Jade. "It was an accident, right? You didn't mean to shoot him."

Jermayne hung his head. "He was so mad when I showed him the gun. He told me again that he was doing everything for me, me and Gran, working hard at school, playing basketball. So he could get us out, you know? And now look what I was doing. He said…he said maybe he should just go and not come back, not if his own brother was going to run with gangs and throw his life down a toilet."

He lifted his head, his eyes so huge and sorrowful Jade had to bite her bottom lip to keep from crying out. "He didn't mean that. Terrell loved me. He was just trying to scare me. So I…I scared him back. I picked up the gun and I said maybe I should just shoot him and then he couldn't leave.

He yelled at me, told me to give him the goddamn gun…and it went off."

"Jesus," Court breathed quietly.

"The…uh…the next thing I remember was how I was lying on my back on the court, all the wind knocked out of me, I guess, and Terrell was lying there, too, all this blood spreading under his head. I called to him, but he didn't move, he didn't get up. But I didn't believe it. He'd get up. He was mad at me, sure, trying to scare me, but he'd get up if I left. I picked up the gun because I knew the gang would want it back, and I ran all the way home and hid in the closet in my room. I kept waiting for Terrell to come home, because I didn't believe it had really happened, you know?"

"But Terrell didn't come home."

"No, he didn't come home. There was this loud knock on the door and I heard voices, and then Gran started to scream and scream and scream. I got up and went into the living room and she was kneeling on the floor, just screaming, while these two cops just stood there looking at her and all the neighbors were trying to see in the doorway, and then they all started screaming, too. Gran kept screaming that Terrell was dead, her baby was dead, and that the person who'd done this would never sleep easy, not while she was alive. She swore it, she swore that on her knees every day after that. She made me get down on my knees next to her and help her pray that they caught the devil who'd killed her Terrell. Every day we'd pray that the one who done it would not rest easy for a moment while she was still alive. Gran's dead now, in the cemetery next to Terrell, so I can't tell her she was wrong. I still don't sleep."

He got to his feet and looked around the room. "I need a bathroom, please. I think I'm going to be sick."

"Come with me," Court said, and Jade watched them leave the room before she slowly got to her feet, moving like an old woman, like Jermayne's grandmother, who'd spent so many years on her knees, praying for the truth. *Thank God she never knew.*

"He's going to be okay," Court said, coming back into the room. "Now, how about you?"

"I've been better," she said, wrapping her arms around him and holding him close. "He told Teddy, Court. He told him the night Teddy died."

"I know, sweetheart. And it explains why Teddy was drunk. He had to have taken the news hard."

She looked at him. If he, if anybody, only knew how often Teddy had been drunk in the past almost two years. But that was her secret, hers and

Teddy's. She'd tell Court one day, because he deserved to know the full truth of why she had come back to Philly so often during their marriage, but not right now. "So now you're back to thinking it was suicide. Jermayne told Teddy what had really happened, Teddy got drunk and felt like he couldn't live with what he knew?"

"It's a theory."

"Yes, but not for long, not once the cops get hold of it," Jade said, sitting down on the couch once more. "Let me run this one by you. Jermayne tells Teddy everything, but then almost immediately regrets it. He leaves, Teddy gets drunk, Jermayne comes back, sees the gun case on the desk. Teddy tells him he has to go to the police, has to tell them the truth about Terrell. There's struggle for the gun. A short one, with Teddy drunk and Jermayne being as big as he is. The gun goes off—that shot into the floor—and the second shot goes into Teddy."

"It didn't happen like that," Jermayne said.

Jade closed her eyes for a moment, wishing she'd learn to keep her mouth shut. "No, I'm sure it didn't, Jermayne," she said, getting to her feet again. "Why don't you tell us what did happen? From the beginning. You went to see Teddy. The night he died."

Jermayne seemed to have himself under control now, as if telling his story again had somehow given him a measure of peace. He perched himself on the front of Sam's desk, his hands braced on either side of him.

"Teddy was on me and on me, about going to school, you know? Ever since I graduated high school last month. He'd call me, he'd show up at my work like you did, ragging at me about how did I want to spend the rest of my life washing somebody's else car, is that what Terrell had wanted for me—like that. Drunk sometimes, I think, but he was okay. Sad, but okay, I thought. I guess I was really upsetting him by saying I didn't want to take any more money from him, that I didn't want to go to that trade school he signed me up for. I disappointed him, just like I disappointed Terrell, just like I always disappointed Gran."

Jade shot a quick look at Court, whose expression didn't give anything away. But he'd heard what Jermayne had said about Teddy, about Teddy's drinking.

"Anyway. He wouldn't leave me alone. And all the time still asking me what else I remembered about when Terrell died. I couldn't take it no more, he wasn't going to stop. So I went to his house that night, late, around maybe ten o'clock? And I told him."

"Teddy was seen on the security camera at Melodie Brainard's house around nine," Jade said. "Okay, that fits. How was he when you saw him, Jermayne? Was…was the gun case on his desk?"

Jermayne nodded. "Yeah. I saw a box on his desk. Big wooden one? I didn't know what was in it, so it could have been a gun. He had a bottle on the desk, a funny-looking one, sort of short and fancy."

"Teddy's Crown Royal," Jade said, nodding. "He saved that for special times, good or bad. Anything else?"

"Anything else? I don't think… Yeah. Yeah, you're right, there was something else," Jermayne said, looking at her again, this time looking a little confused. "He had one of those clear plastic bags on the desk? You know, like for putting food in? Except there wasn't any food in it. Just a hairbrush. I asked him about it, and he said it was a present from a lady and it was going to break something wide open."

"There was no bag or hairbrush on his desk when I found him," Jade said, looking at Court. She felt her excitement building once more. Teddy had been to visit Melodie Brainard again. Had he convinced her of Joshua's guilt? Had she given Teddy her husband's hairbrush so he could get Brainard's DNA? Exactly what had Teddy known that made him go home and pull out the Crown Royal to celebrate—and his service revolver? Because he thought there might be trouble? They were close, so close. And soon it would all be over. "I guess that finishes any more theories on suicide for any reason."

Court nodded, but then went back to the night Jermayne had visited Teddy. "Jermayne, when you told Teddy what had happened all those years ago, what did he say to you?"

"He…he said it was all right. He said it wasn't my fault, that it was an accident. But he said we had to tell. I was crying, like just before, and Teddy, he was crying, too. But we had to tell or else things would never be right. He said I'd never be right with myself if I didn't tell the truth and that…that I'd been carrying a burden for a mistake that should have been put down long ago. He said he carried some mistakes, some burdens, you know, of his own, and he didn't want to see me ending up like him. He told me to go home and pack up my clothes and come back, stay with him until this priest friend of his got home from some vacation he was on somewhere. The priest would talk to me and help me, and then we'd all go down to the station house together and I'd start to feel better about myself."

"Canada. Father Muskie was in Canada. We couldn't even reach him in time for the funeral."

"Right, that was it. Teddy and Father Muskie, they were gonna go with me when I told about Terrell. I still have to do that, don't I?"

"Yeah, Jermayne," Jade said carefully. "You still have to do that. I can arrange a meeting. I know Father Muskie will go with you."

"And you?" he asked, looking scared again. "You'll come with?"

"Sure," Jade said, giving him a quick hug. "I'll come with."

"We both will," Court said. "Along with whatever lawyer Sam recommends. It's going to be all right, Terrell, we promise."

"That's what Teddy promised. That's the last thing he ever said to me. That I wasn't to worry, that he'd take care of everything. I went home to get my stuff and come back, like he said I should. I was feeling pretty good, you know. Lighter? But when I got back to the block, there were all these cop cars and flashing lights. I saw you, Miss Sunshine, standing outside all by yourself, watching them take Teddy away inside that black bag. I didn't know what to do so I just left and went back home. And then the next morning it was on the news that Teddy had killed that lady and then shot hisself. I knew they were wrong. He didn't kill no lady, not Teddy. But maybe he shot hisself because of me, because of what I told him. Maybe it was my fault all over again."

"Teddy was murdered, Jermayne," Jade assured him. "If we weren't already completely sure of that, you telling us about that bag with the hairbrush in it proves it without a doubt. Terrell's death was an accident, and you never made Teddy anything but proud of you. Please remember that."

"I agree," Court said. "But now, unfortunately, Miss Sunshine and I have to leave."

"Not yet," Jade told him. "I had Sam call Brainard's office to reschedule our meeting for after his speech. Back at his house. And Father Muskie is on his way. I don't want to leave Jermayne alone, and Father Muskie will take care of him while we're gone." She looked at Jermayne. "Is that all right with you? You'll talk to Father Muskie?"

"Teddy wanted me to talk to him. Sure, okay."

"Terrific. He's a very nice man. And will you wait for us to get back? Will you stay here tonight?"

"I suppose so, sure. Thank you."

"Don't thank us just yet—I'm also going to hand you off to Ernesto. He'll make sure you get something to eat, and after Father Muskie leaves, he'll talk to you until your ears fall off. But he's a good kid. Jade? I'm guessing we have to go talk to Sam and Jolie now, fill them in on what's going on."

"I know," Jade said, reluctant to leave Jermayne, maybe even more reluctant knowing she now had to tell Jolie about Jermayne. Jolie would cry, and then Jade would probably cry with her. And they'd have to go through that all over again when they told Jessica. Jade hated to cry.

Father Muskie arrived twenty minutes later and he and Jermayne closed themselves up in Sam's study for a good long talk, while Court explained to Ernesto that they had a guest about his own age and maybe Ernesto could find something for the two of them do.

"Sure, no problem," Ernesto assured them. "You think he plays Internet video games? Mr. B has a bitchin' setup in that room of his."

"You're kidding. Sam plays video games?" Court smiled at Jolie, who only shrugged.

"Yes, Sam plays video games," Sam said as he joined them all in the foyer. "Sam is very good at video games. You got a problem with that, cousin?"

"No, I'm just trying to form a mental picture. Okay, got it. It isn't pretty, by the way," he said, winking at Jolie.

"Maybe you'd like my screen name. I'm the Sam-in-ator. Ernesto, just remember to put the controllers back in the bottom drawer of my desk. It seems that Rockne likes to chew on the wires."

Jade glanced at Court, hoping he wouldn't mention that Sunny was following in the Irish setter's footsteps and had chewed on Sam's dining-room carpet. He shook his head almost impercep-tively. Good, at least they could postpone *something*.

What they couldn't postpone, what she didn't want to postpone, was the confrontation with Joshua Brainard.

Jolie excused herself to take yet another cell-phone call from Jessica, who was already downtown at Carpenters' Hall, moaning that she'd been conned into taking the shoot for her station so she couldn't meet them until the speech was over. Jolie made soothing noises for about thirty seconds and then said, "No, we are *not* going to bring him along for you, Jess. Some theories just have to remain theories, okay?" She closed her cell with a snap and rolled her eyes as she headed for the door. "Honestly, some people's kids…"

"Wait a minute," Jade said once she was outside on the drive, suddenly realizing that when she counted noses, she came up with two extra ones—Bear Man's and Rockne's. "What's Rockne doing here?"

"I give up. She'd probably already called Ernesto and told him to sic Rockne on us. She wasn't asking me just now, she was *telling* me." Jolie opened the rear hatch and urged the dog to climb inside. "She says it's a test."

"She's still going with the idea that Rockne was locked out of Teddy's office because the killer was allergic to dogs? Brainard sneezes and she yells *gotcha?*" Jade made a face. "She never gives up, does she?"

"I think it's a family trait," Court said, giving her a kiss on the cheek before opening the rear passenger-side door for her. "Bear Man's driving and Sam already called shotgun, so I get to ride back here with you and Jolie."

Moments later the Mercedes was pulling out through the gates of Sam's sanctuary and heading for the Brainard estate, Bear Man singing along with Queen's "We Are the Champions" until Sam turned off the radio and swiveled in his seat to ask another question about their interview with Jermayne.

Jade just sat in the rear seat, her head back, her eyes closed, Jolie holding her hand on the seat between them, and let Court handle the questions.

She let her mind roam where it wanted to go, which was anywhere but where she was at the moment, because she just wanted this all to be over. She wanted to be with Court, maybe on some small island somewhere, one without phones, without the Internet, without any outside contact. Someplace private where they could talk to each other, hold each other…and heal.

She just wanted to be with him. She needed to be with him.

The Scholar Athlete case was solved, although Jade wished there could have been another solution. They were three for four, Jade and her sisters. Teddy, more often drunk than not, had amazingly done the really hard work, and they had simply followed in his path, one foot in front of the other, fitting the final pieces in the puzzles—or, to be truthful, getting lucky.

HOME?

"YOU KNOW, Miss Sunshine," the doctor said as he put the last stitch in the gash at her temple, just at her hairline, "you're one very lucky lady. Another inch to the right and you might have lost an eye. As it is, we're still waiting on that X ray, to make sure there's been no orbital-rim fracture."

"Then I can leave?" she asked, longing for a hot shower and a soft bed. She felt as if she'd been beaten on by a man with a camera, which she had been.

"We called your father, yes," the doctor said. "He'll be allowed to take you home as soon as those X rays are back. You're still not out the woods on those ribs, either, remember."

Jade tried to sit up, but the nurse put a hand to her chest to hold her still. "You called my father? Why would you do that?"

"Because he's listed on your contact information, Miss Sunshine," the nurse told her. "From when you were in the emergency room a few weeks ago."

Jade subsided onto the uncomfortable gurney. "Oh," she said in a small voice.

"We're very careful, Miss Sunshine," the nurse went on, taping a few Steri-Strips to her sewn-up wound. "There are extremely strict laws now about who we can tell things to and who we can't. Which is why you might want to change your last name on your medical insurance and your contact person. Your husband was very upset when we told him we couldn't give out any information."

"Oh, God." Jade felt tears stinging at the back of her eyes. "Court called here? He's in Greece. How did he find out I was here?"

"I wouldn't know that, Miss Sunshine," the nurse said. "Okay, you can sit up now, but don't get dressed yet. Dr. Hennessey will return shortly with the results of your X rays. I'll send your father back in a minute. He's been pacing out there and driving our reception people crazy."

Jade waited until the nurse had pulled the curtain of the cubicle closed behind her and then gingerly swung her bare legs over the side of the litter and slowly stood up. A soft moan escaped her lips as she felt her bruised ribs—*please, God, don't let any of them be broken*—protest at the movement.

She padded barefoot over to the sink and leaned in close to the shiny chrome paper-towel holder on the wall to get a look at herself. Not good. Besides the Steri-Strips, the skin around her right eye was swollen and already showing signs of turning colors, and there were other bruises along her chin.

She'd gotten in one good leg kick before the enraged husband had managed to grab the strap of her camera, throwing her off balance. He'd hit her twice with the camera, and when she went down, he'd started kicking her. If that squad car hadn't come along, she could be dead.

And if she'd really been pregnant, as she thought she'd been until that ER run ten days ago, she might have lost Court's baby, which, to Jade's mind, would have been worse than dying.

But she hadn't been pregnant, and her silly plans to tell Court the news over a romantic dinner when he came home from Greece had been replaced with the reality of a kind doctor's words that wishing for a pregnancy sometimes makes the body wish for it, too—but sooner or later, reality and nature take over.

She'd mourned the loss, anyway, even as the doctor told her that she needed to relax, not wish so hard, and if, in a year, she still wasn't pregnant, only then would they investigate further.

Jade wanted a baby, maybe needed a baby. She rattled around in Court's huge Virginia home, with him traveling more often than not until this important buyout of another hotel chain was completed.

Court promised her that he'd soon be home more, operating more from his home office and laptop than globetrotting, but that this negotiation had been going on for three years and he had to finish it.

Jade understood that. She understood all that.

But that didn't mean she wasn't lonely. She wasn't made for idleness, for long days spent shopping or having her hair and nails done. If there could be a baby—

"Margaret Mary! Oh, sweet Jesus, I was so worried!"

Jade turned around in time to hold Teddy off so that he didn't try to hug her and finish the job on her ribs that the cheating husband had started. "I'm okay, Teddy. I'm fine." *And stop calling me Margaret Mary. You've been doing it for months and I hate it. I feel like you want me to be someone I'm not.*

Teddy walked over to the gurney and sat down on one edge, the image of despair. "This is all my fault. I was supposed to be out there tonight. I was supposed to be snapping those pictures. Me, baby. Not you. What kind of father am I? Not even a man anymore—"

"Stop that. You didn't feel well, and we knew your boy was going to show up at that motel for his Tuesday-night special," Jade said, picking up her clothing from where it lay folded on a chair.

She immediately saw that her pretty silvery blouse was ripped at one shoulder. But she was pretty sure she could fix it. She loved that blouse; Court had told her that the color did wonderful things for her eyes—and his libido.

Jade smiled, and her cracked lip stung as it began to bleed again.

"I wasn't drinking. I wasn't, Jade, I swear it," Teddy said quietly. "I was only taking a little nap, that's all. You should have woken me up. That husband of yours made me promise you'd only be working on the computer, doing those background checks for me, and maybe some interviews out in the field, maybe trying to collect some of the money owed us. That's all. No running around at night, no pictures, no sneaking up on people. That was the deal, Margaret Mar— Jade. Now I've got to deal with him, too."

"Yes, Teddy. How did Court find out I'm here?"

Teddy hung his head, his complexion pale against the bright oranges and greens and blues of his Hawaiian shirt, the rather purple and red stain that had become more noticeable on the tip of his nose.

He was still a handsome man, but he was looking more and more worn around the edges. He only lost the battle with the bottle "now and then," but the now and then was becoming more frequent since her marriage.

"Oh, that. He called for you just as I hung up with the hospital people. Caught me at a really bad time, when I was half-awake, all blubbering and worried about you and… He said to tell you he's on his way here."

"Oh, no. I wish you hadn't done that, Teddy. I don't need him to see me this way, and there's really nothing he can do for me. Now I've interrupted his important meetings."

"I told him that, I think. I told him what they told me, that you were okay, just banged up, but he just kept saying he'd be here as fast as he could. Jesus, they weren't lying on that one, you look like hell, pumpkin. What are you going to do about that, Jade? What are you going to tell Court? Are you going to tell him it's all my fault?"

"You didn't make me go, Teddy. It was my decision. Court will understand that. Is he flying here or back to Virginia?"

"Here, I think," Teddy said, standing up as the doctor came back into the cubicle. "How is she, Doctor? How's my little girl? Is she going to be all right? I want the best. If you're not the best, then go get the best, you hear me? I can pay."

"Teddy, stop it," Jade said, looking at the doctor, apology in her tone. "How were the X rays?"

"As I said before, Miss Sunshine, you're a very lucky woman. No cracks, no breaks. But you will be hurting soon in places you didn't think you could hurt. I wrote some prescriptions for you, a painkiller, an antibiotic cream for your wounds, and I suggest you don't try to be brave and not take the pain pills. Take them for at least a week, and see your family doctor in five days to check on those stitches. There's only two, so I'm sure he can handle them. The nurse will be in to give you a copy of all those instructions and I'll be back to sign you out."

Jade thanked the doctor, who looked at Teddy one last time before leaving the cubicle.

"Teddy, that was embarrassing. You insulted the man."

"Not if he's good, I didn't,"Teddy said, his smile finally appearing. "Get dressed, Jade, and I'll take you home. Then I can take care of you for a while. That's a turn of the table, isn't it?"

Jade dressed as quickly as she could, signing the release papers, and downed her first pain pill the nurse had brought her before she allowed Teddy to drive her home and help her upstairs to bed.

Either her injuries or the pain pill or a combination of them both combined to let her sleep until well past ten the next morning.

Her first thought upon waking was that she needed to call Court on his satellite phone. But then she realized she didn't know what to say to him that wouldn't upset him, and she probably wasn't yet up to what he wanted to say to her.

For now, she'd let Teddy field his phone calls. That was cowardly, but she wasn't feeling very brave at the moment.

She took a shower, pulled on loose sweats, tied her hair back in a ponytail, slipped her feet into pink fuzzy slippers and went downstairs, following the aroma of canned chicken noodle soup that was coming from the kitchen.

Poor Teddy, he was trying so hard to make it up to her. Maybe he'd made her some bread, butter and sugar bread, her favorite? She'd like that. She hadn't had bread with butter and sugar on top since she was a little girl. The perfect accompaniment to canned chicken noodle soup.

She then fell asleep on the couch in the living room, too sore to think about climbing the stairs again, and when she next awoke it was to see Court standing beside the couch, looking down at her.

If he looked bad, and he did, she must look like she was half in the grave. "Court—"

"Oh, my God," he said quietly, shaking his head. He dropped to his knees beside the couch as she struggled to push herself up against the cushions, doing her best not to wince. "Have you seen your face? No, scratch that. Of course you've seen your face. Where else are you hurt? I want to hold you, but I don't want to hurt you more."

Jade reached out a hand and he took it in his, squeezed it. "Do you…did you ever see those old *Dick Van Dyke* shows on that station that runs old sitcoms?"

Court shook his head, looking puzzled. "No. Is this going somewhere? I've had a long flight—I kept wanting to get behind the plane and push— and unless you have a point here, now I've got to worry that you're delirious."

"I'm not delirious. Well, maybe just a little. I'm taking some pretty wicked little pain pills. Anyway, on one of the shows, Dick Van Dyke goes skiing and falls off a mountain. His wife—I think its Mary Tyler Moore, you know, playing Laura Petrie—wants to kiss him and hug him, but he stops her. He points to his mouth and tells her there's this one spot, at the corner of his mouth. He says she can kiss him there, because it's the only spot on his whole body where he doesn't hurt. I'd say that to you, except I don't think I have a single spot on my body that doesn't hurt."

God, now she was babbling, like Jessica. *Avoiding,* like Jessica. Except she knew her baby sister was better at it.

Court smiled, but she could tell his heart wasn't in it. "Teddy only told me you'd been hurt but you were okay, and that he was on his way to the hospital. But nobody answered the phone when I called from the plane, which just about drove me crazy. I didn't even know *which* hospital. I called every hospital until I found you, and then nobody would tell me anything. Even when I got fairly demented, which I did."

"It's the new laws, the nurse told me. She gave me a copy of them while I was waiting for the doctor to sign me out. The head of a foreign government can ask for and get all my medical records, in the name of Homeland Security and antiterrorism, but they won't tell my own husband a thing unless I've already authorized it in writing. I'm so sorry. Using my maiden name for work probably didn't help."

"Let's not worry about that now. What I needed to know is that you're all right. Whose fault was it, not that it matters."

Jade didn't know what to say. Was it her fault
for stepping in when she'd promised not to do
any even remotely risky fieldwork anymore? Or
was it Teddy's fault, for drinking too much after
dinner last night? Or was it Court's fault, for
marrying her and then expecting her to fit seam-
lessly into his life, even when he left her alone
for a week or more at a time? More than six
months of marriage, and if she counted up all the
days, they'd only been together for a little more
than three of them.

"Jade, honey? The accident. I don't care whose
fault it was. But was anyone else hurt?"

"You…you, uh, think I was in an automobile
accident?"

He looked confused. "I just assumed… Teddy
said there'd been an accident. Jade? You're crying,
aren't you? What's the matter, sweetheart?"

"I thought…I thought you knew. I thought
Teddy had told you." Of course Teddy hadn't told
Court—he knew Court would go ballistic all over
him. "It wasn't a car accident."

"You fell?" Court got to his feet, looking down
at her intensely. "No, you didn't fall. Jade? What
don't I know here? What aren't you telling me?"

"Jade, honey, where in living hell did you put
the Evans background-check file? I've been
tearing apart the office for an… Oh, hello, Court,"
Teddy said, stopping halfway across the small
living room. "I didn't hear you come in. Nice of

you to take time away from that big career of yours to come see our little girl."

"Teddy," Court said, tight-lipped. "Jade was just about to tell me what happened last night."

"Was she now? And how is our girl after her nice long nap? Looks a little the worse for wear right now, don't you think, Court, but she'll snap back fast enough. Won't you, sweetie? Nothing keeps my little girl down for long. Why, I remember that time she went head over ears off her new bike. She had a bump on her head you could hang a hat on, but she was back on that bike the very next day. Brave, or just plain Irish stubborn. I don't know which…"

When Teddy finished speaking, his voice just sort of fading out, the silence in the living room was allowed to grow until even a dead man might have been able to feel the tension. Jade could sense Court's gaze on her.

She cravenly kept her own eyes averted, pretending an interest in the design on the old crocheted afghan pulled over her legs. It was a zigzag pattern in browns and yellows and oranges, pilly with age and too many washings, but her mother had made it in one of her tries to be a Good Wife. It was by far the ugliest afghan in the history of the world.

"You were hurt on the job, weren't you?" Court said at last. "You went out on a job. You took on some drunk in a bar the way you did the night we met, or were trying to grab pictures of some cheating husband outside a sleazy by-the-hour motel."

Her head went up and she realized too late that she had just as good as confessed what had happened. "I'm so sorry, Court. I know I promised."

"Yes, you did promise. You weren't going to do that anymore, Jade. That was the deal. Help Teddy while I'm out of town on business until he can find someone to replace you, fine. I don't expect you to just sit around waiting for me to get this damn deal done, twiddling your thumbs. But *no* fieldwork. We'd agreed."

She'd scared the hell out of him, that was why he sounded so angry. She didn't blame him. This wasn't really anger, it was concern. But still she flinched, his words slapping at her. "I—"

"I sent her," Teddy said, hurrying across the carpet to stand between Court and the couch, as if he would protect Jade if Court tried to hurt her—which was ridiculous.

"Stay out of this, Teddy. My wife and I are talking. This is between Jade and me."

"The hell it is. I'm the boss, she's the employee, and a trained PI, damn it. That's how it works. You don't take on a job and then only do the parts your husband says you can do. What the hell kind of arrangement is that? I *sent* her, just like she went out there a hundred times before you met her and tried to take over her life. You have a problem with how the Sunshine Detective Agency operates, sonny boy, then you have a problem with me, not her."

"Oh, I have a problem with you all right, Teddy, but we'll save that for another time," Court said, his voice cold. He stepped around the man and held out his hand to Jade. "Come on, sweetheart. This isn't helping anything. Time to go home. I'll help you get dressed."

"Are you out of your mind, Becket?" Teddy grabbed Court's arm and roughly pushed him backward. "You don't touch my daughter. She's hurt, she can't be dragged around like some sack of meal because you want to prove something."

"Prove something?" Court shook off Teddy's arm. He actually smiled. "We're married. What else do I have to prove?"

"You *took* her. I challenged you, idiot that I am, and you couldn't stand to lose, so you *took* her. But is she happy? Ask her. Go on, Becket, ask her if she's happy. Ask her why she's here, not waiting for you in your fancy mansion like some prize you won."

"Prize? That's how you think, Teddy, not how I think. She's your daughter, Teddy, not your possession. She has a right to her own life. We have a right to build our own lives, together, in our own way. But you can't stand that, can you? You can't let go of the only one you have left."

Jade struggled to sit up, her bruised ribs catching at her so that she had to suck in her breath at the fierce pain. "Stop it! Stop it, both of you. What are you doing? What are you talking about? My God, what's going on here?"

"You want to answer that one, Teddy?" Court asked, glaring at the man. "You want to tell my wife what this is really about, what it has been about for you from the beginning? That 'loving father knowing what's best for his girls' pile of crap may have worked with Sam, Teddy, but it damn well doesn't work with me."

"Teddy?" Jade was on her feet now, standing next to her father. "What's Court talking about? What worked with Sam? The beginning of what?"

"You selfish bastard,"Teddy said, his voice low and tight. "What do you know about real love? What do you know about being alone? You'd tear out a man's heart. Let me tell you, this girl's been my daughter a lot longer than she's been your sometimes wife. She knows where she belongs."

Even as Jade reached for him,Teddy was on the move, stomping off to his office. He slammed the door and she heard the key in the lock a moment before she heard something hard hit the wall inside the office.

Teddy's fist. She was sure of it.

She looked at Court even as she sat down on the couch again, her legs a bit wobbly from the effect of the pain pills and the ugly scene she'd just witnessed. "What just happened here? For the love of God, Court, what's going on?"

He sat down next to her and carefully took her

into his arms. "I'm sorry, sweetheart, so sorry. I guess that's been building up for a while between Teddy and me, but I sure picked a hell of a time to put it all on the table. Come on, let's go to the hotel. Teddy's right about one thing—you're in no shape to be dragged onto a plane."

Jade extricated herself from Court's gentle embrace. She couldn't actually hear it, but she was sure the bottom drawer of Teddy's desk was sliding open at that moment. She couldn't leave him alone with a bottle, not when he was in one of his black moods.

"The hotel? Oh, Court, I don't think so. I'm such a mess, and the idea of getting myself together and going with you is… Can't we just stay here? I should feel a lot better by tomorrow."

Court looked toward the closed office door. "I don't think that's such a good idea, sweetheart. Teddy seems to bring out the worst in me, and I've already upset you enough. How about we do this—I'll go to the hotel and you stay here and rest. Maybe Teddy will consider that a peace offering or something. I've got calls to make, anyway, and I'm expecting some important faxes…."

"You're so busy with this deal. You shouldn't have come home. I'm so sorry."

"The deal? Right now I don't give a flying…" He kissed her forehead. "Things are going to change, Jade, soon. Once the negotiations are wrapped up, our lives won't be so crazy, I promise. Because you know what, sweetheart? I've figured something out these past months. I'm the boss. And as the boss, one of my jobs is to hire good people I can trust to act in my name."

"Like David Langsdowne? You have forgiven him for that suite, haven't you?"

"Forgiven him?" Court grinned. "I gave him a raise." Then he sobered again. "Are you really going to be all right here?"

"I'll be fine," she told him, resting her head against his shoulder. "And I shouldn't have gone out on that job. It's always the ones you think are harmless that end up being the worst, going all postal on you."

"What I don't get is why Teddy let you go out on the job in the first place."

She hated lying to him. "It's like he said, Court. If I'm here doing the job, I can't pick and choose my assignments."

"Then you won't be back. If Teddy can't see what he's doing, I do. Two days a week, then three. I know I'm gone a lot, Jade, but do you really need to spend all of your time here? Virginia is your home now."

"It is when you're there," she said, wishing she didn't feel so defensive. "Which you rarely are. It's…sometimes it's like we got married just for the sex."

"I didn't know you were thinking that. I'm so sorry, sweetheart. We have to talk about this," Court said, and whether he was agreeing with her or trying to put her off, she didn't know. "For now, I want you to rest, and I'll let you alone to do that. But tomorrow we go home, Jade, all right? I think we need to be at home, just the two of us."

EXCEPT THAT by the time tomorrow came, Teddy was the worst Jade had ever seen him. Hiding in his office, looking through old family photos of when she and her sisters were a lot younger, back when her mother had still been around. He'd actually woken her at four in the morning to make her sit up and look at the photographs with him.

He'd even brought out his case files from some old, unsolved homicide cases that were still open after he'd been injured and had to leave the force. He'd told her about each one, about how they haunted him, how the past was sometimes the only companion he had, the only thing that kept him getting out of bed in the morning.

He'd cried, breaking her heart even though she knew he'd been drinking. In the end, she had helped him to bed, wincing as he leaned against her and set off the pain in her bruised ribs.

When Court called her, she told him she couldn't leave, not just yet. She blamed business, that Teddy was very busy, because how did she tell her husband that she was worried about Teddy's mental state?

Court wouldn't believe her; he didn't like Teddy, anyway, for some reason she still didn't understand. It should be enough for Court to know that Teddy needed her for another few days. Maybe a week. That was all. Then she could feel comfortable about leaving him.

"In another few days, Jade, I have to fly back to Greece to sign the final agreements. You could come with me. We'll have that honeymoon we keep postponing. Please, sweetheart, come with me."

"Looking like this?" Jade told him with a shaky laugh, putting a hand to her face even though he couldn't see what she was doing. "Court, no, I can't. I'll just stay here with Teddy and you can fly back to Athens now, without having to wait around for me to see the doctor again, have these stitches out. Then when you've finished your business we can—"

"Jade," he interrupted, "why don't we stop fooling ourselves? This isn't about what I have to do. This is about the whole bizarre relationship between you and Teddy. You see that, don't you, sweetheart? He's turned our lives into some damn tug-of-war with you in the middle."

Jade hadn't slept. She hurt all over. Her father was falling apart in front of her eyes. Her husband was making demands on her.

All her life. All her life she'd been the one everyone depended on, the one who fixed things; she was reliable, understood everyone else's dreams, everyone's problems.

She was tired. She was so damn tired.

And now her own husband was hinting that

not only was she not holding up her end of their marriage, but that her whole life had been some twisted result of Teddy manipulating her somehow.

"You know what, Court? You don't have to stay here at all. I may look like hell, but I'm fine, I'm going to be all right. Just call me when you get back to Greece," she said, too weary to talk anymore.

"Jade? Jade, listen to me. No, scratch that. I'm coming over. I'll be right there."

"No, Court," she told him, "I don't think so. I think it's best if you just go back to Greece. I'm sorry I got hurt and you had to come home. I…I really don't think I want to see you right now. We're saying things I don't want either of us to say."

"Jade, sweetheart, we don't want to do this."

"I'm not doing anything, Court. You're the one who's saying it's either my job or you. Because that's what you're saying, isn't it?"

"No, Jade. I'm saying that Teddy sees it another way. Not as the job or me, but as *him* or me."

"And how is that any different from what you're asking me to do, Court? Maybe it's time for *me* to decide how I live. Maybe it's time for me to take care of *me*. Goodbye, Court, have a nice trip."

"Jade! Damn it, Jade—"

"JADE? JADE, SWEETHEART, wake up, we're here."

She blinked herself out of her unhappy dream and sat up straight on the rear seat of the Mercedes. "Here? We're at Brainard's house? What time is it?"

"About ten minutes later than it was when we pulled out of Sam's driveway," Jolie told her. "Man, you went *out*. Haven't you been sleeping, Jade?"

"Not enough, I guess," Jade said, avoiding Court's knowing eyes as she climbed out of the car and stood looking at the closed gates to the Brainard estate. "Sam, your place is just as big, but for some reason, it seems five times more inviting than this place. There's just something so…sterile about it."

"Brainard doesn't have Bear Man's smiling face welcoming people to his humble abode," Sam said, smiling. "Right, Bear Man?"

The gatehouse-keeper-cum-bodyguard-cum-chauffeur kicked the toe of his left shoe into the dirt at the side of the macadam roadway. "Now you're embarrassing me, Sam. I'm gonna go take a walk, check the place out."

Jade leaned close to Court. "Nobody ever said. What's Bear Man doing here, anyway? I doubt Joshua Brainard is going to invite us all inside when he gets here."

Jolie overheard her. "Yeah, look at all of us, and Jessica and Matt aren't even here yet. We can't all go trooping inside. We'd look like we were heading for a group toidy or something."

Court threw back his head and laughed. "Maybe we should send Bear Man to quickly hunt up a dozen Vote Brainard buttons to help ease our way inside."

"I'd rather chew nails," Jolie said as she looked at her watch in the light under the streetlamp. "He's probably still talking for the cameras. We're going to be standing around here, waiting, for maybe another hour or so. Why don't we get back in the car and go get some ice cream or something?"

"Ice cream?" Jade said, raising her eyebrows. "My sister wants ice cream? Since when does our weight-watching movie star eat anything that isn't green and has more than ten calories per bowlful?"

Jolie looked across the narrow road to where Sam was peering through the wrought-iron gates at the house, Rockne on a leash beside him. "I get more...exercise now," she said, and then ducked her head when Court laughed again. "Oh, go take a walk, you two. We'll hold down the fort from the Mercedes. I don't need to be seen standing out here, or some helpful citizen will put in a call to the TV stations that Jolie Sunshine is back in town."

"Jolie Sunshine's Back In Town. Sounds like a song title. My heart goes out to you, sis, it really does. It must be such a burden, being a big star," Jade said, giving her sister a playful shove. "Go on, go hide. It's too dark now for those sunglasses to be believable, anyway."

"Come on, sweetheart." Court took Jade's hand, looking both ways before crossing the barely traveled roadway. "If you're done ragging on each other, let's do what Jolie says. If you know what you plan to say to Joshua Brainard, you can use me as your sounding board. You haven't had much time today to rehearse or even build a strategy."

They picked their way down the grassy verge

between the roadway and the six-foot-high, gray fieldstone walls—there were no sidewalks this deep in suburbia—and turned left when they got to the end of the barrier to avoid being caught in the headlights of any car coming up the hill toward them.

"I wanted to be alone with you, anyway," Jade said after they had walked a good thirty feet away from the road. "So much has been happening, and now, soon, maybe even tonight, it's going to be over."

"We hope it's going to be over tonight. If I were a betting man, I'd say our chances are about fifty-fifty. You certainly had Brainard spooked today at the airport. But don't count on it all being over so easily, Jade. The man isn't stupid. He'll know where we're bluffing him."

"I know that. I've pretty much given up the idea of threatening him with DNA evidence we don't really have. We've been lucky so far with the other cases. Although I won't say what happened tonight with Jermayne could in any stretch of the imagination fall under the heading of *luck*. You meant it, Court? You're going to help us walk that poor, scared kid through the system?"

"Any way I can," he said, letting go of her hand and slipping his arm around her back as they kept slowly walking down the slight incline alongside the stone wall to where it ended and a chain-link fence began. "Bad as it is, I have to tell you, Jade, Jermayne would have been much worse off if it hadn't been for Teddy. The way he stepped in back then when Terrell died, took on the responsibility for both Jermayne and his grandmother? That was a hell of a thing to do."

"You're saying something nice about Teddy?"

"We had our differences, but I always knew he only did what he thought was right. I just didn't agree that what he believed *was* always right. I doubt Sam would, either."

"He was human."

"That he was," Court said, and they walked on in silence for another several yards. "He called the divorce lawyer, didn't he?"

"Court…do we have to do this?" She sighed. "Yes, I suppose we do. Yes, Teddy called the lawyer, the very next day after you left to go back to Greece. I…I just sort of floated, *existed,* and let him do what he thought was best. But I never thought you'd sign the papers. I didn't think you'd let me go so easily, not if you really loved me. But you did go back to Greece without trying to see me. I was so…confused."

"Pissed. Admit it, Jade, you were pissed."

She smiled sadly. "All right, pissed. At you. At Teddy. At the whole world, I think. And I didn't appreciate being fought over like I was the prize at some county fair or something. I was hurting, mentally and physically, and I just wanted to crawl into a hole and pull it in after me. And then Teddy swore to me that if I'd just help him, he'd stop…"

"Yes? And Teddy would stop what? His drinking?"

Jade stopped short to look up at Court in surprise. "You knew about that?"

"I smelled it on his breath that last day I saw him—the day he and I almost went ten rounds. It was barely past noon. Yeah, I knew. You didn't trust me enough to tell me, though, did you?"

"Oh, Court," Jade said, stepping in front of him. "I never even told Jolie or Jess. He was such a proud man. Such a sad man. Father Muskie said he was clinically depressed, but even Father Muskie couldn't get Teddy to see anybody, talk to anybody. He lost his wife, he lost the career he loved, and then, one by one, he felt he was losing his daughters."

"You were all he had left, and then I came along."

"I didn't see that then, but yes, I see it now. I've

seen it for some time now. It wasn't all Teddy's fault, how we all behaved. I helped build my own prison and then told myself I was happy. How could I blame Teddy for not wanting to lose what I'd always so freely given him? We even talked about it when he seemed stronger because I was…I was hoping then I might…I might go down to Virginia, to talk to you. But that didn't happen. Teddy died."

"I'm so sorry I couldn't be there for you at the funeral, that you had to go through all that alone."

"My regret is that you and he never really got to know each other. You were a threat to him, Court, to the last little bit of life he felt he had left. Did I think when I came home and saw him that last night, that he'd committed suicide? Because he was depressed, because I'd told him that I wanted you and me to see if we could maybe try again? God help me, Court, yes. Yes, I did. I was so *mad* at him. I was so shattered, I felt so powerless. That's…that's when I went upstairs to my room after everyone had gone and saw the Belleek-china pieces he'd given me. I couldn't stand to look at them. I'd given him everything I could, given up my own happiness for him, and it still hadn't been enough for him, he'd still destroyed himself. So I destroyed every beautiful thing he ever gave me. It…it was the most terrible night of my life."

"Come here," Court said, gathering her close against his chest, kissing her hair. "We can't bring him back, sweetheart. And we couldn't help him any more than he'd let us help him. Not you, not Father Muskie…nobody could fix what broke inside Teddy Sunshine a long time ago. But we're going to do what you and your sisters need to do. We're going to get him back his good name."

Jade let herself melt into Court's strong embrace, trying to draw strength from him, knowing what she felt around her were not just his strong arms, but the force of his love for her. The love she'd thrown away, if there really had been love between them when they were together a lifetime ago.

There had been immediate attraction, wild and urgent and undeniable. On both sides. But had there been love? Or did *real* love need time to grow, to mature? If they had gone more slowly, not rushed in like fools had rushed in since the dawn of time, would there have been a different ending to their story?

She'd wanted him then, believed she could not exist without him. But she had existed without him this past year. Existed, not really lived. The man who had stepped back into her life only a few weeks ago was not the same man who had walked out of it a year earlier. She wasn't the same woman. What she felt for Court Becket now was light-years away from what she'd felt for him back then. Deeper, wider, truer.

How strange. Their love hadn't seemed to be able to withstand the short separations during their marriage, but it had grown a hundredfold in the long year they'd been apart.

"By tomorrow this could all be over," she said at last, her voice muffled slightly against his shirt-front. "What happens then, Court? What happens to us?"

He put his hands on her upper arms and held her slightly away from him, the better to look down into her face, deep into her eyes, she imagined, making sure she was listening. "If you close a door, I'll break it down. If you run away, I'll find you. I'm never letting you go again. You're my life, Jade. More now than ever."

"If…if Teddy hadn't died, then would you…"

Court slowly shook his head. "Check the date on our divorce papers, Jade, before we burn them. On the fifteenth of next month that date would be exactly one year ago. I promised myself when I signed on the dotted line. One year, I'll give us both one year. One year for us to get our heads on straight, for me turn over more of the daily operations of Becket Hotels and a few other things to competent managers, because I wanted to be a husband, not just a lover. Time for you to make your peace with Teddy and not feel as if you'd just suddenly abandoned a very loved, but very needy man."

Jade blinked back tears that stung at her eyes. "And then? What were you going to do when that year was over?"

His smile made her heart skip a beat in her chest.

"Do you remember our little slice of Sodom and Gomorrah out in Vegas?"

"I could hardly forget it," Jade said, sure she was blushing in the near-dark. "What about it?"

"The grand opening of the Jade Tower Casino and Spa is set for the fifteenth of next month. I think you'll like it. It's mostly glass, jade-green glass, of course. I'd already arranged with Teddy for the two of you to be flown to Vegas on the company jet to cut the ribbon."

Jade staggered where she stood. "You *what?* You? And *Teddy?*"

"It takes a big man to admit when he's wrong, or at least that's what we told each other. He also told me he was about to call me if I hadn't contacted him first. He loved you, *Margaret Mary*. And, for some strange reason, even after I'd acted like such a horse's ass the last time we were together, he'd decided that his little girl truly loved me."

Jade's bottom lip trembled uncontrollably as the threatening tears spilled down over her cheeks. "She does," she managed, her voice breaking. "Teddy's little girl loves you very much."

"That's good," Court said, smiling almost sheepishly. "I was sort of counting on that. I wish we could go somewhere and be alone for two weeks at least, but we can't, not until this is over. I understand that. And there's something else you need to know now, before we move on with our lives. When we spoke, and we spoke a few times, Teddy told me he was, as he said, cleaning up his act, and he wasn't going to wallow in self-pity any more."

"He *was* getting better," Jade told him sincerely. "He hadn't had a drink in weeks, as far as I knew. And he seemed happy, even though the business was pretty slow."

"You helped there, Jade. He was taking back his life, starting with some unfinished business he'd been neglecting. He was going to close the agency after you left—he believed we'd get back together. He'd live on his police pension and devote himself completely to some cases that had haunted him for a lot of years. So no, I wasn't surprised when you told me about the cold cases or that he'd been pursuing them pretty actively. The hell of it is, by taking steps to take back his life, one of those cases ended up getting him killed."

"He died a cop," Jade said quietly, tears threatening again. "Not a failure, a cop. It's what he would have wanted." She looked up into Court's face. "Thank you, Court. You just gave me back my father."

He caught her sob with his mouth, holding her tightly as she slipped her arms up and around his shoulders, glorying in the sense of coming home, of finally being where she belonged. There was no passion in the kiss, not the sort of electrically charged physical reaction she was more accustomed to with Court. What she felt was an ache easing, an emptiness filling up. Two hearts, healed, another heart at last laid to rest.

There, in the dark, Jade and Court took their first step toward a new beginning.

But first, there had to be an ending….

"Come on, sweetheart," Court whispered in her ear. "We should be getting back. It'll soon be too dark to see anything out here, anyway."

By the time they'd returned to the roadway, Jessica and Matt had arrived, Rockne was doing his usual I-thought-I'd-never-see-you-again frantic greeting and Jessica's clear laughter was brightening the darkening sky.

"Hey, youse guys," Jessica quipped, seeing them, "you missed it. Old Man Brainard did another one of his fainting acts when a cracker-jack reporter—that would me *moi*—asked a particularly probing question from the peanut gallery. I mean, he didn't actually grab his chest and swoon, but he did go sort of pale all over and get up and leave the stage. This time Joshua stuck around, though, and held down the fort. I guess he figured the same dodge wouldn't work twice."

"You never make things easy, do you, Jess? We've been invited to the man's house to speak with him," Jade said, shaking her head. "Did you have to go after him in public? What did you ask him?"

Jessica rolled her eyes. "Well, I didn't ask him if he killed his wife, if that's what you're thinking."

"She came close, though," Matt said, slipping an arm round Jessica's waist. "Don't worry, I gave her a little nudge and shut her up."

"Right, a little nudge. My ankle is going to be

black and blue." Jessica turned to look at Sam and Jolie. "Glad you're back. So you're not just hanging around here for moral support? We're all going to confront the guy together? Isn't that pretty close to a group toidy?"

"I think I heard that line somewhere before a little while ago," Sam said, at which time Jolie glared at him. "But you're right, Jessica. There's too many of us. We're the ones who showed up late, so we'll go. Jolie? You agree?"

"I guess so, if Jessica here promises to behave. None of us are on the man's Christmas-card list, Jade, but he really isn't happy with either his old golfing buddy here or me, so we'll wait in the Mercedes again. Don't ask me to go any farther away than that."

"Good," Jessica said, obviously pleased. "But Rockne stays. I still say my theory has merit if Brainard takes one look at him and says he can't have him around because he's allergic. Matt and I didn't get close enough the night we slipped inside the fence. But it makes sense that that's why Rockne was locked out of Teddy's office that night."

"She's like a dog with a bone," Matt grumbled, shaking his head. "All right, Jess, Rockne stays, for now. But once we're inside and Brainard doesn't react, you're going to have to take him back to Jolie and Sam. Agreed?"

"Agreed," Jessica said reluctantly, but then almost immediately brightened. "It's showtime."

Jade turned to see two sets of headlights approaching up the winding hill, Joshua Brainard and his hangers-on or bodyguards or whatever the heck was the reason for the second black SUV.

They stood back and the lead car pulled in front of the gate, but then stopped with the gate still closed.

The blacked-out rear passenger-side window slid down and Joshua Brainard's handsome, solemn face appeared. "I asked to see *you,* Ms. Sunshine. I don't think it is in our best interests to turn this into a…into a…"

"Group toidy," Jessica whispered, thankfully quietly.

Jade secretly agreed with the man, and quickly offered a compromise. "If you'll allow Mr. Becket to accompany me, I'm sure everyone else will be willing to wait here. Is that agreeable?"

"I just want this unpleasantness over with, Ms. Sunshine, and for all of you to promise to go away. All right, you and one other may come in." He stuck his head out further and looked at Jessica. "But not her."

The window slid back up, hiding Joshua Brainard's face once more, and the gates opened. Both SUVs slipped inside.

"I'm almost flattered," Jessica said, grinning at Matt. "The man's afraid of me."

"Jess, honey, everybody's afraid of you," Matt said, deadpan. "It's probably why I feel better carrying a gun."

"One other?" Bear Man said. "That would be me, right? I go with her?"

Sam and Court exchanged smiles before Sam answered, "Actually, Bear Man, I think Jade would like Court to go with her. You can guard us out here. How's that?"

"Fine," Bear Man said, waving his arms as he walked away. "Fat lot of good I'm going to do out here..."

"Who do you think was in the second vehicle?" Jolie asked.

"My money's on the old man, Cliff Brainard," Matt said, taking Jessica's hand. "They're not quite joined at the hip, but you can usually find one when you see the other. If Joshua told him you were meeting here with him tonight, Jolie, he would also want to be here. Come on, Jess, back to our car. You can pretend you're a big bad cop on stakeout."

"Ha-ha, funny man. Jade? Here, sis, take Rockne's leash. I'm telling you, Brainard starts to sneeze and we're halfway home."

"Jess, I'm not going to—"

"I'm betting Brainard still didn't fix that slice in his chain link," Jessica interrupted. "I bet I could still get inside, eavesdrop from the patio."

"I knew I should have brought my handcuffs," Matt said, looking apologetically at Jade.

"Oh, just give me the damn leash, Jessica Marie," Jade said. "I'll take him in with us, but then I'll bring him back out the first chance I get. And you'd better be waiting right here at the gate to take him."

"Okay, that works. See? It doesn't take a lot to make me happy."

"Which explains her ecstasy over the size of the diamond in her engagement ring," Matt said, earning himself a jab in the ribs from his beloved.

You'd think they were at a damn party, Jade thought. Maybe they all just felt it, smelled it in the warm night air. *Victory.* All because of Joshua's reaction to hearing Tarin's name at the airport, that and a missing hairbrush in a plastic bag. Combined, they were the last two nails in Joshua Brainard's coffin.

Jolie gave Jade a hug for luck and then everyone else returned to their cars while Jade and Court headed up the drive on foot toward the well-lit front door, which was only fifty yards or so from the gates.

"I can't believe I just got away with that," Jade said as Rockne nosed ahead of them, sniffing at the grass. "The last thing I wanted was to have Jess in here with us."

"I sensed that, yes, and I think Jolie did, too. Deferring to the oldest, or something like that. I think the jury's still out on who won, though, considering we've got the dog. Are you really ready for this?"

She squeezed his hand. "More ready than I was an hour ago, yes, thanks to you."

They walked up the semicircle of marble steps to a wide portico and the almost-as-wide man who was standing with his back to the slightly open door.

"Leslie," Court said, just as if the two of them had been formally introduced. "You want to stand there making faces like a constipated grizzly, or do you want to take us to your leader?"

"Wow, what got into you?" Jade whispered as they followed the bodyguard into the large foyer.

"I think he's the one who made the threatening phone calls, disguising his voice," Court told her quietly. "And then there's the way he chased us the other day. He's not my favorite person, and I wanted him to know it."

"No, that's not it," Jade said, looking at Court, seeing a part of him she hadn't seen before, hadn't known existed inside the button-down business-man. "You want to make him mad. You want to make him take a swing at you. Don't you?"

"I wouldn't mind. He scared you, and he said *knotty pine.* I don't think he shot Teddy, but he knows too many details not to have been in on it somewhere. Mostly, I don't like that he scared you."

"That's very nice of you, Court, even very macho, but just in case you haven't noticed, the man's built like a brick sh—"

"Shh, here we go."

Jade turned her attention to the double doors Leslie was pushing open with a flourish and the room they entered behind him. It was time to remember that she wasn't only Teddy's daughter; she was a trained private investigator. It was time to push emotion aside and put her game face on.

She was pretty sure Leslie wasn't going to pull a trumpet from out of his backside and announce them, so she just kept moving, her eyes shifting right and left, taking in her surroundings, until she saw Joshua Brainard standing in front of one of several sets of French doors that overlooked the well-lit pool, a short, fat crystal glass holding some brown liquid in his hand.

"Ms. Sunshine. Mr. Becket, is it? Yes, of course, Sam's cousin. I saw you today at the airport." He shifted his gaze back to Jade. "You enjoyed that this afternoon, Ms. Sunshine? Inflicting pain?"

Jade wondered for a moment if this would be easier if Joshua Brainard didn't look like such a nice guy. Handsome, born to money, personable. He was, she thought, sort of a cross between an earnest, younger Robert Redford and Matt Damon at his most vulnerable. Hardly the face of a killer.

Yeah, well, as Jessica would say: tough beans. If the man was looking for some sort of apology, he might as well know now that an apology wasn't going to happen.

"You won't deny, Mr. Brainard, that you recognized the name. Tarin White."

Joshua walked over to a grouping of chairs and motioned for Jade and Court to join him. "No, I don't think there would be any point in that after the way I reacted to your little trick. Nice dog— what's his name?"

"Rockne," Jade said, tugging on the dog's

leash. Rockne had decided to sniff the stranger—the stranger who wasn't sneezing. "You've got Leslie, I've got Rockne."

"Right, Rockne's the muscle. I'm only here for the floor show," Court said sarcastically, again surprising Jade. Amazingly, she had never really thought about Court's life outside the two of them. She had a feeling he could be a real bad ass in the boardroom.

"He doesn't look much like a killer," Joshua said, Rockne now sitting at his feet. "You know, now I remember seeing him before. The night your sister and the police lieutenant trespassed on my property? I never could have a pet. Allergies, you know."

Jade watched as Joshua rubbed behind Rockne's ears, the dog's tail banging against the carpet in ecstasy before Rockne sank lower onto his haunches as if prepared to make a night of it at Joshua's feet. "Maybe, then, I should get him out of here."

"No, no, it's all right, leave him. It wasn't me who was allergic." Joshua sat back and crossed one leg over the other. "So how much do you know about Tarin?" He got to his feet once more. "Oh, wait. I'm a terrible host. Let me get you two something to drink."

Court also got to his feet. "I see a few bottles over there, Mr. Brainard. Allow me. I don't want to infringe on your conversation. Here, let me refresh that for you. Single malt?"

Joshua looked at his glass and then handed it to Court. "Uh, yes…thank you. That would be very nice."

It was a subtle move, and Jade folded her hands together so as not to applaud it. Smoothly, deftly, Court had reversed roles with Joshua Brainard, putting himself in the position of host. And it worked. As he sat down again, Joshua wasn't looking quite as at home in own house as he was a moment earlier.

"Becket Hotels, right?" Joshua said, gesturing over his shoulders with his thumb as Court headed for the small bar located on the far of the large room. "I think he may have played in our member-guest tournament with Sam a few years ago. So it's you and Court Becket, and your sister Jolie and Sam? Is that what they call keeping it in the family?"

"Does it matter?" Jade asked coolly, more than willing to fall in with Court's idea to keep the man off balance. "Why don't we get back to Tarin."

"Yes, all right, back to Tarin. How did you connect me with Tarin?"

"I didn't. My father did. You should have met with him when he wanted to see you, Mr. Brainard. Things may have turned out differently if you had."

"I don't see how, not if he knew about Tarin. Not unless your father was looking for a payoff, for hush money."

"Teddy wouldn't take hush money or try to blackmail you over something that happened so many years ago. We're not talking about an extramarital affair here, we're talking about murder. So why don't you try again?"

"You're an angry woman, Ms. Sunshine, but you're directing that anger, and your suspicions, at the wrong person. Tarin and I were such a long time ago, as you said. A lifetime ago. I don't want to play twenty questions with you, Ms. Sunshine, so why don't I just tell you what I think you want to know. Besides, the Fishtown Strangler case has been solved. We both know that."

All right, time to drop the first bomb. "Tomorrow morning's newspapers will report that Herman Longstreet confessed to five murders, not six. He swears he did not kill Tarin, and the cops believe him. So why don't you do as you suggested and just tell us what you know."

"He…" Joshua pressed a thumb and forefinger to the bridge of his nose, shook his head. "No, that's not possible. Of course he killed Tarin. He killed all of them. I don't…"

Court returned with two tall glasses filled with ice and ginger ale and sat down beside her once more. He hadn't brought Joshua's glass back, deliberately taking away the man's crutch, or his weapon, as it had been a very heavy, lead-crystal glass.

"Jade might not have told you, Mr. Brainard, but I'm her ex-husband, a condition soon to be remedied. Which is why I insisted upon accompanying her here tonight. In other words, Jade lost her father and she deserves answers, and I'm here to see that she gets them."

Joshua seemed to recover, sitting up straighter once more. "I understand. And I asked Ms. Sunshine to come here because she and her sisters have been, to put it bluntly, harassing me to the point where my father has become ill. I want it stopped. I've nothing to hide, unless you're out to destroy me out of pure vindictiveness. In this age of *gotcha* politics, I suppose going public about Tarin could cost me the election. But that would be Philadelphia's loss, not mine."

"You're a real savior, I'm sure. It might help move matters along if you stopped thinking about the election, Mr. Brainard," Court told him. "The subject here is murder, not your political ambitions."

"Could you just start at the beginning, Mr. Brainard?" Jade couldn't believe how cool the man was, how composed. Did he really think he was going to get away with murder after all they'd learned?

"All right, I'll choose to take your word that there's no hidden political motive here. For the moment. Let's talk about Tarin. I met Tarin my last semester of grad school. I was researching a paper and she was working part-time in the library to earn money to continue taking college courses. I was already engaged to Melodie, before you ask, and I'm sure you would have. I kept seeing Tarin off and on, and…and my father found out."

"He didn't like that she was black?" Jade asked him as he fell silent for a few moments.

"I don't know about that, I'd not like to believe that. He didn't like that she wasn't Melodie. Melodie was perfect. The former Olympic swimmer. Beautiful, intelligent, well-spoken, daughter of a good family. We'd always known I'd go into politics eventually. Melodie would make the perfect wife for a politician. We looked good together. I loved her. She was a good person."

"But you kept seeing Tarin?"

"But I kept seeing Tarin, yes. Even after the wedding. I'm not proud of that fact, but there was just something about her. She was so…so *free*."

"You paid for her dental work," Court said quietly.

"I did. I paid for her apartment, too, miserable as it was. She'd allow the dental work, but she hated that I paid for her apartment, so she refused to move out of this small, miserable place above a beauty shop. I hated sneaking around, I hated all of it."

"You were hiding from Melodie," Jade said, nodding her head. "I'm a private investigator, Mr. Brainard. I've seen lots of love nests paid for by married men. Tarin White was far from taking advantage of you."

"It was the other way around, Ms. Sunshine. May I call you Jade?"

Jade nodded her agreement. Anything to keep the man talking.

"Thank you, Jade. Please call me Joshua. What was I saying? Oh, yes, it was the other way around. For three years Tarin and I snuck around like criminals, until I'd finally had enough. I wanted to marry her. But only two days after I told her I was going to leave Melodie, and to hell with any idea of a political career, she was gone. I went to the apartment and she wasn't there. She didn't leave a note, nothing. She was just gone. I never saw her again."

Jade bit her lips together as she looked at Court for assistance.

"But she did show up again, Joshua," he said helpfully. "She showed up several months later, as one of the victims of the Fishtown Strangler. Excuse me, alleged victim."

"Alleged victim." Joshua Brainard looked at Court levelly, and then at Jade, figuratively pinning her to the chair with his intense blue gaze. "Now I see what you're after. This has nothing to do with the fact that I'm running for mayor."

"It never did, Joshua. We couldn't care less about your political ambitions," Jade said, believing she could almost hear the proverbial penny drop inside the man's brain as he finally came to the correct conclusion.

"But you're wrong. I did *not* kill Tarin. I loved her. I know what you're trying to do here. You're trying to say that I killed Tarin and then I killed Melodie and Teddy Sunshine to keep from having my first crime exposed. Not the affair, a murder. I'm not an idiot, I can see where this is going. I'm no saint, either, and I'll admit to that. I cheated on my wife. Hell, I never should have married

Melodie. It wasn't fair to her. It wasn't fair to me. But I did not *kill* anybody."

Joshua had raised his voice, and Rockne got to his feet, barking his displeasure at being woken up. Jessica would say he was coming to Jade's defense, but Jade knew better.

"Let me take him outside, Joshua. I'll be right back. Come on, Rockne, let's go see Jessica." She walked back through the foyer, pretending not to notice Leslie standing there, his massive arms folded across his chest.

Jessica must have been watching for her, because she met her at the open gate, her expression eager. "So? Did he react? Did Rockne make him sneeze? Did he tell you to get him out of the house?"

"He rubbed Rockne behind the ears and Underdog here lay down with his head on the man's shoe to take a nap. He said he'd never had a pet, but that's because somebody else in the family was allergic to animals. Happy now?"

"Not really, no. Who else in the family? It's the natural follow-up question. You did ask, right?"

"Wrong. It was a stupid idea and I don't know why I listened to you."

"What's up, Jade? Isn't it going well in there? Because it's starting to rain out here, in case you didn't notice, and I could still go in there with you and—"

"He's lying," Jade interrupted. "You remember how you said you can tell someone is lying if their eyes go left and down? I ask him a question and his eyes keep going left and down, so he's got to be lying. Except that my gut tells me he's telling the truth."

"Uh, about that?"

Jade had already turned to head back up the drive; she wasn't sure she could trust Court to be content making small talk until she got back. She turned to her sister impatiently. "About what?"

"About the shifting-left-and-down thing," Jessica said, smiling weakly. "I think I had that wrong."

Jade stomped back down the drive. "You think you had that wrong? What do you mean, you think you had that wrong?"

"Down girl," Jessica said, holding up her hands defensively. "Okay, okay, I know I had it wrong. Right brain, left brain—it gets confusing. But I think when someone looks left and down, they're examining their memory maybe? Not looking for a lie. Is that a problem?"

"A problem?" Jade wanted to scream. "No. Not a problem. I shouldn't be relying on that kind of hocus-pocus stuff, anyway."

"Except you said your gut's telling you he's telling the truth, and what's that if not hocus-pocus, and maybe gastric juices?" Jessica reminded her. "So now what? We've been wrong all along?"

Jade shook her head, shaking off that idea. "No, we can't be wrong. Teddy was on to something. He had to be, or he and Melodie Brainard wouldn't be dead. I've got to get back in there."

LESLIE WAS STILL standing in the foyer, but now he was smiling. That smile gave Jade a bad feeling as she walked past him, back into the room where Joshua and Court waited for her. It was as if Leslie knew that she was striking out and that the Brainards had won.

Both men were standing at the French doors, looking out over the pool where Melodie Brainard's body had been discovered. Joshua had his glass again, and the two men seemed almost friendly, which was weird.

"Who found her?" she heard Court ask as she joined them.

"The housekeeper," Joshua said. "The woman'd been out for the evening, and when she came home, she wanted to get a drink of water and... and the window over the kitchen sink looks out onto the pool. Melodie always liked to keep the area lit. The housekeeper has since quit and gone back to Guatemala, saying it wasn't safe here, but I can put you in contact with her if you feel it's necessary."

"I'm sure if the police allowed her to leave, they were satisfied with her story," Jade said, also looking out over the pool, its surface broken by large, plopping drops of rain, imagining what it must have been like to see a body floating in that beautiful, clear blue water. Probably as bad as seeing your father's brains blown all over knotty pine... "Who do you think killed your wife, Joshua?"

"I'm sorry," Joshua said, returning to his seat. "The police are confident your father killed Melodie. My affair all those years ago has nothing to do with Melodie's murder. Your protests to the contrary, I think Teddy Sunshine discovered that Tarin and I had had an affair, and he was trying to blackmail us. I wouldn't see him, Melodie said or did something to make him angry, and he stran-gled her. Having once been an honorable man, he couldn't live with the fact that he'd taken a life, and he went home and shot himself. Family loyalty is one thing, Jade. But facts are facts."

Again, Jade believed him. Was he that good at

being sincere, or did he also believe he was telling the truth? She had no choice but to pull out her last weapon.

"Well, thank you for seeing us, and for your honesty," she said, holding out her right hand.

"You're welcome. Let's hope we've settled something here tonight. And again, I know your pain. We've both suffered a great loss."

Still holding on to his hand, Jade said, "Yes, I agree. Tell me, though. What happened to the baby?"

His hand didn't tighten on hers. He didn't drop his hand back to his side. In fact, he didn't react at all. "I beg your pardon? What baby?"

She let go of his hand and feigned innocence—Jessica, without the *girls*. "Oh, I'm so sorry. You didn't know?"

Joshua looked from Jade to Court and then back to Jade. "What's going on here? What are you talking about? I told your sister that Melodie and I couldn't have children. There was no baby."

"We're not talking about you and Melodie," Jade said, pushing on because there was no going back now. "I don't have my notes with me, so I can't be exact here, but the autopsy report showed that Tarin had given birth only a couple of months before she died. My notes also show that, counting backward as we all do, Tarin had to have been pregnant when she left that apartment you set her up in and say is the last place you saw her. So what baby, Joshua? *Your* baby."

"No," he said quietly. "No, that's not possible. She wouldn't have…she never…*oh, my God.*" He sat down all at once, as if his legs couldn't support him, and looked up at Jade and Court, his eyes tortured. "Where? Where's the baby now? No, not a baby, not anymore. Where's my child? Tarin left me. She was out on the streets, she was prostituting herself and got herself killed. Wasn't that bad enough? What did Tarin do with my child? Is that what your father learned? Was he trying to tell me I had a child somewhere? Where? Did she give the baby up? Is the child in some foster home or been adopted? I have to know!"

"We don't know," Jade replied. She believed him; nobody could fake that kind of shock. She'd just delivered one hell of a blow to the man. "Not for certain. But we do have a theory. Teddy had a theory. Joshua, I sincerely apologize for believing that you killed Tarin. But now you have to help us. We still have a lot of questions."

"Ask me anything," he said, collecting himself. "I don't know how I can help. My God, *Tarin.*

Why didn't she come to me? Why did she go out on the streets like that?"

Jade racked her brain for a question, one of the loose ends that had been bothering her, settling on, "Your father was a part of the mayoral task force set up to catch the Fishtown Strangler. Did you ask him to join it? Because you can see how we might think that's how you knew the MO of the serial killer and then imitated him when you killed Tarin."

"I did *not* kill… I'm sorry, you're only explaining how you came to your conclusions. What was the question? Oh, my father and the mayoral commission. Yes, Dad was on that. He's always been active in the community, that's not a secret. And yes, when Tarin became one of the victims I did read any files he brought home, hoping to learn more about what had happened to her, where she'd gone, where she'd been living." His eyes got hard. "I didn't use the files as a primer for murdering the woman I loved, the woman you're telling me was the mother of my child. That's obscene."

"Teddy believed it, though, we think. We think that's why he wanted to get close to you, and to Melodie." Jade looked to Court, who just nodded. "We know that the night Teddy was killed he had been to see your wife, and that she gave him a hairbrush, which he put in a plastic bag and took home with him."

"What? Why? I don't understand."

"We think we do. We think Teddy wanted to see if you were a match to another cold case he'd been working on all these years. We believed that Melodie then told you what she'd done and you strangled her the way you did Tarin, and then killed Teddy in order to get back that hairbrush."

"That's insane. It's…it's just insane."

"So you say. We were trying to solve a murder, Joshua, several murders. We gathered facts, we reached…conclusions. The Baby in the Dumpster case," Court said, carefully putting himself between Jade and Joshua, just in case the man reacted violently. "Teddy believed—we'd come to believe—that the murdered baby was your son, Joshua."

"No," Joshua said, his expressive eyes now showing unimaginable horror. "No. That couldn't be. It just couldn't be."

Jade took up where Court had left off. "We concluded that Tarin had decided to blackmail you by threatening to go to your wife and show her your baby, and that you killed them both, staging Tarin's murder to look like she was just another victim of the Fishtown Strangler, and then storing your own son's body in a freezer somewhere for several months so that when the body was found, nobody would connect dead baby to dead mother. I'm sorry, Joshua. But you can see why we decided you were the most likely suspect. It's even why we brought Rockne here tonight. Rockne was locked out of Teddy's office that night, and my sister Jessica thought it was because the killer was allergic to dogs. But you're not."

"No, Jade, I'm not," Joshua said dully, getting up from the couch and walked over to the French doors once more, standing with his back to the room. He stayed there for a full minute, then another minute, while Jade and Court watched, and then, finally, he turned to face them once more.

He looked as if he'd aged twenty years in those two minutes. "No, *I'm* not allergic to dogs. I think I need you both to leave now. If you'll please excuse me. Leslie will show you out."

"Court…" Jade said, putting her hand on his arm as Joshua brushed past them, heading for the foyer, "what do we do now?"

"Follow him?"

By the time Joshua had reached the bottom of the stairs, he seemed to have come out of whatever

tightly wound mode he'd been in, and was calling
for his father. Each word he said was louder than
the last one, the tone more frantic, fiercer, a man
rapidly losing all control. "Dad? Dad! Where are
you? Goddamn it, *where are you? What have you
done?*" He put his hand on the railing and ran up
the staircase.

Leslie put his wide frame in front of Jade and
Court to stop them from following. "Time to go,"
he said, his voice deep, coming from somewhere
low in his belly.

"Yes, I think so, too," Court said, and the next
thing Jade knew, Leslie was on his back, his eyes
rolling up into his head as he lost consciousness.

"How—"

Court pulled out his cell phone and called Matt,
told him to get Bear Man and come to the house,
to make sure Leslie stayed where he was and to
alert the police while he was at it. He then took
Jade's hand and they ran for the stairs. "I saw you
take down that guy in the hotel bar the night we
met, remember? I couldn't have a wife who could
do that when I couldn't, so I took few lessons. It's
a man thing, I guess."

Jade looked down at Leslie's inert form as they
pounded up the winding staircase. "Graduated top
of your class, I bet. Where do you think they are?"

But Court didn't have to answer, because they only needed to follow the sound of Joshua's loud, tortured voice as he confronted Cliff Brainard in one of the bedrooms.

"It was you. It had to be you. Nothing else makes sense. They thought it was me, but it was *you*. My own father. You killed Tarin? Melodie? You murdered *my son?* Why? *Why?*"

Cliff Brainard was in bed, sitting up against a small mound of pillows, the cream-colored sheets and his navy blue silk pajamas only accentuating his pale, stricken face. "Your *son?* Your *mongrel,* you mean."

Joshua was standing at the bottom of the large four-poster bed, swaying where he stood, looking as if he might pass out. "My God, I went to his funeral, sat in the pew next to you, played the whole thing for some damn photo op you said we had to do—and didn't know he was my *son*. He was my blood. He was *your* blood."

"No. He was the end of any political ambition you had. I didn't want to do what I did. It destroyed my health. Look at me—I'm nothing but a sick old man now. But I don't regret what I did. I did it for you, Joshua, then and now. I did it all for you, son."

"No," Joshua said, slowly shaking his head as

he backed out of the room as Matt walked in, his pistol drawn, his gold lieutenant's shield visible on the pocket of his jacket, and walked to the head of the bed. "No, old man, you did it all for *you*. Officer, please. Get him out of here."

TUESDAY, 3:45 A.M.

JADE ROUSED herself reluctantly when she heard Jessica call out Matt's name, having fallen asleep with her head on Court's shoulder as they'd waited in Sam's living room for Matt to return to the house. Ernesto and Jermayne were both upstairs in guest rooms, asleep.

"So?" Jessica asked Matt as he collapsed onto the facing couch. She handed him a cup of coffee. "You said he'd waived his right to legal representation and wanted to make a statement. Did he?"

Matt rubbed the back of his neck. "As far as I know, he's still talking. He's one of those guys who doesn't shut up, even when the people listening to him just want to go to the can and vomit. I had to get out of there, and since Brainard's who he is and the top brass are falling all over each other to have their names connected to the bust, they let me leave."

"Oh, my poor baby. It was bad?"

"It wasn't good. And the guy still thinks he was justified. I see an insanity plea in Clifford Brainard's future, I'm sorry to say. Even refusing a lawyer could be seen as being nuts, a smart guy like him."

Jade took the cup of coffee Court had poured for her and leaned forward on the couch. "Can you tell us what happened? I think we've got most of it, but some things still don't make sense."

"Let me give you what I've got," Matt said, and Court took Jade's hand in his as if to help her through the rough parts that would come when Matt told them exactly what had happened to Teddy.

Matt filled in the history, beginning with the day Joshua Brainard had informed his father that he was leaving Melodie to be with Tarin. Clifford Brainard had gone to Tarin, explained that she would be ruining his son's bright political career and he'd one day hate her for it. He'd given her enough money to go somewhere and finish her degree, and because Tarin loved Joshua, or for the money—no one would ever know the real truth, probably—she immediately left town.

But once her son was born she came back. Again, whether it was because she felt Joshua should know he had a son or to blackmail him with that son, no one would know. Cliff Brainard said she'd come back for more money, but as Matt said, who was going to believe him?

Cliff was already on the mayor's task force, knew the details of how the Fishtown Strangler operated, and saw his chance to be rid of Tarin. He met with her at his penthouse condo, just to talk, he said, and drugged her drink.

He'd planned to strangle her while she was unconscious, but while he was in another room drinking up some courage, Tarin woke up, grabbed the infant and tried to get away, tried to escape through the kitchen of the penthouse.

"She fell down a flight of cement service stairs while holding the baby. The baby died in the fall," Matt told them. "Again, this is what Brainard says. He swears he had planned to leave the baby on a doorstep, but do I believe him? Anyway, he strangled Tarin, then did his best to simulate the rest of the Fishtown Strangler's MO postmortem, the bastard."

"The simulated rape," Jade said, nodding. "We couldn't figure that one out, Matt, remember? And the drugs in her system?"

"Leslie, loyal Leslie, moved Tarin's body to a dump spot in Fishtown. But Leslie wouldn't touch the child's body, so Brainard put it in the bottom of an extra freezer in a basement storage room that belonged to him. The freezer, one of those deep, horizontal ones, was supposedly only used to store deer meat during hunting season, so his housekeeper never went into it. Somebody already went over to check it out, but it's long gone by now, I'll bet. Anyway, he left the body there until he could figure out what to do with it."

"And the Baby in the Dumpster was the result," Jessica said, wiping her moist eyes. "What a ghoul."

"I can't wrap my head around something like that. Your own grandchild, packed away in a freezer for months, and then dumped like garbage. Brainard said the whole thing nearly killed him, which it damn well should have. He hadn't planned on the Dumpster. He'd planned on the Delaware, figuring what the freezer didn't do the water would, but he started to feel sick and had to dump the body quick before he drove himself to the hospital, where he had his first stroke. He hasn't been a well man since."

"My heart bleeds for the bastard," Court said, pouring himself another cup of coffee. "So all right, years pass, Brainard thinks he's pulled off the perfect crime and saved his son's political career. But then Teddy entered the picture."

"He'd always been there," Jolie said, sighing.

"He worked those old cases twice a year, isn't that right?"

"More often lately," Jade said as Court squeezed her hand. "He was a man on a mission, I think. When he found Tarin's dentist and discovered who'd paid for her implants, all the pieces started falling into place for him, just like they did for us, and he went to see Joshua Brainard."

"And Melodie Brainard," Matt said as he continued his story. "Where, according to Clifford Brainard, he found a vengeful, vindictive woman who was more than happy to hurt her husband. And gosh, after all the Brainards had done for her. Cliff chose her friends, her clothes, the charities she could support. He did everything for her to make her into the perfect candidate's wife. But she wasn't grateful, you understand, she didn't appreciate all his efforts. So in case you're wondering, the bit the shampoo girl heard and told us about the bruises, Melodie saying she wasn't going to take it anymore? I think we can be pretty sure who was responsible."

"Again the father, not the son. Why on earth did she stay?" Jolie asked, clearly confused.

"Maybe she loved her husband," Sam suggested, and Jolie glared at him. "Hey, don't look at me like that, it's just a theory. More likely, it was the glory of being the candidate's wife."

"Mayor today, governor in four years—two terms, the limit—and then the White House," Matt told them. "Good old Cliff had it all figured out."

Jade sighed. "Everything but one determined, retired cop."

Matt took up the story once more.

Teddy had been convinced he had his murderer in Joshua Brainard, and worked on Melodie to help him. Her mistake was telling Cliff about Teddy's visits, asking his advice. So Cliff had made a visit of his own to Teddy's house to try to talk him out of ruining his son's life with false accusations. But Teddy wouldn't play ball, and over the course of the next two weeks Teddy had either pretty much convinced Melodie that his theories were correct, or else she'd given him the hairbrush to help prove him wrong.

But Melodie, through fear, feelings of revenge— who knew?—had also felt some pressing need to tell Cliff everything Teddy told her. She'd signed her death warrant, and Teddy's, when she told Cliff she'd given Teddy Joshua's hairbrush so he could get DNA from the hair on it.

"Cliff knew where the security cameras were located and how to disable them, and he knew Melodie took a swim every night, like clockwork," Matt told them as Jade curled up closer to Court, because the worst was coming, soon.

Cliff entered the estate, his former home, through the cut in the fence and approached Melodie as she swam laps in the pool. He kept her talking, her back to the trees, as Leslie advanced on her, grabbed her, strangled her and tossed her into the pool.

Then they drove to Teddy's house to get the hairbrush.

"Was the door locked? Was the security code set?" Those two questions had been driving Jade insane since the night Teddy died.

Matt told her that the alarm had been active, but that it had also been active that afternoon, when Cliff first confronted Teddy, and Teddy had grumbled to him that his daughter was always nagging him to use the damn code and he couldn't be bothered remembering useless numbers, so he just used his birthday, which drove his daughter crazy.

"Why did Teddy even talk to the man?"

"Good question, Court," Matt said. "Brainard says it's because he'd come to him, father to father, to ask that he not jeopardize his son's bright future with an old scandal, a youthful love affair that couldn't possibly mean anything anymore.

Anyway, later, it was simple enough for Brainard to find out Teddy's birth date and let himself, and Leslie, into the house after Jermayne left. They saw him leave—Jermayne—and then waited about an hour before they made their entry."

"Giving Teddy enough time to fall off the wagon after Jermayne told him what he told him."

"Right, Jade," Matt said, looking to Court as if for permission to continue. "According to Brainard, Teddy was pretty drunk when he and Leslie opened the door to his office. Teddy managed to grab his service revolver out of the box on his desk, but Leslie was too strong for him. One shot into the floor, the other shot…well, Brainard admits he gave Leslie stage directions. *In his mouth,* he said, so it would look like suicide. Oh, and if I said Clifford Brainard is talking, it isn't any more than Leslie's talking, trying to cut himself a deal. Leslie's story varies a little, as in, he killed nobody, just cleaned up after the boss."

"You okay?" Court asked Jade quietly.

"No, Court, I'm not. Teddy never brought out his gun except to clean it. If he had the gun out, it was because he expected trouble. But even then, he couldn't fight the bottle when he took a hit of bad news."

"Jermayne's confession," Jolie said, resting her

head on Jade's shoulder. "But would things have turned out differently if he and Jermayne hadn't had that last healing talk? If Brainard and Leslie were intent on killing him, getting back that hairbrush, framing him for Melodie's murder—would the ending have been all that different?"

COURT WALKED OUT of the bathroom, a towel wrapped around his waist, to see Jade sitting cross-legged on the bed, watching the DVD Jessica had made and they'd watched earlier—a lifetime ago, when Jade first had seen Jermayne's silhouette outlined against the trees at the cemetery.

"Jess is going to talk to Father Muskie tomorrow about another ceremony at the cemetery," she told him as she hit the power button, turning off the television. "And Matt says he thinks the department will agree to some sort of tribute. After all, Teddy not only died in the line of duty, but he died a real hero. Jess even wants a wake at Teddy's favorite watering hole. Jokes, stories, Irish songs, laughter, toasts to Teddy's memory. What do you think?"

"I think the word is closure, and I think it's a very good idea," Court said, sitting down on the side of the bed. "I don't even mind putting off our second trip to Elvis-impersonatorland until we're back from visiting Morgan in England, since the Jade Tower isn't quite ready for us to occupy the honeymoon suite just yet."

"How did you know I'd want to go back to that same awful wedding chapel?"

"I took a wild guess," he said, sliding more fully onto the bed so he could nuzzle her neck. "You're a bit of a traditionalist, you know."

She tipped her head slightly, to give him better access. "Mmm, I think you're right. In fact, maybe we could go visit our friendly Elvis impersonator once a year, just so we have an excuse to stay in the honeymoon suite. Is it still pink?"

"If it is, David's fired," Court told her, easing her back against the pillows. "The entire time I was in that suite I felt like I should be wearing a blue bow so I could remember I'm a man."

"And I know just what we could have tied it around for the best effect," Jade said teasingly, snuggling into the pillows as she drew him down to her. "Love me, Court. Hold me, make love to me. Please."

He knew what she needed. She needed to be held, to feel alive, to go someplace that took her away from all the ugliness she'd lived with since the night Teddy died.

There was a time for talk. Later. There was a time to plan for their future. But not now.

Now, she needed him. Now, he needed her.

He kissed her hair, her cheeks, her soft, willing mouth. He eased her nightgown over and off her shoulders, his mouth following where his fingers blazed the way, driven on by her soft moans of pleasure.

She reached for him, but he only caught up her hand and kissed her palm, each fingertip. His pleasure would be found tonight in her pleasure. Her release, her escape, her tumbling climax.

He worshiped her small, perfect breasts, glorying in her response, in the soft, hesitant way she said his name over and over again as he captured her nipple in his mouth and suckled her, circled her hardening bud with his tongue.

Fly away, he told her inside his mind, *fly away to the clouds, dearest Jade, where there is nothing but this, nothing but us.*

They'd made love so many times, in so many ways. Hard, and fast, and fierce. Teasing love. Adventurous love. Even dangerous love.

Standing just inside the front door of his Virginia house, their clothes hanging off them, her back against the wall, because neither of them could wait for the climb up the stairs to their bedroom.

Their short honeymoon stay in Vegas. He, watching her learn him. She, watching her own reaction as his fingers drove her to ecstasy.

That rainy afternoon Jade had been looking in his library for a book to read and found a copy of the *Kama Sutra* Court thought had been thrown away after college.

They'd definitely had the passion, the carnal-pleasure portion of the program, down pat.

That hadn't proved to be enough, for either of them.

But this was different. How he felt about Jade was different now; deeper, more a mental union, a sense of sharing, of caring, that had little to do with what had first attracted him to her.

He could exist without her. He'd proved that.

He couldn't *live* without her.

Without words, he told her now how much she meant to him. With each touch, each slow, tender caress, he hoped she knew how much he loved her.

Fall into me, his touch told her. *I'm here, I'll always be here.*

When he finally levered himself between her legs, his arms braced on either side of her so that he could look down into her face, it was to see tears in her eyes as she returned his gaze.

"I love you, Court," she whispered, reaching up

for him, to pull him down, to press her mouth against his.

He blinked several times, fighting his own emotions, his arms tight around her, glorying in the way she clung to him in turn.

And then they flew with each other, fell into each other, their simple, ages-old union—a man and his woman—at last making promises they both could keep.

To love, forever…

TWO WEEKS LATER

"SORRY TO KEEP you waiting," Sam said, walking into the foyer, where everyone else was already gathered. "That was Joshua Brainard on the phone."

"How is he doing?" Jade asked. "No matter what, his father's death must have devastated him. Suicide in a jail cell? Not exactly the way anyone would think the great, politically powerful Clifford Brainard would die, huh?"

"Personally?" Sam said, shrugging. "I think it was a relief for Joshua, not having to go through the horror of a trial. He's already had to give up his political ambitions, and he just now told me that he's leaving the state, moving permanently to the family ranch in Colorado, or wherever it is. He only phoned because he read about the graveside ceremony this morning and wanted to tell you all one more time how much he regrets what his father did."

"He's arranged for a scholarship for Kayla Morrison's daughter," Jessica informed them. "Did you guys know that? The last victim, after Tarin? We did a small piece on it on last night's show. Kayla was the only one who left any children behind, and Brainard said he felt he owed the survivors something, because if his father hadn't confused the investigation, maybe the Fishtown Strangler would have been caught before Kayla became a victim. He's trying. I don't think it's working, but I'll give him points for trying."

Jolie looked at Jade, shrugging. "I still like him. He's a likable guy, the perfect politician. But maybe more real now."

"A hell of a way to get real, finding out your father is a monster," Sam said, taking Jolie's hand. "Come on. The three of you have been thinking about this day for a while. You don't want to be late."

Jade hung back with Court as the others headed for the cars. "Teddy wasn't perfect," she said quietly.

"None of us is, sweetheart. Teddy was a complicated man. He had his faults. But he did the best he could. It's all any of us can do. Bottom line, Jade, he raised three pretty wonderful daughters.

Now come on, it's almost eight o'clock. It's time to say a real goodbye."

"Jessica insisted on this ungodly early hour even after the wake last night that went on until the bar closed. She's hoping for a morning mist. I don't know why."

"And you were afraid to ask?"

Jade smiled, her heart almost light. "You got it."

The drive to the cemetery was uneventful, but as they passed through the gates and into the cemetery it was to a sea of blue uniforms lining either side of the roadway. Teddy's honor guard, men and women he had worked with, fellow officers from Philadelphia and a half-dozen surrounding communities, all there to pay their belated respects to a fallen comrade.

"All right, *now* I'm going to cry," Jade said as they approached the grave and she saw the color guard, the flags, the trumpeter waiting to play taps. But the crushing sadness was gone, the ripping grief that had not that long ago been so raw, so new.

Even Rockne, once more with his Notre Dame scarf tied around his neck, padded across the freshly cut grass with his head held high, Sunny scampering along behind him.

"Oh, look, Court. It's Morgan."

They walked over to Court's cousin, who kissed them both hello, and then they introduced her to everyone, including Jermayne, who looked huge and nervous as he stood there in his new suit beside Ernesto, who had actually left his intricate calculator in his pocket as a show of respect.

Jermayne was going to be all right, Jade and Court would see to that. They'd walked him through the system, and when he gave the police the names of the three boys who had given him the gun to hold for them, he'd been told to go home, he'd done enough. One of the boys, now a man, had been arrested the next morning, and the other two were already in jail on other charges.

All three had been convinced to plead guilty in favor of a lesser charge, although they could have been tried for murder for having given the gun to Jermayne in the first place.

The Scholar Athlete case was closed. Jermayne started trade school in three weeks.

"Court told me about the ceremony when we spoke the other day," Morgan said as she smiled at Sam, a cousin she had not yet met till now. "I couldn't resist. I hope nobody minds? Besides, this way I can make a personal appeal that you all come visit me at Becket Hall."

"Close your mouth, Denby," Jade overheard Jessica tell Matt. "We already know she's beautiful."

"Hey, I'm engaged, not dead," Matt answered, and Jade bit her bottom lip as Jessica warned him that he'd *pay for that remark later.*

It was amazing how different a person could feel standing in the exact same spot they'd all stood in just a few weeks earlier. Three women, alone. Rockne, grieving. That day they'd buried Teddy in disgrace. Today they would figuratively lay him to rest in glory.

Here we are, Teddy, your girls, your babies. Don't worry about us, please. We're going to be just fine. Jolie's with her Sam, and Jessica is going to drive Matt happily crazy. And Court, Teddy. I'm so glad you two were able to talk, come together, get to know each other a little. He loves me, Teddy, and I love him. We're going to be all right. We're all going to be all right. We love you, and we'll never forget you. But it's time for us all to put that one foot in front of the other the way you always told us, and get on with our lives. God bless, Daddy, and Godspeed.

"Sweetheart?" Court whispered. "Are you all right?"

"Oh, yes, I'm all right." She smiled up into his

beloved face. "We're all just fine. I love you, Court."

"I love you too, sweetheart. And I'm so proud of you. I'm proud of all three of you. Teddy's girls, doing right by their dad. You're a pretty re- markable bunch."

Father Muskie arrived and kissed each girl, and then hugged Jermayne, having to stand on tiptoe to do so, before he took up his place behind the newly laid brass marker and indicated that they should all make the sign of the cross.

He spoke about Teddy's booming laugh, made a joke about those horrible Hawaiian shirts. He told a quick, funny story about a time they'd gone fishing together in Canada, and the day Teddy had kissed the Blarney Stone in Ireland.

He spoke of Teddy's love for his daughters, the contributions he had made to the community in his long years of service with the police force, and his dedication to the victims he represented.

Jade stood very close to Court, his arm around her waist. Occasionally he'd lean down to kiss the top of her head or murmur something comforting into her ear.

They all flinched involuntarily at the rifle salute and shed a few tears as the honor guard presented Jade with a folded American flag.

And then, at last, it was over. She'd made a promise, they'd all made a promise, and they'd kept that promise. Teddy could now rest in peace.

Jade turned to leave, but Jessica grabbed her arm. "Wait. One more thing. And we've even got the morning mist rising from that creek over there. Remember, Jade, Jolie? Remember what Teddy always said he wanted?"

Jolie nodded. "A blanket of red roses like he'd just won the Kentucky Derby and a piper playing 'Amazing Grace' on the bagpipes. He said, if we were lucky, a good stiff breeze would come along and lift the piper's kilt a little, just to take the edge off everyone's sorrow. How could we forget?"

"I don't know how," Jessica said, smiling up at Matt. "I didn't."

And then, as if on cue, a piper dressed in full regalia stepped out from the line of blue uniforms and began playing "Amazing Grace."

He walked past the headstone, nodded to Father Muskie and then proceeded past everyone, heading for the slight hollow in the distance, leading down toward the small stream of fresh-flowing water that was still shrouded in morning mist.

Jade took the handkerchief Court pressed into her hand and wiped her tear-wet cheeks. When she looked up again the piper was nearly gone; the symbolism of him moving off, alone, impossible to ignore.

The pipes, faint now, could still be heard.

Her mind put the words to the music: *I once was lost, but now I'm found...*

Jade closed her eyes as a feeling of great peace filled her. As if he could sense the change in her, Court put his arm around her shoulders and pulled her close, pressed a kiss against her temple.

No, Jade realized with a sigh and a smile, she was not just found... she was *home*.

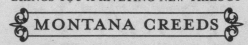

REQUEST YOUR FREE BOOKS!

2 FREE NOVELS
FROM THE ROMANCE/SUSPENSE
COLLECTION PLUS 2 FREE GIFTS!

YES! Please send me 2 FREE novels from the Romance/Suspense Collection and my 2 FREE gifts (gifts are worth about $10). After receiving them, if I don't wish to receive any more books, I can return the shipping statement marked "cancel." If I don't cancel, I will receive 4 brand new novels every month and be billed just $5.49 per book in the U.S. or $5.99 per book in Canada, plus 25¢ shipping and handling per book plus applicable taxes, if any*. That's a savings of at least 20% off the cover price! I understand that accepting the 2 free books and gifts places me under no obligation to buy anything. I can always return a shipment and cancel at any time. Even if I never buy another book from the Reader Service, the two free books and gifts are mine to keep forever.

185 MDN EF5Y   385 MDN EF6C

Name _____ (PLEASE PRINT)

Address _____ Apt. #

City _____ State/Prov. _____ Zip/Postal Code

Signature (if under 18, a parent or guardian must sign)

Mail to **The Reader Service:**
IN U.S.A.: P.O. Box 1867, Buffalo, NY 14240-1867
IN CANADA: P.O. Box 609, Fort Erie, Ontario L2A 5X3

Not valid to current subscribers to the Romance Collection,
the Suspense Collection or the Romance/Suspense Collection.

Want to try two free books from another line?
Call 1-800-873-8635 or visit www.morefreebooks.com.

* Terms and prices subject to change without notice. N.Y. residents add applicable sales tax. Canadian residents will be charged applicable provincial taxes and GST. Offer not valid in Quebec. This offer is limited to one order per household. All orders subject to approval. Credit or debit balances in a customer's account(s) may be offset by any other outstanding balance owed by or to the customer. Please allow 4 to 6 weeks for delivery. Offer available while quantities last.

Your Privacy: Harlequin is committed to protecting your privacy. Our Privacy Policy is available online at www.eHarlequin.com or upon request from the Reader Service. From time to time we make our lists of customers available to reputable third parties who may have a product or service of interest to you. If you would prefer we not share your name and address, please check here. ☐

BOB08F

Kasey Michaels

77318	MISCHIEF BECOMES HER	___ $6.99 U.S.	___ $6.99 CAN.
77291	DIAL M FOR MISCHIEF	___ $6.99 U.S.	___ $6.99 CAN.
77127	EVERYTHING'S COMING UP ROSIE	___ $6.99 U.S.	___ $8.50 CAN.
77059	STUCK IN SHANGRI-LA	___ $6.99 U.S.	___ $8.50 CAN.

(limited quantities available)

TOTAL AMOUNT $ _____
POSTAGE & HANDLING $ _____
($1.00 FOR 1 BOOK, 50¢ for each additional)
APPLICABLE TAXES* $ _____
TOTAL PAYABLE $ _____

(check or money order—please do not send cash)

To order, complete this form and send it, along with a check or money order for the total above, payable to HQN Books, to: **In the U.S.:** 3010 Walden Avenue, P.O. Box 9077, Buffalo, NY 14269-9077; **In Canada:** P.O. Box 636, Fort Erie, Ontario, L2A 5X3.

Name: _____
Address: _____ City: _____
State/Prov.: _____ Zip/Postal Code: _____
Account Number (if applicable): _____

075 CSAS

*New York residents remit applicable sales taxes.
*Canadian residents remit applicable GST and provincial taxes.

HQN™

We *are* romance™

www.HQNBooks.com

PHKM0409BL